TRANSGRESSIONS

Vaiju Naravane is a journalist, broadcaster, lecturer and publisher. Based in Paris, she is the Europe correspondent of *The Hindu* and Foreign Fiction Editor at the French publishing house Albin Michel. This is her first novel.

Transgressions

Vaiju Naravane

HarperCollins *Publishers* India

First published in India in 2014 by
HarperCollins *Publishers* India

Building 10, Tower A, 4th Floor, DLF Cyber City, Phase II,
Gurugram Haryana – 122002, India
www.harpercollins.co.in

ISBN: 978-93-5029-651-6

2 4 6 8 10 9 7 5 3 1

Typeset in 11/14.2 Goudy Old Style
Saanvi Graphics Noida

Printed and bound at
MicroPrints India, New Delhi

For my son, Sanjay d'Humières,
for my mother, the grandmother he never saw
and
Rajni Kumar, teacher and friend

Belshazzar's grave is made,
His kingdom passed away,
He, in the balance weighed,
Is light and worthless clay;
The shroud, his robe of state,
His canopy the stone;
The Mede is at his gate!
The Persian on his throne

–'Vision of Belshazzar', Lord Byron (1881)

Prologue

Paris, August 2007

Kranti looks at her flat with silent satisfaction.

Those cherry red sofas are just the thing, she thinks. She likes the way they pick out the gold-braided crimson drapery in the old family portrait of Nana Phadnavis, statesman, poet, child molester – one of several flawed ancestors, and the deeper red in the pale lemon of her Tree of Life carpet.

The portrait that once belonged to her grandfather is the first thing you see on walking through the door. Sharp, penetrating eyes, gaunt, aristocratic features, the caste-mark worn proudly across the forehead, a diamond and emerald-tipped turban that barely hides his Brahmin's shaven head – a fist-in-the-solar-plexus kind of effect, she concedes.

The window at the far end of her curved salon is open, letting in the pellucid light of a late summer evening. It's an elongated, double drawing room crowded with plants, carpets, paintings and furniture that nevertheless conveys a sense of space and delicacy, of airiness.

She has dusted and cleaned with a vigour she had forgotten she possessed. Her nostrils feel ticklish and a sneeze hovers somewhere between her nose and throat. Kranti sniffs inelegantly, wipes her nose with a small rough hand, the index checking the rim of her nostrils for lingering droplets. *Les mains d'une cuisinière*, her ma-in-law would have said, a kitchen maid's hands, ugly and red from constant cleaning. And now from cracking open spiky poison pods, Kranti would have added.

From her antique swivel chair near the window that gives on to the rue Chardon Lagache, she has an unencumbered view of the avenue de Versailles as it culminates in the roundabout at the Porte de St-Cloud. As she twirls around, the fading orange light catches the red henna streaks in her dark hair. She is of indeterminate age. Most people place her at between forty (on her best, dolled-up, sari-clad days) and forty-five (at her panda-eyed worst). She is fifty, if a day, a fact sometimes given away by the faint parchment crease lines that form on panda-days at the base of her neck.

The gilt and black Andalusian looking glass above the fireplace throws back her own reflection. A dusky, far-away face, a mere smudge in the mirrored landscape, as usual ticking off 'Things to do' lists. Her afternoon of labour was not ill-spent, however. What stares back is a picture of quiet beauty and ordered calm. Exactly, but exactly what she needs today.

She showers, pulls on a long, soft purple dress in brushed satin she has worn only twice before, both times to the opera – once, to a magnificent Russian production of Prokofiev's The Fiery Angel at the Scala and the second, to a pathetically poor Madame Butterfly at the Viennna Staatsoper. She has chosen the gown because of the satin slippers that go with it. 'Now I'm squeaky clean both inside and out,' she thinks, rubbing cream into her hands before painting her nails a strong dark red.

'*Et voilà ma p'tite Kranti*, you have the hands of a duchess now,' she mimics the ringing, over-enunciated tones of her ma-in-law. Ex. Not quite, since they were still married in the eyes of the church, she and Guillaume de Lorel, or weren't they?

Many years ago, in Milan, she was summoned by the Ecclesiastical Tribunal to talk about a possible annulment. Guillaume's new wife Celestine, a fervent Catholic, was desperate to be married in church, but the groom had travelled that path before. It had taken all the Lorel connections to get the Church to even consider the matter.

Everything, of course, hinged on whether or not she had been baptised. The Holy Father could, at his discretion, annul the marriage between a Catholic and a heathen, celebrated on the strength of a Papal waiver, what the French call a '*dispensation spéciale*'. It simply meant the Bishop of Rome was snatching back a favour he had, in a moment of kindness (or was it weakness?), bestowed upon a non-Catholic. But what if the poor soul had been saved, the non-Catholic baptized in the meantime? Would the Holy Father not be repudiating a member of his flock?

'*Lei è stata battezzata o non battezzata?*' the hostile priest detailed to deal with her case kept asking. For him, that was all that mattered. Kranti had played her cards close to her chest, parrying his questions cunningly, leaving him frustrated and angry.

'When I agreed to marry Guillaume, I was warned there could be no divorce. How come the Holy Father is changing his own rules?' she asked, her eyes round and innocent.

'One does not ask such questions of His Holiness,' the priest snapped. At the end of the session, he still did not know if she had been '*battezzata*', but she led him to believe that that could have been the case, given the conversion fever that regularly gripped the Catholic nuns who ran the boarding school she had attended in India. He had found her obstreperous, stubborn, rude and not a little stupid. Finally, after three hours of extremely confused and confusing testimony, the old priest made her sign a document and led her out, visibly happy to see the back of her. She never heard from the Ecclesiastical Tribunal again. Nor did Guillaume and Celestine, who, to Kranti's secret joy, continued to live in sin.

Kranti reaches across to the small chest of drawers that stands near her desk and pulls out envelopes of neatly stacked photographs, striking off 'see family pix' from her 'Things to do' list.

There are about a dozen or so pictures of her marriage and she has to admit she and Guillaume make a handsome pair. The wedding was an absolute coup and Kranti can again savour the triumph of over twenty years ago. But it's a triumph now tempered with regret and a hint of bitterness. Bitteness at all the cruelty, intentional and otherwise; regret at her inability to stand up and say no. The demure Indian daughter-in-law agreeing to everything they asked. A church wedding? Yes, all right, if you insist, especially since the Holy Father has agreed to bless the union.

What could they say afterwards? They had wished it upon themselves. The bride was dressed not in virginal white but in gold-threaded scarlet silk with lots of heavy Indian-style jewellery. Not Debussy but Ravi Shankar and Jean-Pierre Rampal – East meeting West poured out from the speakers.

Her readings were from the Ashtavakra Gita, Chapter Twenty, a definition of God by negation.

'I am Shiva, the Unconditional, the Absolute Good. I am neither Guru, nor Disciple. Why speak further? Nothing emanates from me, neither existence nor non-existence, neither unity nor duality resides in me.'

Intoned in French, the words sounded particularly sacrilegious, blasphemous even, as they travelled up the cavernous walls of the church to crash upon the burnished organ pipes behind the altar.

A penniless, coloured divorcée marrying into the French aristocracy at the chapel in Versailles. It was Madame, not Mademoiselle Goray, who took her place to say 'Oui' beside Comte Guillaume-Marie Jean-Jacques de Lorel. Her effrontery struck them dumb. They had been foolish enough to insist upon a church wedding. She had scored with unerring accuracy – like a guided missile latching onto a powerful source of heat.

Very few of the Lorels turned up for the wedding. '*C'est une divorcée*'. The three little words did the rounds of the tightly-knit clan, and it was mainly Guillaume's distaff side, lesser nobility tinged with more than a swab of Swiss blood, that made up the congregation.

When it was all over, and the enormity of what she had done finally dawned, Kranti felt a grudging respect for the doughty old countess and her gentle, pious husband. Agreed, they had given her no choice and she had been uncharitable in return, but they had accepted the calamity with stoic calm, taken it on the chin. Blue blood and *noblesse oblige*. They never spoke of the wedding again.

From a large Manila envelope, Kranti pulls out two photographs, places them side by side on the table. The first is an obvious enlargement and the picture has a blurry aspect, as if rubbed out by time. It shows Guillaume's parents standing at the head of the tilleul alley in front of the family chateau in Auvergne, a carpet of yellowing autumn leaves at their feet. They look every inch the retired military couple, the General and his countess wife. He, with his toothbrush moustache, she, with her lacquered *mise en plis*, ne'er a hair out of place.

The other picture, a sharply focused studio shot in black and white, over half-a-century old, is of an Indian husband-and-wife pair looking self-consciously, even earnestly, into the lens. But for slightly protruding teeth and a certain lack of height, not evident in the picture, the man would be spectacularly good-looking. He obviously knows his best angles and offers them to the camera. His light brown eyes seduce. Look, he says, look at my strong jaw, long curling eyelashes, deep, perfect dimples. Come, run your fingers through my dark, wavy hair, admire how it falls over my wide intelligent forehead, touch my sensuous lips. Desire me, and you shall possess.

The woman, clearly uncomfortable, has anxiety writ large on her face. She has haughty, clean-cut features and a small, neat nose but narrowly misses being beautiful; and not just because the nose is ever so slightly to one side. Her face has an odd, monkey-like cast, as if distorted in infancy by a severe bout of whooping cough. There is a disconcerting absence about her, a stony emptiness. Her eyes, not her best feature, are small, opaque, unseeing almost, with sparse eyelashes. Dead mutton eyes, Kranti once called them.

The back of the photograph has been rubber stamped in violet ink. 'Prabhat Studios, Deccan Gymkhana, Poona.' The date, hand-written in fading brown sepia is 18 May 1950. She is wearing a square-necked, puff-sleeved blouse, a yellow silk sari with gold embossed dahlias on a bottle-green border. The neck is cut wide and her collar-bones show, stark and cruel. Although the picture is in black and white, Kranti has no trouble seeing the colours of her mother's sari or the hazel in her father's eyes. Aayee is 24, Baba 27. This is their wedding day.

Other pictures tumble out of the envelope. Kranti as a fat, smiling baby; with Aayee and Tai, her older sister, in the garden of her grandfather's house in Poona. Aayee, tall and willowy, the girls, hair bound in fat sausage curls, identically dressed in ankle-length *parkars*, clutching at their mother's sari; Kranti, in Baba's arms, holding aloft her favourite doll, and here, dressed up as a Bharatanatyam dancer with nose rings and a hundred roses in her hair. And then, more recent photos, maybe a decade old. Posing nude on the rocks near Stromboli, her small round breasts pointing upwards to meet the sky. Eating pizza on the zodiac, one foot trailing in the water, her naked sex resting casually on the boat's taut grey rubber, eyes challenging, caressing the lens, much as Baba's had done over fifty years ago.

The sight of the pizza awakens her dormant stomach, which gives an audible rumble. She has eaten nothing since the morning. This has been a day of fasting, of purification and retreat, starting with a ritual washing out of her stomach and intestines. Castor oil and an intestinal 'douche', which is nothing but a sophisticated way of saying enema.

Kranti does not want embarrassing, fetid smells to escape her body when they find her. '*If the body is properly prepared, cleansed inside and out before passing into the other world, putrefaction will be reduced, avoiding unseemly gases that could mar the ultimate moments,*' states her *Guide to Self-Administered Transcendence*.

'*Undertake this final journey only if you are very sure the time has come for you to sever your bonds with the present. Self-administered death should take place in a spirit of calm detachment. Make sure you leave no loose ends behind. Write letters to your near and dear ones explaining your decision. Do not forget to contact the gas, telephone and electricity agencies, asking them to cut your connection. Make your will. Leave nothing to chance. Look at your family photos. Memorize the faces of your loved ones. You will need them by your side on your journey through the worlds. You should not leave this earth a troubled spirit ...'*

A couple of weeks ago she had tried to obtain a copy of *Suicide, mode d'emploi*, scouring the quayside bouquinists and calling up her journalist and fashionista friends. But the banned guide to suicide that caused such a furore in France has vanished from the market and Kranti has had to make do with an irritatingly sanctimonious tome written by a self-styled Indian professor, a certain Acharya Zen Mahalingam.

Kranti has worked all morning to extract the eighty drops of colourless liquid that lie warming between her breasts, still and calm in a small glass vial. The tiny test tube, less than five centimetres long, with its tight-fitting cork stopper, dangles delicately at the end of a thin gold chain.

Long ago, the tube was filled with fine gold dust, brought back from Somalia by one of her itinerant journalist lovers, and Kranti wore it everywhere, day and night, as her lucky charm. One day she awoke to find the lover gone, the cork missing and the vial empty, the gold dust spattered across the pillow, clinging to her hair and cheek. Her luck escaped along with the cover and the gold, and the bottle, chain and errant stopper have lain discarded in her jewellery case until now, when she has found a new use for them. The chain, freshly washed in *ritha* water, feels clean, cool, the weight of the liquid a constant reminder of what lies ahead.

'Mad apple, thorn apple, moonflower bright,
Ferry me across but hold me tight.
Let the devil smoke his weed, let him have his due,
Row me to the far side, to a morning new.
Green dragon, nightshade, now help me sleep,
Blow the angel's trumpet loud or I shall weep.'

Kranti sings breathily, touching the chain around her neck. Her voice is soft and off-key. She made up the ditty while preparing her decoction this morning and set it to the tune of an old Irish ballad taught her by the nuns when she was little. *Tumty tumty tum tum, tum tee-ee tum, tumty tumty tumty tum, tum tee tum.* And now she can't get the silly tune out of her head.

The little pods were bright green and spiky when she picked them off a clump of wayside bushes in Kerala's tea-garden town of Munnar, peremptorily commanding the startled driver to 'Stop the car at once' on the winding hilly road. The translucent white flowers with their webbed wafer-thin petals wilted like beached jellyfish almost as soon as she placed the foul-smelling branches on the seat. The pods took their time, going from bright to dull green, the spikes hardening, then splintering, as brown spots pitted and shrank the surface between them. 'They look like those deadly bomblets in Antonio Prohia's Spy vs. Spy comics,' she thought.

That was several months ago, during her last trip to India. Since then, the poisonheads containing fatal quantities of atropine, hyoscyamine and hyoscine have been waiting patiently for their day to dawn, locked up in a transparent jam jar.

Datura stramonium L. (thorn apple). Also known as mad apple, moonflower, devil's trumpet, angel's trumpet, green dragon, stinkweed, jimsonweed, locoweed, toluguacha, apple of Peru and sacred datura, one of the oldest poisons known to humanity, famous for its aphrodisiac, mind-altering and medicinal qualities; famous also for its unerring ability to kill.

Her fingertips are roughened from the spikes, the skin torn and punctured, as if she has just finished yards of embroidery, without the protection of a thimble. When she broke open the pods this morning, the insides reminded her of a dried up pomegranate or an oversized cardamom. A crackly yellowish membrane separated the four chambers packed tight with seeds, some black, some brown. On close examination, they looked nothing like the cardamom's perfumed offerings, but had a curious, uneven matt texture with a kidney-like shape that made her think of deformed, hunchbacked bodies. Some 600 seeds in all. Enough to kill a fair-sized horse.

Kranti drummed her fingers on the tiled tabletop in her kitchen. They must be crushed, then boiled. But which pestle and mortar to use? The brass one reserved for khada masala, or the small wooden one with a crack in its side, kept aside for garlic? They had both been used before and would not do. Instead, she opted for the smooth white newness of a marble pestle and mortar bought, it seemed like an age now, at the oldest apothecary's in Budapest.

She crushed the seeds with measured, regular taps of the pestle, sniffing occasionally as the grains disintegrated to become a coarse brown-flecked powder. This she tipped into a saucepan placed on low heat, containing half a cup of water. Ten minutes later there were just a few spoonfuls of water left. She strained the precious decoction into a coffee cup, carefully transferring the liquid with a plastic dropper into the glass vial, counting out loud as the drops fell into the bottle one by one. More than enough, she thought, as she held up the stoppered bottle to the light before slipping it around her neck. The vial swung back and forth as she bent over her chores, coming perilously close to breaking, so she slipped it under her dress, savouring for a moment its coolness against the heat of her body.

On her list only one item is now outstanding. Written in French, it says: *passer à l'acte.* Do it.

There are fresh flowers in every room and the flat has the heady smell of an airless funeral parlour. The pestle and mortar have been put back in the drawer, the rubbish taken down, the bin lined with a clean plastic bag, the laundry washed and put away. Her letter is written. It stands, neatly folded in a thick ivory envelope, by the mirror in the living room.

Professor Mahalingam's final words echo in her ears: '*You must pay attention to how you look when you are found. Remember you are courting death in a serene, detached manner. No point in startling or frightening those who discover your mortal remains. Choose a posture that will reassure you in your last moments, allow you to go in peace and which will, at the same time, convince your loved ones that death has indeed been for you a joyful departure, a voluntary throwing off of the mortal coil.*

Kranti has settled on the classic pose that decorates the tombs of departed kings, queens and assorted clerics in big and small churches scattered across Europe – hands folded over the chest, gracefully flowing robes that reveal as much as they conceal, smooth silk slippers that hide unsightly bunions and calluses, a blissful, even beatific smile playing about the lips.

She lines her mouth with lipstick, and fixes a wig upon her head. It fits like a tight skull-cap. The thick fringe highlights her large chocolate-coloured eyes, imparts an appealing roundness to her face. Black and snake-like, it cascades down her back, its weight giving a proud tilt to her head. She switches off the bathroom light and moves to her bedroom, where three lily-scented candles are burning.

Kranti hesitates, decides not to discard the specially made satin slippers. Her dress is an off-the-shoulder affair, with a richly embroidered train that falls to the ground. A clever Bombay tailor made it from a *jamavar* sari, copying the pattern from *Dépêches Mode*. She settles herself on the bed, arranges the folds of cloth gracefully around her body, the train fanned out dramatically beside her. Fishing out her necklace, she uncorks the vial, proposing an invisible toast.

Tears gather in her eyes. Her smile is wobbly, her voice shaky but determined. 'If this were mere coincidence, those in the know would probably call it poetic justice. But we know this is no coincidence, do we not, my sweet philtre? To us, Baba. To you, my father, my tormentor. To your magical poisonous ways, and to me, your darling Revolution,' she declaims. Then she swallows the draught in one straight gulp.

The liquid is bitter beyond belief and a shudder goes through her body. Her mouth suddenly feels dry, robbed of saliva, and she falls back on the bed, fighting for breath. 'Dry as a bone', she mumbles, trying to recollect the mnemonic by which physicians remember the symptoms of datura poisoning. 'Blind as a bat, mad as a hatter, red as a beet, hot as a hare, dry as a bone, the bowel and bladder lose their tone, and the heart runs alone.'

Her heart is in fact thudding like a drum and she puts a hand over it in an attempt to calm its runaway beat. She sees an astonishing cloudburst of colour, a Diwali fireworks of a kind she has never seen, hears a din of voices; a clanging, clashing cacophony as hundreds of faces, some known, some alien, crowd her vision. Her eyes are wide open, the pupils dilated, glittery as jet, her fixed smile slipping just a little at one side.

Satin slippers pointing vertically upwards, hands fluttering at her breast, she looks like a long-dead queen carved in stone atop a sarcophagus.

A dense fogginess clouds her mind. She is floating down the river. Ophelia? The Lady of Shallot? The faraway wail of an ambulance pierces the thick tempest of snow that is numbing her mind. It's a train whistle and she is now with her family, with Baba, Aayee and Tai, on their way from Aurangabad to Lucknow in their own little compartment-for-four with mangoes, melons and tender coconuts cooling in a tub of ice. The pounding of her heart moves in rhythm with the wheels of the locomotive: *Kasha sathi, pota sathi, Khandalyacha ghata sathi* ... *Kasha sathi, pota sathi, Khandalyacha ghata sathi* ... a chorus of children gleefully bellowing out the old Marathi nonsense verse.

She now knows what she has been trying to tell her parents all these years. It has been hiding forever, teasing, tantalizing, in the folds of her brain, to finally surface, like cream rising on milk, or a slow moon climbing the dark night sky. Oh, how could she have been so stupid! It's all crystal clear and must be told, now, this very instant, before she loses it again. 'Aayee, Baba, Tai ...'

From the labyrinthine depths into which it has sunk, Kranti's will to live surges up, a diver without an aqualung coming up for air. Blindly, her hand reaches for the telephone by the bed. Her fingers brush the keys, looking for the right digits to press. She turns over on her side but her fingers have already stopped working. Curled up like a foetus, eyes shining but unseeing, she has slipped away, the telephone clutched to her stomach, its wire stretching out from her navel like an uncut umbilical cord.

1

The Savic Family Discovers a Corpse

August 2007

Olga Savic took a full four minutes to climb the 67 steps that led to her third-floor Paris flat. Her heartbeat was jumpy and she was out of breath.

'Those boys, they'll kill me one day,' she thought, her anger further shortening her breath.

They were polite enough, those children. If she climbed up another two flights to point out that they had left the lift door open once more, they would mumble an apology and promise to be careful the next time. But she knew it would happen again.

'Probably on a Thursday,' she muttered.

It was not a difficult climb, but Thursday was soup day. And though August was not the best of months to buy leeks or turnips, Ivan was adamant. He would not do without his soup. So Olga Savic's shopping bags were filled with leeks, carrots, celery, tomato, fennel, parsley, thyme, a chunk of stewing beef and a bit of shin bought at the weekly open-air market.

There had been too many people crowding the only nearby café open at this time of year, and so she'd had to skip her customary halt to hurry back home. And now she was twitching for a cigarette and the cup of coffee she knew she couldn't have upstairs. At each floor, she put down her heavy shopping bags and paused to catch her breath, cursing in her native Serbo-Croat, glancing incuriously through the stairwell window at the grimy inner facade of 100, rue Chardon Lagache towering above the courtyard with its ancient paving stones, bicycle shed and green, blue and yellow wheely bins – one for bottles, one for paper and plastic and the third for 'biodegradable' refuse, thanks, or rather, no thanks to the new Mayor. 'Multiply and prosper,' she thought sourly at the thought of having to separate her rubbish.

It was a harsh, stiflingly hot morning and the sun was high enough to light up the windows of the flat across the courtyard. Unwashed windows. Ivan would not tolerate that; nor would she, Olga Savic reasoned, seeing a vision of her sparkling panes overlooking the avenue de Versailles.

She could feel beads of sweat gather at the tip of the hair in her armpits, run down her arms and fall in quick succession on the nylon tights and closed shoes she wore under a pale cotton dress, light blue jacket and beige raincoat.

In the old days before the war, in her native Croatia, she had run with her sisters and cousins, sandaled and bare-legged in summer, their mouths and hands deliciously fragrant, sticky and red from berry-picking. After the war, as a desperately poor and passably pretty young refugee from Eastern Europe, she wore rough knitted stockings to hide her hairy legs and give herself an air of mystery. A heavily powdered face, a slash of red lipstick and black clothes. Always.

Ivan had been intrigued. He thought she had 'held a position' back then, by which he meant, been a spy or something. When he found out she'd been a 'steno' in Dubrovnik, it was too late. They were married and Peter was on his way.

Although she had abandoned her 'forever black' dress code, she felt naked and uncomfortable without her tights and sweater and she took off her heavy clothing only at night, slipping into comfortable white flannel nightgowns that she ran up, in the old-fashioned way, on her ancient Pfaff.

The mystery had long since evaporated. The intriguing angularity of her face was now mere gauntness and her streaked grey hair, though still thick, looked lank and greasy. 'I'm like a tough old chicken. Stringy. Wouldn't put me in my own stewing pot,' she reflected with dour satisfaction, the thought popping up with suspicious regularity on Ivan's soup days.

Olga Savic put down her bags and felt for her keys in a small purse she wore crosswise across her shoulder, where her double pack of Marlboroughs fought for space with lipstick, Kleenex, a cigarette lighter, loose change, keys, lists, a boiled sweet and other oddments.

'Is that you, Olga?' Ivan's complaining voice wafted down the corridor even before she had the door fully open. 'There's a peculiar smell here. I'm sure there must be a dead pigeon or something on the balcony.'

'I'll take a look, Ivan.' She half dragged the bags into the kitchen. It was almost eleven o'clock and although she was gasping for coffee, Olga made hot chocolate for Ivan and herself. Since his illness, he was forbidden coffee and the smell of her brew would only drive him to greater verbal excess.

Sitting up in bed, unshaven and still in his pyjamas, Ivan Savic frowned at the sight of his wife. Despite his stroke, he continued to rule his little world with as much discipline as his weakened state would allow. The flat was suffocating. No question of opening the windows though; too much noise, too much dust.

Last Monday, two weeks after his return from hospital, he had spent an hour explaining the details of the filing system to Olga, who had nodded and said 'yes, yes', assuring him she had understood what needed to be done.

His lips had gone blue with the effort and Olga had insisted he stop. Partly out of concern, but partly, as Ivan suspected, because she was simply bored. Since then, she had put off any discussion about his work. 'Take it easy. We don't have to worry. Peter's just sent this big cheque to the bank. So we're doing quite nicely, thank you,' she told Ivan.

'I don't want that little pouter's money. I brought him up and fed and educated him. I am man enough to look after my own old age,' he had fumed. But he knew that the business was doing badly, that he no longer had the strength, nor, worse perhaps, the will to carry on fighting what he already knew to be a battle lost. How could an old-fashioned mail order business selling cheap gadgets from Eastern Europe survive in this age of the internet and competition from millions of little yellow and brown men?

During Olga's trip to the market, he had gone to his small study and was almost felled by the force of a truly impotent fury. His desk was piled high with invoices, bank notices, commercial brochures, professional magazines, creditors' notes, a huge jumbled heap. She had said yes, she understood, and then she just hadn't bothered, quite happy to live off the generous hand-outs of their homosexual son. He was sure Peter knew the business was suffering, but continued to support it anyway, mopping up the losses from one year to the next. 'It gives Baba something to do,' Ivan had overheard him tell Olga.

An intense feeling of humiliation had washed over Ivan. Peter. His pictures were all over the place – the house in California, the boyfriend – a Romanian this time, the Porsche, the Ferrari, the crazy clothes. For Olga, his room had become a goddamn shrine. She kept a scrap-book with his baby pictures, locks of downy hair, his letters, written in a hand that had changed from roundish to raffish and clippings from the gutter press showing him in the company of film stars. There was a special album devoted to the launch of Peter's very own PeterS brand of cosmetics with photos of the parties in LA and New York, interviews in Vanity Fair, Cosmopolitan, and other glossies, even some of his product ads that appeared in fashion magazines. Every so often, he had heard her laughing over them with their neighbour, that strange Indian lady he couldn't figure out. A Hollywood make-up artist, that's what Olga had produced, Ivan thought, someone who cruised around with actresses and poncey rent boys. What did it matter if Peter was famous and rich as Croesus?

Once, when Peter was visiting, Ivan had gone through his 'professional gear.' He had found a suitcase filled with what he disdainfully called 'paint' – boxes of powder, foundation, creams and oils, fake nails, eyelashes, make-up palettes rubber face masks, glue, beards and mustaches and other instruments of disguise. But it was the other box, a rivet-studded Louis Vuitton affair, that made Ivan yelp in disgust – stacked to the brim with different coloured wigs, blue, blonde, black, red, gold, straw, chestnut – dead, repelling masses of women's hair.

Peter's affection was reserved for Olga, of course, his adored Mamimou. She had taken him to galleries and museums, introduced him to her fake arty friends, paid for private piano and art lessons. Little wonder the boy had become a randy homosexual. Ivan felt the bile rise in his throat.

As his wife came in with a small silver tray with tiny coconut wafers and the thick, dark, Viennese-style chocolate she made to perfection, Ivan fought hard to contain his anger. His hand shook and he felt a fresh wave of irritation at Olga's solicitous smile. 'I wish she'd stop treating me like a cripple or an idiot with that beatific look. Play acting as always, bearing her cross with fortitude. What does she think she is, a bloody saint?' he thought.

There, he'd got a whiff of that smell again. Stale and sickly sweet, like some dead animal. 'I told you, there's a smell. Will you look?' he growled.

Without a word Olga Savic moved to the window. Pushing aside the translucent white drape that softened the August glare, she pulled open the airtight aluminium frame that held the double-glazing in place, to be greeted by a blast of heat and traffic noise. Nothing. The window-ledge was bare, still relatively clean from the vigorous sweep she had given it a week ago.

She turned to Ivan, a small pitying smile at the corner of her lips. Sad that life should be made up of such small victories now, she thought. 'There's nothing there. It's all in your head. I can't smell anything,' she said.

'It's there, I tell you. The smell is in my nose and I can't get it out of my head.'

Nature moves in strange ways, she thought. The stroke that had turned poor Ivan's face crooked with a droopy lower lip had also done something miraculous to his sense of smell. He could sniff out anything now – mineral or vegetable, raw or cooked, animate or dead as dodo. Better than Bijou, the concierge's smelly poodle that trained its rheumy nose on her shopping bags every time she came in. 'Didn't I tell you the salt has to be put in last? Salt increases the cooking time!' he had yelled the other day, enthroned on the toilet seat. A few minutes earlier, she had heedlessly thrown salt in with the meat and vegetables for his potée.

He stumbled out of bed and moved unsteadily towards the kitchen. 'It's here. The smell is stronger here. Are you sure you didn't leave the window open? Maybe a mouse got in somehow. Maybe it's trapped behind the cooker'.

She felt fear clutch at her heart. 'Ivan, Ivan, get back to bed. You mustn't walk about like that. You'll have another collapse. I promise I'll look. Now come back, please,' she said, helping him down the corridor.

Fuming, Olga Savic spent her entire afternoon hunting down the source of Ivan's elusive, mysterious smell without success. She pulled out the cooker, the refrigerator, the cupboard. Nothing. Nevertheless, there was something frightening about Ivan's insistence and when he began retching, her ironic comments about something rotting in the Kingdom of Savic died upon her lips. The smell, he complained, was unbearable and getting stronger by the minute.

'Is he mad? Am I mad? Or is it the smell of his own death that has begun to haunt him?' she asked herself.

Seeing Ivan bent painfully over the toilet bowl she rang the hospital. Then she gave him two brimming tablespoons of Primperan and put him to bed before setting about cleaning up the mess in the toilet. 'If this carries on, I shall have to call Madame Benoît', she thought, not relishing the prospect of the concierge's superior stare. Her neighbour was away, she knew, having tried Kranti's bell yesterday and this morning.

100, rue Chardon Lagache was an impeccably maintained Haussmann-style building of the late 19th century whose lift and banisters smelt of beeswax. In the large foyer, a cherubic cupid stood ready to shoot his hard, stone arrow at the heart of an unsuspecting lover-to-be. In bygone days he had gracefully peed into the marble fountain over which he so naughtily presided. But the tap had been turned off a couple of years ago and Madame Benoît, the ageing concierge, a blowsy bottle-blonde whose hair showed dirty-grey at the roots, now lavished her love on three large ficus plants that bloomed dense and green under her knobbly care.

Madame Benoît had been the concierge at 100, rue Chardon Lagache, for almost forty years. She knew every square inch of the building as well as she knew the pockets of her buttoned-up, navy cover-all and had witnessed births, deaths, marriages, divorces, surreptitious love affairs and all kinds of other goings-on, some spicy, some not, like those of the third-floor Yugos, for instance, who secretly operated a mail-order company – in a residential building, if you please. She would happily report them to the police or to the building's manager for unauthorised trade were it not for the hefty cheque the Savics slipped into her unresisting fingers every Christmas.

On two occasions she had had to call the fire brigade – when the cellars caught fire and when poor Madame de St Jacob, shivering in her nightclothes in the dead of winter, threw herself off her sixth floor balcony. She died in hospital after a week's agony. Madame Benoît had sent flowers but did not go to the very private funeral. It was a case of suicide, after all.

There were twelve large flats in all, two to a floor, mostly occupied by the owners, with maids' rooms on the seventh floor that could be reached via the service sataircase at the back. Only the old people were left now, grandparents most of them. 'I wonder what will happen when I retire, when they die. These flats are meant for receptions and large families. They will surely be sold, may be chopped up into two or three smaller ones per floor,' she told Bernard, the butcher, who was her special friend.

He would not be averse to the changes. His best custom no longer came from 100. That had dwindled since the children grew up and left. Old people tended to eat less meat. They also grew stingier with age. Madame Lavergne who used to buy at least a couple of chickens, a good side of roast, strings of fat Lyon sausages and several types of pate every week, now came in only for a bit of ground steak or thin veal cutlets. 'We eat more fish now,' she told him apologetically the other day. He knew it wasn't true, but he continued to treat her with his usual deference and courtesy, paying her compliments, like in the old days, when he had gently flirted with this very attractive older woman.

There was only one good customer from 100, the Indian lady who threw champagne dinners for all sorts of strange people, or so Madame Benoît told him. She always wanted the best – lamb, usually, or free-range Bresse chicken. Money was no object, it seemed.

C'est un drôle d'oiseau, mused Bernard, a very strange bird indeed. Not at all like the embassy wives who dropped into the shop once in a while when their flunkeys were away. Those vixens rarely spoke French and when they did, it was in loud loathsome foreign voices. They parked their four-wheel drives arrogantly on the zebra crossing in front of his shop, their spoilt brats quarrelling over expensive video games in the back.

Not this one. She came by herself, an old-fashioned straw shopping basket swinging on her arm. At odd hours of the day, avoiding the morning rush of housewives and the evening queues of harried working mothers stopping by to pick up steaks for dinner.

Figure-hugging slacks, thick cotton, usually gabardine, never jeans; Cashmere sweaters, worn loose over her lanky frame, a long Indian scarf thrown carelessly around the shoulders. Casual chic, no great shakes, really.

Until the day he saw her all dressed up. Then Bernard understood what Madame Benoît meant. 'That one's no immigré. You can tell. Not like those Yugos who live next door to her. I should know, I "do" for her', she had said.

She had reminded him of a distant, exotic bird when he saw her that day, all colour and light. It was just before closing time when she came rushing in, her electric-blue Indian dress swirling around her feet, words tumbling out, tripping over themselves. He didn't recognize her for a moment – the hair drawn back, a red dot on her forehead, eyes bigger and blacker than he had ever seen, long diamond earrings swinging from her ears.

'*Bonsoir*, Madame. You look beautiful like this. What do you need?' He had blurted out the compliment.

'*Soyez gentil*, Bernard. Give me six more lamb chops. Quickly, please.' Unexpected additional guests, she said, likely to arrive any minute.

Hands gone suddenly unsteady trimmed the edges of the chops just the way she liked them. Ears barely heard the clink of the porcelain piggy accepting her tip. As he handed her the package, Bernard's hands brushed lightly against her fingers and he felt his ageing loins stir. That one must be a helluva expensive *poule* to maintain, he thought, looking speculatively at her departing back. He wondered who the lucky man was and how much she cost him per month.

The question intrigued Madame Benoît too, he knew. Like any good concierge worth her salt, she kept a sharp eye on her 'flock' and usually had newcomers down for what they were in less than a week. 'It's my *pif*,' she would say, tapping her long Breton nose.

But years after entering Madame Goray de Lorel's employ, she was still scouting for answers. There were lots of visitors and many of them were men, she said. Of course, there was the good *docteur* too, more frequent and regular than the others. But that did not prove anything, or did it? She had married the MP Guillaume de Lorel and she must've got a pretty good divorce settlement to live in such luxury. 'That funny name is real enough. She uses it on her personal cheques. It must be genuine or she'd be hauled up by the *Banque de France* double quick,' Madame Benoit had mused.

'And then those dinners and all that wine', she told Bernard with knowing looks. Madame Benoît was assiduous about counting bottles, keeping a tab on how much was drunk and by whom. And there were always several empties of champagne and good Bordeaux the day after *la dame Indienne* entertained. 'Well,' she said archly and not without a twinge of envy, 'some people have all the luck! Now only foreigners enjoy the good things that France has to offer. I have seen gift hampers from Le Nôtre, Daloyau and Fauchon. Snails and truffles, foie gras and champagne. You should see the bouquets sometimes. Just one of them would cost me my entire salary. You know, *mon cher* Bernard, I may not have any of that, but one thing I can say for sure, whatever I have, I've come by honestly!'

Olga Savic went to bed, her head a buzzing hive of doubts. There had been no news from Peter for a week and she was worried. Ever since she'd heard of Gianni Versace's murder at the hands of his gay lover and this other, more recent and hideously gruesome homophobic killing just outside Paris, her sleep had been troubled, plagued by disturbing, violent dreams in which she stood by, often a helpless, hand-wringing bystander, as Peter was bludgeoned or kicked to death.

Tonight, he was on his knees, bleeding from the head and nose, murmuring '*Maman*, help me *Maman*...' and she just stood there, feeling hot in the California sunshine, looking ridiculous in her thick stockings and blue cardigan as slim, almost naked Hollywood starlets with bare alabaster arms strode past, smiling, not looking, not caring about this crazy East European mother and her fatally wounded son.

She struggled awake. It was 5 a.m. Ivan was snoring beside her on the mattress, his breathing loud and regular. Olga Savic went into the kitchen to make herself a cup of camomile tea. Mug in hand, she moved to the salon to lay out a game of solitaire on the dining table and it was there that she got the first, insidious whiff of the smell, of death and decay, rotting flesh; putrefaction.

'It's not Ivan's death I'm smelling, it's Peter's,' she thought, panic overtaking her. She knew now that Ivan was on the mend. He had been fractious and ill-tempered throughout his meal, complaining that the soup was too salty, demanding cream, knowing fully well it was forbidden. And for the first time in fifty years of marriage, Olga Savic found herself wondering what it would be like to leave him, set up house on her own, to be free like Kranti next door, who had jettisoned unwanted husbands and lovers to soar like a bird in the open skies.

That smell again. It seemed to be coming from near the front door. Still in her nightgown, Olga Savic stepped out onto the landing, hesitated before her neighbour's door. She knew Kranti rose early to do yoga, but was five thirty too early? How many times had she told Olga to wake her up if she needed something, especially during Ivan's illness and never mind the time? At first Olga Savic knocked timidly, then she rang the bell in one long continuous jab, her finger stuck to the button, pushing hard, willing the door to open. There was no answer.

She knew Kranti was not in. She had tried before. The smell overtook her again as she turned to cross the landing. Her mouth filled up with saliva and she felt her stomach rise up to meet her throat. A cold sweat broke out on her forehead and lips. She felt giddy and sick. She knew. Knew what lay behind that resolutely closed door and she was terrified. As frightened perhaps as she had been during the war, when, with a terrible sense of foreboding, she had run with her Serb mother to flee the murdering bands of Ustasha.

Ivan found her lying on the living room couch a couple of hours later, fast asleep. She looked small and vulnerable. Moved by an unaccustomed tenderness he made her a cup of chocolate, sloshing half of it in the tray as he shuffled to where she lay.

'Ivan, we must call Madame Benoît,' Olga said as he shook her awake. 'Something terrible has happened to Kranti next door. That's where the smell is coming from. She's dead, Ivan, I know.'

'Don't be ridiculous!' he snapped. 'What could ever happen to that one? Nothing ever happens to people like her. Must've left the window open. There's probably a rat or a pigeon in there. Careless woman, always getting others to do her dirty work for her!'

'No Ivan, Kranti's not like that. You don't know how much she helped you, me – when you were in hospital. It couldn't be a rat or a pigeon, the smell is too strong; it's got to be something big.'

'Maybe. But I want nothing to do with it. She has encouraged our no-good son in his silliness, swanning around town with him every time he's here. I don't like that bitch. She has this peculiar hold over you. You're always scurrying to do her bidding. And even if there is something, I don't want to get involved. The place will be crawling with policemen. They'll want to question us; they'll poke their fat noses into the business and you know we're not licensed here.'

But Olga Savic was a stubborn woman and there was no stopping her now. Bijou sniffed at her ankles and the concierge lifted an unbelieving, supercilious eyebrow as Olga Savic, confused and incoherent, urged her to open Kranti's flat. '*Un accident*. You must go in, *entrez, entrez*,' she urged.

'*Mais non*, Madame Savic, *mais non*,' the concierge responded, an unpleasant smile on her lips. 'One can't just enter someone's house like that.'

Olga Savic refused to budge. 'It costs you nothing to check. In any case you have the keys; it's not like I'm asking you to force open the door.' With an exaggerated, very Parisian shrug, Madame Benoît gave in, but refused to ride in the lift with the Croatian, letting out expressive sighs as she climbed the stairs.

The smell hit them the moment the door swung open. Bijou skittered off as Madame Benoît held up her handkerchief to her nose and tiptoed into the bedroom. She was out of there in a trice. '*Il faut appeler la police, et vite*,' she said, rushing in through the open door of the Savic flat. In quick succession she called the police and the fire brigade then asked to use the toilet.

'*Oh mon Dieu*, I,'ve never seen anything like that!' she told Bernard later. '*Et la puanteur*!' The stench of it. Only the Yugos next door could have gone so long without having noticed it. 'And Madame Goray de Lorel all tarted up like a low dive harlot. I had always found her so nice. Just goes to show how little you really know people, especially foreigners,' she said.

2

An Act so Terrible...

For weeks the police seals remained in place. Interminably, it seemed to Olga Savic, who came to the conclusion it had something to do with Kranti being foreign. I suppose they'll send the body home to India, she'd thought in those early days.

She had wanted to ask Kranti's boyfriend what was happening, but he always looked grim on the occasions she glimpsed him entering the flat. Moreover, he was in the company of policemen who broke the seals when they entered, then put new seals on before they left. She knew they were policemen, even though they weren't in uniform, by the way they walked, that wary look they had.

'I don't know what it is exactly,' she said to Ivan. 'But something strange is going on.'

'The less we know the better,' he replied with such finality that they stopped talking about next door. But Olga Savic could not stop thinking about what Kranti had done. How often had she tried to imagine her friend, lying stiff and frozen in the city morgue. She knew they had probably cleaned her up after the autopsy, removed that awful wig, maybe even washed her;

but she couldn't think of her any other way. Nor could she get up the courage to go see her. Once in that state was more than enough. And she found herself crying bitter, bewildered tears at how easily her friend had left her without even saying goodbye.

When it finally took place, Kranti's funeral turned out to be a strange and awkward affair. Unreal. Surreal.

As if by magic, in the midst of miserable weather, the sun appeared. It was so stiflingly hot that Olga sweated profusely and took care to stand apart from the others, lest she begin to smell. There was no question of Ivan accompanying her and she had gone alone, taking a taxi to the crematorium at Puteaux, putting up with the abuse of the sullen driver who swore at every passing motorist, too tired to argue with him about the roundabout route he had taken.

Press and TV cameras seemed to materialize out of nowhere. Essentially, she presumed, to cover Kranti's ex-husband, Guillaume de Lorel, the charismatic centrist MP, solidly tipped for a ministerial post, but also for the glamour crowd who would provide juicy snippets for the gossip pages. The Indian ambassador drew up in his chauffeur-driven Mercedes with CD plates. They have come not to mourn but to be photographed, to see and to be seen, Olga Savic pressed her lips tightly together. Maybe Kranti would have laughed. Perhaps she's laughing now.

There were several models whose clothes she knew Kranti had designed and other familiar faces from the fashion world. None of them wore mourning and Olga felt herself shrinking into her black suit and patent leather pumps. She recognized a man from Dior who had featured in last week's *Elle* magazine. He's elegant but does he have to be so terribly camp with that high collar to hide his chicken neck? Peter's gay but he doesn't wear it on his sleeve like that! Olga desperately missed her son's confident, reassuring presence. He'd have known how to fix them with his Alain Delon looks, she thought fiercly. She spotted Dr Perrin, Kranti's boyfriend, at the back of the crowd, head down, eyes inscrutable behind dark glasses, studiously avoiding the photographers, not quite succeeding.

Many of the mourners were whispering, greeting each other with exaggerated kisses in the air. No emotion, not a tear. Scant respect. It had been a sad, sad day.

Long afterwards, Olga Savic would remember the grinding noise of the electric crematorium, its invisible flames eating up the coffin behind the uncompromising metal doors of the furnace. Waiting in silence for forty minutes for Kranti to be burnt to ashes in the cold, impersonal hall fixed up to look like a secular church.

Guillaume de Lorel had made a speech, his voice lost in the bare room, just about audible above the noise of the incinerator. 'We will miss you, Kranti. None of us is able to quite understand just why you chose to leave us the way you did, and we are all still coming to terms with what could only have been punishment for our failure to love you enough, to make you understand the depth and extent of our love. But know, wherever you are, that we love you still and miss you.'

Olga Savic was not impressed. How banal he sounded. Compared to the fiery speeches he made in the Assemblée, this was lifeless, like a disagreeable duty, which perhaps it was. But given his knowledge and position, he could surely have done better.

Why, even she could have talked about Kranti's love for life, the jokes she told, how crazy, how generous she could be. The food she cooked, her many different personalities. He said nothing, absolutely nothing about her painting, her talent, energy, zest, madness, selfishness. A good quote from Shakespeare, Rilke, Dante or any of France's literary giants, Victor Hugo or Rimbaud perhaps, would have been easy for him with his fancy degrees. We might not have understood it all, but it would have been nice. Not like this, talking down to us and to her, as if we were all dolts, she thought.

When the grinding stopped, they walked single file into the garden, where the furnace-man sprinkled some of Kranti's ashes, collected in an elongated steel container, on the rosebushes, much in the way of fertilizer or manure, and Olga Savic wondered why, with so much food in them and on them, the roses looked so undernourished, so anaemic.

Goodbye, Kranti, she sobbed quietly, quick tears chasing each other down her cheeks. Dr Perrin walked up to plant a chaste kiss on her forehead. 'She liked you a lot, you know,' he said.

And those words comforted Olga Savic, who laid the wan pink rose she carried on top of Kranti's ashes and went home hugging his words to her like precious stones.

She found herself reading Kranti's farewell note many times a day until it began to tear along the folds. It had become almost a part of her, like the handkerchief that always accompanied it for the tears that were certain to flow. The folded paper had taken on the shape of her hip as it made its way from skirt pocket to skirt pocket, acquiring a smooth patina coloured by the different types of dyed wool with which it came into contact. All these weeks later, she still didn't know what to think. She could only mourn.

'*My darling Olga,*' Kranti had written. '*I know you will find it hard to understand or accept my decision and I do not expect you to find excuses for what I have done. As a friend, I think I owe it to you to give you some sort of an explanation.*

'*You have always seen me happy, busy, active, on the go, doing things. And that is the way I would like you to remember me. I am going away serene, certain in the knowledge that I shall keep in touch from wherever I am.*

'*You have always held me in very high esteem, my darling Olga, and for that I am exceedingly grateful. Truth to tell, I am neither as talented nor as virtuous as you believe me to be. If I have decided to end my days, it is by way of expiation for some terrible things I did in the past. These last couple of years, I have tried to make up for my own misdeeds by living a life of kindness. But my guilt has not lessened; only grown. I have lied, cheated, perhaps even stolen. But those are minor misdemeanours compared to this other thing, an act so terrible that I cannot utter the words to describe it.*

'*And so all these months, you have been talking to an evil being, befriended someone who does not deserve to live.*

'*Guilt is a burden I can no longer bear. I must pay back with my own life. Nothing less will do. I hope you find it in you to forgive me and pray for me, although I do not myself believe in prayer. Tell Peter I love him.*

Your friend, Kranti.'

3

The Ivory Princess

From Kranti's living room window, Robert-Pierre stared absently at the lit-up cylinder of the Sofitel hotel, its sign a distant neon scream now misted over by powdery rain. Kranti never failed to comment on how its tall stem marred the low-slung elegance of the skyline. He had always vaguely demurred, giving in to what he had shrugged off as 'Kranti's normative diktats'. He quite liked that faraway beacon with its promise of an entire mini-universe. There was something intriguing about those blinking lights making fairy patterns in the sky as guests wandered in and out of their rooms.

Through the open window he could hear the slick of tyres on wet tarmac and the deep, angry growl of an impatient bus eager to finish its Sunday run at the Porte de Saint-Cloud two stops away. High summer had given way to a sodden autumn and at four-thirty it was already dark.

He pulled off his glasses giving them a ruminative wipe with the end of his yellow silk tie as if to clear a peeping space through the heavy grey-black outside. Turning away from the window, he took a few steps to stand before the mantelpiece.

'But of course you're still here, *n'est-ce pas, ma princesse*,' he said, addressing the carved ivory head of a negress, the latest addition to the clutch of objects above the fireplace. He'd had a devil of a time sneaking the six-kilo sculpture past the customs on his return from Senegal over a decade ago. Now he was glad he'd taken the risk.

She was a laughing negress, her unseeing eyes turned flirtatiously upwards. High cheekbones, flared nostrils, a wonderfully mobile mouth and hundreds of tendrils of kinky hair, the twisted ivory ribbon around her forehead frozen mid-flutter.

But it wasn't the face itself that held Robert-Pierre's interest. Reaching behind one ear, he released a clever little catch concealed by the mass of curls and the top third of the face sprang up to reveal a small, scooped out hiding place.

He peered at the contents. Kranti's small, perfectly formed porcelain molars winked back at him from their bed of slate grey ash.

'It doesn't really matter whether you're Indian or African, now, does it? You're stunning, *résplendissante, comme toujours*,' he muttered, unconsciously adopting the Franglais that had become their lingua franca.

Staring at his face in the gold-and-black Andalusian mirror, he pushed back a stray lock of hair and adjusted his glasses, bending forward to check the progress of a small red spot at the end of his nose, noticing for the first time how his hair had greyed these past two months.

The dead red lilies had disappeared from the copper vase, which was placed chastely at one side of the mantel. Silver gleamed quietly in the pale yellow haze cast by the table lamp's parchment shade. It was as if Kranti, still in residence, had stepped out for a minute to pick up the dinner loaf.

He bent down, drawing a finger across the sheer glass coffee table. Not a speck.

Someone's been here cleaning up the place,' he thought. 'It was swathed in dust the last time I came'. It couldn't have been Madame Benoît who had refused to come near the flat once the body had been removed.

The timeless and tiresome Olga Savic must have wheedled the keys out of the concierge again.

The last couple of months had not been easy. He had spoken to Kranti's ex-husband about the formalities and the funeral, and like Guillaume de Lorel, evaded questions from inquisitive tabloid reporters on the scent of Kranti Goray de Lorel's 'ritual Indian suicide'. He had met bankers, lawyers, taxmen and prying Indian embassy officials while trying to handle the unaccustomed froideur of Sophie. His wife.

It had of course shattered his long-harboured illusion of the 'perfect understanding' he shared with her. Their marriage was not as neatly arranged, as open or meticulously compartmentalised as he had assumed.

He knew what caused her coldness and distress, of course. That phone call from the police, so polite and cordial at first. Would Docteur Perrin like to step over to the Police Judiciaire to answer a couple of routine questions?

Walking down the never-ending corridors of the police headquarters on the Quai des Orfèvres with the Seine glinting just outside; how often had he imagined that labyrinthine building in the countless Inspecteur Maigret novels of his adolescence.

'You are an eminent man, Monsieur. So how do I address you? Professeur, Docteur?' Inspecteur Laporte began and Robert-Pierre found himself wondering whether the deference was genuine or a mere put on.

'Oh, either will do,' he said, although personally, he far preferred Professeur.

'Let's see. You qualified as a doctor in 1971, then specialised in psychiatry. So what were you doing in '68, manning the barricades?'

'Something like that,' Robert-Pierre found himself relaxing.

'Whereas I was a stripling of 19 on my first assignment, a foot soldier you might say, sent in to quell high class revolutionaries like you,' Laporte's smile was more of a grimace.

'I wasn't high class. My father was a postmaster,' Robert-Pierre protested.

'Yes, but educated. Educated. My father was a mill hand. My mother could barely read. You guys throwing stones were the educated elites. We belonged to the lower orders.'

'But we were fighting for you, for your rights too...'

'Not true, *Docteur*. You were fighting to get access to the girls' dormitories. Not the same thing. But no matter. And now you are *Professeur* and *Chef de service* in Psychiatry at the Hôpital Sainte Anne. That's a very important job. You also have a private practice and patients who are quite well-known. I've seen you on television amongst the talking heads. You're good, really very impressive. It is sad that you should be mixed up in this strange business. So, shall we go over your relationship with the deceased?'

'I am as baffled as you by what happened. There's nothing to tell, really. We are, were, just very good friends,' he said.

'You say you first met Madame de Lorel what, four years ago? We think it was more, certainly more. Would you really describe your friendship with the deceased as "just good friends"?

'Yes, really.'

'Really? She doesn't fit the type does she? I mean most of your other friends are either writers, thanks to your wife, whose books by the way I admire greatly, or members of your profession or academics or ... celebrities. You were never seen in public with Madame de Lorel, were you?'

'No, not really. She didn't enjoy going out.'

'Yes? That's not what we've been told. She was quite a party person, it appears, especially with the fashion crowd. But not with you. Never seen with you. And you are often spotted in the company of women other than your wife. But you were a frequent visitor, were you not, at Madame de Lorel's place? In the afternoons, mainly, sometimes several times a week? Now, let's see, the concierge says you were there as often as two or three times a week. Were those professional house calls or was there something else?'

The questions were courteous but cold, vaguely menacing. He sweated. A lot. It was August, after all. The Inspecteur had soft, doughy hands, surprisingly feminine on one so burly, and they rested casually on Kranti's notebooks, which were sealed in transparent plastic with a label bearing an official stamp.

Robert-Pierre tried to maintain an outward calm. 'I did know Madame de Lorel quite well. We were good friends. There was a relationship once, but it ended a long time ago,' he said.

The Inspecteur shuffled some papers in a pink folder. 'Is that so? Then why would someone leave all her possessions to "a good friend", not to her family, or to a lover? Perhaps you could explain this entry in Madame de Lorel's diary dated 15

November 2006: *"Venice again with 'R'. I have him all to myself for four glorious days. Sleeping cuddled up against his warmth. Bliss,"* Laporte read aloud. 'That was not even a year ago. The "R" is you, I presume? There are many other entries of a similar nature. Really, why do women keep diaries?' he said.

Robert-Pierre winced, remembering that passage.

Kranti had read it out to him just before they went to bed, lulled by the songs of gondoliers and the lapping of the lagoon. He had felt flattered but also embarrassed at the thought of a fifty-year-old woman making teenage confessions of puppy love.

The inspector studiedly consulted some notes. 'And the deceased figures on your patient list. Her name is in your appointment book. Now, let me think, when was that? When you first met? You know having sex with a patient could cost you your career if it becomes known?'

And the bank statements Inspecteur Laporte was so deliberately turning over were his, Robert-Pierre saw. They must list the hotel payments in Venice. How have they obtained those? But that means they've found out I haven't declared all my income to the tax guys. I might have to go to jail, he thought, frantically going over the list of clients who payed in cash and whose names never appeared in his official appointment book. They have that too, and Kranti's name is in it. They have the dates, they've put two and two together.

He stopped pretending. They knew everything, so why bother to deny it? But his admission that he was Kranti's lover did not put an end to the questions. If at all, the interrogation became tougher, repetitive. On and on went Inspecteur Laporte, now cajoling, now conspiratorial. And if there was ever a threat in his voice, it was so quickly veiled that Robert-Pierre wondered if he'd imagined it.

How long had he known Madame de Lorel? Had *Monsieur, pardonnez-moi, Professeur Perrin*, ever prescribed her sleeping pills or any other drug she could have used? Why had she willed him her property? Was he aware of the will? Did he know that he would be her sole heir? Had he seen her will? Was she depressed? Did he know the name of the substance she had taken or how she could have procured it? What was the state of his finances? Was he in debt? When was the last time he had met Madame de Lorel? What was he doing the night before she died? Did Madame Perrin know of his illicit liaison?

Slowly, with increasing dread, he understood what was happening. He was their chief suspect. Kranti's death, they believed, was not an innocent suicide, it could be murder. And what better assassin than a fully qualified psychiatrist who could legally prescribe a basketful of deadly drugs to a fragile, suggestible and lonely woman? In a rising panic he realized they would speak to Sophie, check his story out with her.

'Do you gamble? Does your wife know of your affairs? Are you in need of money?' Inspecteur Laporte rapped out again.

'I am in need of a lawyer,' Robert-Pierre said.

'You can call one if you like. You're here not as an assisted witness, just someone helping us with our enquiry. But go ahead if that's what you want,' Laporte said, pushing the telephone forward.

Robert-Pierre hesitated. He could of course call Alain, but he was essentially Sophie's family lawyer and could not be trusted or even expected to keep silent on a matter as serious and sordid as this. The only other lawyers he knew were patients of his and that was entirely out of the question.

So he submitted meekly to Laporte's questions. They returned, each time, to the same essential point – Was Kranti depressed? Had he manipulated her, drugged her, encouraged or pushed her to do what she did? In short, was he a party, an accomplice to the crime, if crime there was one.

They can't pin anything on me. There's no evidence, he tried to reassure himself. And yet the feeling of fear persisted, even after the questioning stopped. What lay hidden between the covers of Kranti's diary, he had wondered. And yet, months later, with the notebook now in his possession, he had not dared open it.

And here he was, back at the flat, alone again, like a murderer returning to the scene of crime. He had dumped everything returned by the police in one big, messy pile by the side of the door. The small pouch containing her watch, gold chain and earrings was nowhere in sight and the bunch of letters the inspector had waved tantalizingly under his nose also appeared to have vanished, but the notebooks she had left him were stacked in a small, neat pile on the coffee table.

Made of thick, ruled, margin-less paper, they were identical except for their different-coloured leather covers which bore the address of an obscure stationer's in Venice. Their edges tooled in gold, they were claret red, moss green, navy blue and black.

He remembers Kranti, emerging triumphant, eyes sparkling, laden with packets from the untidy shop in a lane behind the Fenice, just before its destruction and resurrection. It was a bright December day, the trip to Venice his present for her fiftieth birthday.

'This is exactly what I've been looking for. I'll be able to start writing now. This is what will help me write. I never thought I'd be so happy on my birthday. But doors are opening, not closing.'

'You need patience and determination to write, not fancy stationery,' he'd laughed.

'It's important to have everything just so. I can't write on foolscap or in ordinary notepads. The paper has to be special, the pens too. "*Pour écrire il me faut du satin jaune*" – so, it's yellow satin or nothing,' she said, quoting Oscar Wilde.

Of course she'd bought the notebooks; also, funny-shaped bottles of blue-green and black ink, delicate Venetian quills made of multi-coloured hand-blown glass, pads of onionskin, thick ivory letter paper with lined envelopes. But for a long time after the frenzied shopping spree, writing continued to elude her. He teased her so much, she stopped telling him how far she'd got.

He found himself caressing the smooth leather, slowly turning the pages. Only two of the notebooks were filled – the red and the black. The red contained an annotated and lavishly illustrated manuscript he presumed was for children. It showed two little girls, sisters from the look of it, playing together in a grand old house set in a garden dense with foliage and a sunburst of flowers. The unfinished story petered out into a kind of scrapbook with notes, newspaper clippings, random jottings and some lovingly rendered, extremely detailed watercolours of exotic plants.

The black notebook contained no drawings, just hundreds of lines of closely written text, mostly in her trademark blue-green ink, with long passages in bold black and sepia. In death as in life, she was brassy, overstated, clamouring for attention, shouting out her existence. And these dead pages of prose bore testimony to that.

He knew Kranti had been trying to write. But she'd been secretive about it of late and he had assumed she'd dropped the foolish idea. Subconsciously competing with Sophie, he'd thought with a snort. He hadn't realized she'd written so much. It was days before he could bring himself to even flick through the red notebook, the one without the personal pronouns. He had read the first few pages of the so-called novel, and found himself lingering over the water colours.

It was a simple, even simplistic narrative, told from a child's perspective, the story of Kranti and her sister Shanti. Very obviously autobiographical.

What struck Robert-Pierre most was not the tone of wonderment or the strong sense of place her writing evoked, but the numinous quality of the sketches that seemed to dance off the page. Her touch was light and assured, her palette made the girls come alive as they played amid banks of flaming orange blooms. The colours were Kranti's hallmark hues; he would have recognized the drawings anywhere. She could have become a very successful book illustrator, had she tried. God, what a waste, he thought.

There were other pictures. Some, capturing a family drama in progress, where the girls bore expressions of fear or sorrow, as did their extraordinarily beautiful mother, while others displayed a wild exuberance, celebrating, it seemed to him, the very essence of life. How strange then, that a woman who could produce so much joy and beauty on a page could also kill herself deliberately, vengefully.

The black diary, the most painful part of her legacy, he had been unable to touch. He could not deal with the 'I' factor just yet.

'Why did you not tell me? Would it have hurt to give me a hint?' he said aloud, addressing the ivory negress, the anger snaking up from his stomach where it had lain coiled tight these past weeks.

All his knowledge, his training and decades of experience as a practicing psychiatrist had been of no use. She had pulled the rug from under his feet with a ruthless finality that had sent him hurtling into an abyss. He felt inept. Emasculated.

The embassy had contacted Mrs Shanti Aiyer, Kranti's sister and only immediate relative, about repatriating the body. The return message had surprised, even offended Mr Sharma, the Indian consular officer. Mrs Aiyer was saddened and shocked by the news but was unable to meet travel or repatriation expenses. So could the embassy arrange a local cremation?

'What sort of a family is this?' Mr Sharma frowned, nodding his head. 'If it had been my sister I would have taken out a loan to meet the expenses. But these modern westernized families, they don't care for traditional values. So this unpleasant task now falls to you, since you are the legal heir. Ms Goray's former husband does not want to handle the formalities. Let the legal heir do all that, he said. But he will attend the funeral, it seems. So now it is up to you. The embassy has dealt with the demise of Indian nationals before. If you like, I can give you the procedures to follow.'

Robert-Pierre had done what Mr Sharma, with his superior experience in these matters, had advised. It took him back to the funeral of his father in the tiny hamlet outside Rouen. The rough-hewn village church full to overflowing, his own voice, so tight with tears, reading out the eulogy, his mother beside him, the genuine sorrow of neighbours and friends at the passing of an ordinary, upright man. And the sheer physical effort it took to lower the coffin into the grave. He never thought his father's small, shrunken body could weigh so much. He recalled his muscles, strained, knotted and stiff. But it was something he had wanted to do for a father who had appeared remote but was, in fact, very much a part of his being. This was altogether different.

He'd sent Kranti's sister a long letter of condolence along with copies of the will and the police certificate, which listed the cause of death as *suicide*. The will, written in English and French, had been witnessed and signed by her lawyer and his clerk and named Robert-Pierre as the beneficiary.

He thought of the sister now, wondering how long he could put off calling her. 'Is this your guru? I've seen posters of her all around town,' he'd asked Kranti once, pointing to the photograph of a large, traditionally dressed woman stuck on the notice-board in her office.

'I don't have a guru,' she'd laughed, 'and this is not the famous Jyotika Amma, that you're thinking of. This is a picture of my sister, Shanti. When we were children I had to call her Tai, or elder sister. Everything rhymed and chimed together for us as children. She was Shanti. I was Kranti. We wore identical frocks, shoes, hairstyles and people took us for twins practically into our teens. She does look a bit like that overfed Amma, the so-called Singing Saint, now that you mention it. I don't believe in such people; charlatans all, I say. But my sister does. She married someone from a very traditional, religious family and observes all the fasts and rituals.'

With a resigned sigh, Robert-Pierre sat down on Kranti's – now his – cherry-red velvet sofa and dialled a number written on a blue post-it stuck to the side of the telephone.

'Ah, *les colonisés*,' he mumbled, startled by the ring-ring sound from the receiver.

'Hello,' a male voice answered.

'*Allo*, can I speak with Madame Aiyer? I am calling from Paris please,' he said.

Without replying, the unseen man, Madame Aiyer's husband he presumed, began calling, 'Shanti ... Shanti...'

An answering shout was followed by the sound of approaching feet, then clunky noises of the telephone changing hands, before a slightly breathless voice said, 'Hello, Shanti Aiyer here.' The connection was excellent, without the usual long-distance hum. Mrs Aiyer sounded as if she were speaking from the flat next door.

'My name is Robert-Pierre. I am calling from Paris.'

'Oh, hello. Thank god you called. We were wondering how to get in touch with you since there was no address. We got your letter after the embassy had contacted us. I hope you got ours, sent care of the Indian mission?'

'I got it. Thank you for your sentiments.'

'That was the best we could do. I wanted to come. But it's so expensive and then we thought, what was the point? Better to get the ashes, in order to immerse them. Then we can have the final ceremonies here. It's been a terrible shock as you can imagine; such horrible news. My poor sister. What happened? Can you tell me what happened?'

Except for her accent, which was thick and Indian, her voice was remarkably similar to Kranti's. She spoke in a curious sing-song, and Robert-Pierre tried to visualize the broad face in Kranti's study – the forehead dominated by a huge vermilion mark, the colour of her sari, the podgy upper arms, as they emerged like a pair of fat sausages from the tight confines of her short-sleeved blouse.

'I think it was depression... I am very sorry.' Robert-Pierre found his English suddenly deserting him.

'It's so difficult for us to believe. She was the most fun-loving person in the world. I've never seen her depressed. What did she do, how did it happen?'

'*Empoisonée* ... she took ... *comprimés*, for sleep,' Robert-Pierre struggled.

'You mean tablets? Sleeping tablets? Oh.' A pause. 'Where is she now? I mean, what have you done with the body? I hope it's not lying in some morgue somewhere.'

'She was ... *incinéré* ... by burning. Do you want ashes? I have ashes...'

'That was going to be my next question. So you have kept the ashes. But they shouldn't just be kept like that. There are rituals to be followed ...We are Hindus, you know, so the ashes must be immersed in the Ganges. Can you not at least bring the ashes here so I can give my sister a decent farewell?' Shanti's voice had suddenly acquired an edge.

'She did not want. Kranti did not want *cérémonie religieuse*. It was how she wanted, very simple.'

'That's all very well, but you see, we believe that her soul will have no peace unless her ashes join the Ganges,' Shanti Aiyer said slowly but firmly. 'Why don't you bring the ashes here so we can get the ceremonies performed? Then Kranti can finally be at peace?'

'I don't think, it is not possible,' Robert-Pierre began cautiously. 'I have much to do. It is very difficult. Maybe later.'

'Your letter did not really say who you are. I mean, what was your relationship with her? You see, we don't know anything. I have to be frank with you. For the last several years, we did not have much contact. My sister, as you know, was a very independent woman and we tried not to interfere in her life. We are simple people and sometimes it was difficult for us here in India to understand what was going on. For a family like ours it was embarrassing. The divorces, the liaisons, each time a new man with her.'

'I understand, I think ...' Robert-Pierre said, but Mrs Aiyer was merely drawing breath.

'It is hard in our society. We have to think of neighbours and friends. So we tried to keep away as much as possible. But that said, she was my sister and I loved her. Your letter said nice things about her, but it gave no details about how it happened or your relationship. We could not understand the death certificate – it's in French. But the will is quite clear.'

'Yes,' Robert-Pierre said.

'And you're the sole heir. I understand she left behind a lot of property. Those paintings alone are worth a fortune, I notice. I find it all rather strange...'

'You think something is wrong? You think something not okay...?'

'All I am saying is that she was a very jolly person, very fond of her nieces, especially my elder daughter. It's strange she should have left her nothing. She always treated her like her own little girl. That is all I am saying. Are you sure you cannot come here with the ashes, then we could talk about all these things?'

'Yes.'

'Yes what?'

'I will try. Is not possible for the moment. I have much work. But later...'

'Well, I suppose I should have expected this. You are all like that. Our religious feelings mean nothing to you and why should they? Why would you want to come? What do you care if my sister's soul never finds rest, if her family is deprived of what is rightfully theirs...'

'But I am caring. I am caring deeply.'

'Do you? Do you really? I must say I am hurt. Not for myself, I don't want anything for myself, but I am upset about the way my daughters have been treated. Don't you have a Napoleonic code or something? She was telling me about it. One cannot be disinherited in France.'

'That is correct for the children, but there are no direct *héritiers*. You know she made a testament which has signature of the lawyer and his assistant.'

'Yes, but there is something called moral obligation, isn't there? At least, so far as her remains are concerned? It is not so much the property that I am talking about. You will be hearing from us. At least do something about the ashes...'

'I will try. Yes, of course we can discuss... I am sorry I have to go. But we can discuss...'

'What is there to discuss, really? You only have to fly over...'

Robert-Pierre could hear the voice continue, torrential, unchecked, as he quietly cut in to say goodbye and replaced the receiver with fingers that shook.

'And you, blind fool, why did you not see? *Quel con, mais quel con!*' he savaged himself, articulating for the first time, the question that had tormented him from the moment he'd entered the bedroom. Forced himself to see the blue-black face, made blacker still by the swarm of busily feeding flies.

It smells just like the lion's cage at that country circus she took me to near Bombay, the thought had gone through his head. A wet, mangy lion lying on its side by a hunk of water-logged, rotting meat, emitting a roar more piteous than frightening as the monsoon rain lashed its flanks through the rusty iron bars of its cage.

Or like that time in Africa when he had travelled to the Great Lakes region as a volunteer psychiatrist to help victims of the Rwandan massacres. A river clogged tight with bodies, thousands of naked cadavers lapping its banks like a giant black wave. Up and down, up and down, bobbing gently – closely-knit clumps of putrid human hyacinth. The living were the real dead, he'd discovered, numbed by terror, carrying the silence of the massacred in hearts turned to stone. They had no need for his advice, his solicitude, his doctor's bag of magic pills.

There was no getting away from the stench. It was in his hair, on his tongue, his teeth, his brain, and no amount of bathing, scrubbing or changing of clothes could erase it. Finally, in his hotel room, he had called for a large bowl of crushed ice, and emptying his bottle of Azzaro aftershave, plunged his head into the stinging, icy chips, drawing the artificial fumes into his nose and mouth, pressing down with cheeks and chin until his eyes burned and his face felt wooden with cold. He'd bullied his way onto the next flight home.

He could see that lion's cage now, as clearly as he could the undulating bodies, the translucent, black-tipped maggots dancing on the purple satin of her dress, that ridiculous wig, the bloated face, the Madonna smile under layers of caked foundation – oil sludge fouling a tranquil beach. The images superimposed, yet separate, clearly visible, like a grotesque computer collage. And that odour, sick, sweet and rotten. He was that lion now, wounded and whimpering, with a stench up his nose that no amount of cologne could banish.

And then, nothing. No letter. No explanation. Just the will, the red notebook with its unfinished novel, its illustrations and clippings and the black diary that he hadn't dared read. Despair? *Ah non*, his trained psychiatrist's mind rejected that immediately. Not an impulsive gesture but a planned *mise en scène*, ritualistic, meticulously prepared. Revenge? Punishment? Only the diary could tell him that now.

It was not a quiet death. Not a quiet death at all, thought Robert-Pierre, with a shake of his head, and he felt a mixture of love, pity and anger welling up in sudden salty tears.

He saw her now, with her galaxy of writing instruments, a few of them outrageously expensive, performing the rituals of mixing inks, filling pens, wiping the nibs carefully with a stained georgette rag that was once powder blue. Oddly-shaped hands with their dwarf-like little fingers, the left wrist encircled by three tight silver bracelets she claimed had once belonged to the ten-year-old slave mistress of an Ethiopian warlord.

Their first meeting couldn't have been more banal – a reception at the ministry of culture in honour of a visiting Indian dance troupe. A gasp and a giggle next to him, both immediately suppressed, made him turn. Around the corner from where they stood, the legendary bosom of the French culture minister was making its appearance before the rest of her came into view.

'O *mon Dieu!*' he exclaimed as they both watched the majestic advance of Catherine Gentille's monumental breasts. The culture minister's snowy peaks, proudly revealed by a plunging décolleté, jiggled and shook.

'Like blancmange,' Kranti said, her eyes bright with malice.

'Blancmange? You mean blancmanger, *sûrement*?'

'Is that what it's called in French? I've never seen the stuff. But I think of it as something wobbly, like jelly.'

They watched Ms Gentille's advance with shared amusement. 'I can't bear this woman's books though; too pretentious, too much pseudo-philosophical showing off. All fluff, no substance.

And she pretends to know India, but makes stupid mistakes, especially in the iconography. And then there's this thing about French intellectuals that gets me – I find them verbose, laboured and often, quite honestly, ridiculous!'

'You are so Anglo-Saxon,' he said. 'But one day you will understand the French and then you will know we're not quite so bad, so *ridicule*.'

'What do you do?' she asked.

'I'm a psychiatrist,' he said. 'And you?'

'Oh, this and that. I make sketches for a fashion magazine. I dabble in paint. I read, curled up in bed mainly.'

'You must spend a lot of time on your back then?'

'Side, on my side, like a foetus,' she said, studying his card. 'Robert-Pierre. It's unusual, isn't it, in France? I mean, I've known Jean-Pierres, Jean-Claudes and I've even met a Jean-Charles...'

On your back or on your side? he thought, his eyes scouring the deep V of her blouse beneath the flimsy veil of chiffon.

'... but never a Robert-Pierre.'

'True,' he smiled. 'My mother studied the French Revolution and she was a great admirer of Robespierre. But, of course, she couldn't possibly name her son after such a discredited historical figure. So she made up the slightly odd but perfectly acceptable Robert-Pierre.'

'And do you admire your bloodthirsty namesake?'

'It must have had some effect. I was a Maoist in my twenties.' He lunged at a passing waiter's tray, grabbed two glasses of champagne, handed her one.

'Strange,' she said, taking it absently. 'My father was a communist. Of the armchair variety. And guess what my name, Kranti, really means? It's Hindi and Marathi for "revolution".

Isn't that funny? In fact, he named my sister Shanti, which means "peace", and so he could introduce his two children saying: "Here are my daughters, Peace and Revolution", or something like that! He'd read practically all there was on Marxism and you couldn't argue with him about communism – you couldn't challenge him about the invasion of Prague say, or Hungary. He'd bark: "Have you read Anti-During? Don't talk to me if you haven't." And there the argument ended. Most frustrating.' She sipped tentatively, made a face.

'And have you?'

'Still not!' She laughed.

'And what does he say now?'

'He died in 1989. Before I got a chance to say "I told you so", just as the Berlin Wall was beginning to tremble and shake. But it wouldn't have mattered. We'd stopped talking to each other long before that. Have you read the *Livre noir du communisme?*'

'The one that chronicles communist atrocities? I have. The research is remarkable but I disagree with the editor's premise that communism and fascism were more or less the same.'

'So do you have a lot of wealthy suburban housewives gracing your couch in the afternoons?' she asked.

The suddenness of her attack surprised him. He detected an unexpected vein of bitterness in her and felt his defences rise at the prospect of yet another life story pouring into his reluctant ears.

'What do you think?' he parried.

She gave him an appraising look. 'I'm sure you do. But to be fair, I'm also sure you get rid of the idle and the vain in the space of a session and a half. I can't see you extending much sympathy to self-indulgent, empty-headed women whose only problem is a surfeit of time and money.'

'Why do you assume suburban housewives in France are idle and rich?' he said, suddenly passionate. 'That's an image borrowed from America. In France, when you have money, you try to live in the heart of the city, whether Paris or elsewhere, not in suburbia. Also, why do you assume the women are the worst offenders? I've come across far more ignorant and bigoted men than I have women. But you're right. I try to keep my idle, rich patients to a minimum. Where you're wrong is about the suburbs and small towns. It's not just a case of ennui and what accompanies it, but also what that ennui produces. I go every Thursday to Versailles and spend an afternoon a week in Mantes-la-jolie, a "difficult" suburb. That's where most of my clinically challenging cases come from, not my Parisian practice. There's unimaginable ferment out there – as much in bourgeois Versailles as in working-class Mantes. Incest, rape, drugs, crime, racism, social failure. I've seen it all.'

The avalanche of words appeared to take her breath away. She looked at him with wide-open eyes, as if mesmerized. The whites had a bluish tinge.

'I'm sorry. I didn't mean to put you on the defensive. What's your connection to India?' She asked.

'None. I happen to be friends with someone in the ministry. I should be saying hello.'

Some of her easy self-assurance had evaporated then. She put down her half-finished glass of champagne on a nearby table and made her excuses. Once or twice, during the evening, he spotted her green and blue chiffon sari weaving through the crowds, but she had not glanced his way again. That night, he looked her up in the phone book. But neither of them attempted to make contact.

4

An Oriental Odour Tinged with Spices

Yes, she had consulted him, and yes, he had transgressed.

'For the first and only time in my professional life,' he had confessed to Inspector Laporte. 'I cannot explain what happened. I had no control over it. I was not thinking rationally. In my defence, she did not remain my patient for long. I stopped the sessions immediately.'

'Only to continue the other stuff, eh?'

'I was not violating professional ethics then!'

'That is not the point. You broke your code, your doctor's oath. You slept with a patient and later you continued to have an affair with her in order to keep a hold over her psyche. How do we know you did not push her to do this?'

'But the sessions lasted barely a week. Then I put a stop to it. I did not meet Madame de Lorel for weeks after that, until she invited me to her house for a dinner party, which I attended as a friend. We became lovers much later. But there was an interval when I did not see her at all! Besides, our relationship lasted several years. If I wished to push her to suicide, why would I wait so long?'

Sitting in Kranti's drawing room, Robert-Pierre relived the feeling of uncontrollable lust that had overtaken him at the sight of the elegant figure in the tight-fitting Alaïa suit sitting demurely in his outer office.

A waft of vaguely familiar perfume. The same one that Sophie wore. But on this dark- haired woman it smelt different. He'd never dealt with an Indian before; a few Germans, an Italian or two, but the vast majority of his patients were French.

She was certainly not the person he'd been expecting and he had no way of knowing that the Madame de Lorel pencilled into his diary would turn out to be not an ageing, be-ringed French artistocrat but the Indian woman he had met at that cocktail. Her card simply said Kranti Goray. Where did the Lorel name come from? And was there any connection to the family of Guillaume de Lorel? What did she want, why was she here? He could not deny the sexual undercurrents already swirling aroud them. 'Do come in and take a seat,' he said, leading her in to his consulting room and pointing to the patient's chair. He struggled to remain professional.

'I shall need your details of course, date of birth, address, medical history, especially if there is any history of mental illness in the family. We do not start the analysis straight away. Initially we sit face to face, in conversation, if you see what I mean, until we come to an understanding of what we are going to do together. I shall need to know why you decided to consult ... is it something you have been contemplating for a while or was it a spur of the moment decision because you ran into me?'

'How often will we have to meet?'

'Twice a week initially. Perhaps more later, when you are on the couch.'

But it had proved impossible to keep up the professional façade. The air between them was electric, incandescent with lust. Her responses to his questions were laconic. 'I have issues with my mother. I treated her badly when she was alive. I do not sleep well and I cannot paint. All I do is make fashion sketches.'

'How wrong she was,' Robert-Pierre thought, recalling the vivid sketches in the red notebook.

It was not for a consultation that she had sought an appointment. That became clear soon enough. Her invitation was blatant and the boldness of her approach acted as an aphrodisiac. By the second session, he understood she had no serious desire to delve into her past, examine the demons that plagued her, at least not with him.

Professionally speaking, they were getting nowhere. The sexual tension between them was like a stretched guitar string. A greater force had pulled him to his feet, made him draw her up from the chair facing his. He ran a tentative finger down her cheek, waiting for a response. When it came, it belied all expectations.

Their coupling was frenzied, animal. He drank in her smell, a rich, oriental odour tinged with spices. Even the sweat that poured out of her armpits had that un-French, foreign smell. In wonder and trepidation, he stroked her long cinnamon shanks. Could this really be happening to him? What did this strange, sexy woman really want? He cancelled his appointments and for a week they made love on his consulting couch, furiously, as if each time would be their last.

Sanity returned after that week of ferment. He wore his best three-piece suit to their session, the waistcoat buttoned up, the tie in place, covered up like a priest, he thought.

His gaze was fixed on the square of blotting paper on his desk. 'This has to stop. You know I have breached professional ethics. I cannot take you on as a patient. I have never done this before and I have no intention of it ever happening again. I must apologize, it's my fault entirely. I can give you the name of an excellent colleague who could work with you,' he said. He could not meet her eyes, but concentrated instead on writing his referral.

She had spoken little during that week. Even during their frantic lovemaking on his couch, passionate and panting, she had made little noise.

'I understand perfectly,' she said, much to his surprise. 'It must be very difficult for you. Perhaps we could meet otherwise, as friends.'

He shook his head.

Her chutzpah staggered him. He had geared himself for protest, perhaps a few tears. Her poise and control were startling. She took her referral and left. Although he was tempted to phone her several times, he bit back his desire and waited. Two can play the game, he thought.

After a decent interval, she called to invite him to dinner. Her voice was friendly and warm without a hint of what had transpired between them. Starting on a clean slate, as if nothing has happened, he thought.

An ambassador, a banker and his rather boring wife who claimed to paint, a retired American columnist who regaled them with stories of Nehru in Indonesia – a small, studied party of eight. He'd asked his secretary to inform her he'd be coming alone and it turned out, whether by design or accident, that he was the only 'unattached' male to her female. He'd lingered deliberately after dinner, angling for some of the fine cognac he had spotted among the bottles.

She wore an embroidered sari in heavy biscuit coloured silk, with dangly earrings that made her face look small and oddly compact, feline in its concentration. Once the kitchen help had left, she kicked off her shoes to settle back sideways on the long red sofa, her knees rising up like pyramids beside him.

'That was nice, wasn't it? Although I always wonder if it's worth the effort,' she said.

Between sips of cognac, he began rubbing her feet, congratulating her on the meal, the excellence of her Indian-style lamb chops. She'd opened up an entirely new culinary universe to him, he said, allowing his fingers to travel under her sari, over her knees and up her thighs.

She sat there serene, giving him a quiet lecture on Indian spices, not a hint of tensing in her muscles, a little smile playing about her lips as she spoke.

His exploring hand jerked back, scorched. Instead of the usual barrier of silk and lace, his fingers had encountered a tussock of wiry pubic hair. '*Mais, qu'est ce que c'est que ça?*' he asked, his glasses at an angle.

She sat up laughing, her eyes like bits of darkened glass and he hid his confusion as best he could, his face a comical slew of questions.

'It isn't as if modern Indian women don't wear underclothes. But traditionally, under the sari, at least in the villages, women don't wear panties. That's a European invention. So when I wear saris, I don't. It's much easier when you live in India to just lift up your skirts to pee. Or do other things,' she said, giving him a conspiratorial grin.

A surge of desire shot through him. Once again, the absence of prudishness or shame both shocked and excited him. Where did it come from? Weren't Indian women supposed to be demure and submissive? Not brazen, not bold, like this, as if she were the man and he the woman.

He did not go home that night but spent it tangled in her white linen sheets. The next day, he gave her a lingering kiss at this very front door he was now facing, promising to call her again soon.

If only I could understand what led her to it. What despair, what anguish did she keep bottled up inside? What lay behind that gay, mocking façade that treated life like an elaborate joke? 'We're all players in a farce, that's what life is, a farce', she'd said once.

Robert-Pierre's professional brain took over. He knew she hungered to belong to his other self, the sphere of ideas he inhabited, envying his familiarity, even friendship with Derrida, Bourdieu, Foucault, Latour and other French intellectuals, his editorship of an avant-garde psychology magazine that gave him a ringside seat at every major ideological debate in the country, his eminent position at the hospital. It was his world, of concepts and abstractions, books and 'the intellect' that fascinated her, held her in its thrall. But it was a side of him that belonged to Sophie. She knew that. He had made it clear at the outset, and snob that he had become, he had kept Kranti out of his public life, savouring her privately in their small hidden world.

There had been some terribly shabby moments in her life, he knew, hurts not easily forgotten. Making a splash in Parisian society had appeared easy at first, she'd told him on one of those rare days when talk of her past life was permitted. 'I used the Lorel connections to the hilt,' she said with a hoot of laughter, as if it had all been a gloriously wicked prank. With her name listed next to Guillaume's in the *Bottin mondain*, the

French equivalent of *Debrett's Peerage*, she had revelled in her new-found status of Madame la comtesse, her entry further eased by Guillaume's cousin, a top model who graciously allowed the use of her name. She would never be fully accepted by the upper echelons of France's rigid aristocracy or its fabulously wealthy and utterly mannered haute bourgeoisie, but the fashion world with its fads and fantasies, its worship of the exotic had embraced her, if only for a moment. 'Its love could but be transitory, such is its nature,' she shrugged.

Forever on the lookout for fresh icons to place on a pedestal, the better to pull them down, the Paris demi-monde had feted *la comtesse indienne* for her style and beauty, featured her in *Elle*, *Marie Claire*, *Madame Figaro*, then taken her apart, bit by bit, lovingly, as if peeling an onion, baring her life to its core, especially after it became known that she and Guillaume were no longer together. The very people who had appeared so kind, so *enchanté* by her *joli* French accent, were mocking her gaucherie, cutting her dead. Within the space of a few months she had become passé, a has-been, to be pitied perhaps, but not really worth a second glance.

'I don't care any more. I did once. But Guillaume was essentially my passport to the West. I wonder sometimes if I ever really loved him. I know I desperately tried to convince myself that I did. I played the good wife who received his political friends and gave perfect dinners for over a decade. If that isn't devotion, what is? But when I look back, it was a marriage of convenience – mine,' she laughed.

He'd been taken aback by her candour, her hardnosed pragmatism. So she was just an economic *immigré*. She used her charms to snare an unsuspecting man – and not any man. Someone from the *crème de la crème*! The thought, quickly suppressed, had gone through his head. But he'd marvelled nevertheless at her insouciance, her nonchalance.

As the sheen of her love affair with the French fashion world wore off, she withdrew, emerging slowly from her isolation to become a freelance consultant with a couple of fashion houses. With their India-inspired lines doing remarkably well, she earned good money, working with noble fabrics, rich silks and brocades, intricate hand embroidery. Her meticulous artwork, executed with strong fluid strokes, won high praise and she was much in demand, but her heart was no longer in it. Fashion had become mere commercial art, a means to earn her bread and butter, especially after her break-up with Guillaume.

'They shrugged me off, so I shrugged them off. That's all there is to it,' she said dryly when he tried to question her further and he left well enough alone, happy not to get sucked into a discussion of her *état d'âme*.

In those early idyllic days, he would call her at odd hours, seized by a sudden desire for her taste, her smell, anticipating the hot, humid response his hands and lips would elicit. Often he would find her lost in books on Indian art and sculpture, well-thumbed tomes that gave details of temple bas reliefs and traditional motifs. Her knowledge of fabrics, of weaving and printing techniques and the history of apparel won his respect. But so convinced was she of doing 'commercial stuff' that she brushed off his praise, accusing him of humouring her, calling his admiration false, insincere at best.

And although he knew her to be deeply troubled, he could never persuade her to drop her guard. Not that he really tried. She ground her teeth and cried in her sleep, he'd noticed, the first time they went away together for a weekend. But to be honest, he hadn't probed enough. He got too much of that sort of thing in his practice. And she had appeared game for a deeply physical but emotionally distant, lighthearted affair, at least in the beginning.

And then, wham! She had knocked him out of his condescending superiority, turning the tables with the reckless folly of her act. Was it all for nothing, just the Freudian death wish in spate, leaving chaos and destruction in its wake, or was she there somewhere, jeering at his discomfiture from on high?

Appalled by what he saw as his own egotism, his inability to see beyond his immediate concerns, he grew desperate to know more. He wanted to shake her until her teeth rattled in her head, make her talk, spit it out. A sickness gripped him. Kranti was gone. He could never see, touch or feel her again. A handful of ashes was all that was left. Perhaps the black diary would help him get behind the mask. I hope it isn't a boring list of what she ate, what time she rose or slept and the people she saw, he thought.

5

The Black Notebook

Paris

16 November 2005

I wonder what R will feel if he ever reads this. Betrayed, surely, when he understands I have been cohorting with the enemy. But hasn't he only himself to blame? I have joined the enemy camp and I must say, the satisfaction is great.

Sometimes I hate R. I hate him because I love him and he does not love me back. I wonder if he will ever be capable of real love.

Pierre Keller. I picked him because of his voice, his name and because of the way he argued with R on that televised debate, giving as good as he got. He could become my Pierre...

Sophie calls him Pierre whereas I am stuck with Robert... 'Sophie is the only one who calls me Pierre. You are both so different, so call me Robert,' he said.

Well, one day Keller could become my Pierre. His voice has that gorgeous, deep, sonorous timbre. No contempt or scorn for the lower orders. Sheer empathy. Lovely shock of grey-black hair, strong, leonine face. Nice waiting room – all paintings and wood panelling. Must earn a packet. I could fall for him in a big way if it weren't for the teeth. Too yellow, too long. Gum trouble probably. So I guess he will never become my Pierre. Why am I so hung up on teeth and oral hygiene? Lovely thing about R is his smile. It's like a sunburst of light. He has the sweetest, most wonderful mouth. And his eyes truly twinkle.

Terrible first session. I just lay there, stiff as a board, incapable of speech. I'd got the timing all mixed up and turned up a quarter of an hour late. So finally he said: 'Why are you here?' I mumbled something about being unable to sleep and Aayee and R and me. Can't remember now exactly, but I sounded all confused. It came out in a garbled rush and then I went dumb again. That was six months ago and the sessions that followed were more of the same – unable to talk, with tears that flowed unchecked.

I think he began losing patience with me at some point. We were getting nowhere. He had let me take my time and despite that gorgeous encouraging voice, I just couldn't bring myself to talk or if I did, I would 'intellectualise', discuss safe subjects like painting or sculpture or books. Make things so abstract that my feelings were kept strictly at bay. I was also trying to impress him, I think, projecting myself as this charming, elegant, intelligent beauty who so easily straddled two cultures, unconsciously putting him at a disadvantage.

None of that cut any ice with him. One day, he said: 'It seems more than just lack of sleep, don't you think? I need to know about you. Not much, just a few facts.' And as I nodded, still all choked up, he said: 'Can you bring in some photographs, pictures, portraits of your family, your home, your colleagues, of places where you have lived? Your paintings, maybe?'

So I took out all those old snaps. Aayee and Baba's wedding picture where he looks like a professional seducer and she like a scared country goat. And then those early years, in black and white, when Tai and

I were so close, living in each other's heads, the twins they called us. Pix with Guillaume; Italy with Giovanni. Of course I didn't take any photos of R with me. Pierre knows him so well and Sophie and all their smart friends.... I am going to have to keep R's identity secret although I don't know how that's going to be poss. One is not supposed to spin yarns to one's analyst! I'll make R a lawyer or journalist or something like that so I won't be lying exactly, but I shan't tell Pierre he's a psy!

Then Pierre asked me to tell him about my early childhood and again, it was as if I'd been struck dumb although there were a million images rushing through my head. The problem is, when I try to talk about it or write it down, it goes all brown on me, leached of colour... A still, sepia photograph. A dead past. Just dead.

Thank God Pierre speaks such wonderful English. When I blurted out, 'I go off into this brown study', he understood perfectly and didn't miss a step: 'Brown, because of the sorrow?' So gentle.

And I started telling him. Bits here, bits there. Very disjointed. Making no sense. Not to me. Not to him. One moment I was fifteen, the other I was three and a great chasm of brown lay in between. It isn't always like that; only when I try to put those thoughts into words, when I try to reason, to rationalize. Something stops me dead in my tracks, an inner governor or something.

We talked about that too. That terrible break. At fifteen. Aayee falling ill. All that had come before. The happy family stuff. The innocence. How it all shrivelled up. 'It dies when I try to talk of it or put it down on paper...'

'And have you tried to paint?'

'There's no point. I do only commercial stuff. I gave up on the serious business long ago. And when I try, it comes out all wrong.'

'That's not evident from the work you've shown me. But you are holding back. Who is watching over your shoulder as you write or paint, do you think?'

I wanted to turn around and look at him at that point, to see his eyes. He had so startled me. Because I know who constantly looks over my shoulder at all hours, all times, no matter what I do.

So it caught me off balance when Pierre asked me point blank like that. No wonder they say he is the best man in town. I wanted to see his eyes, search his soul. But I only got that divine voice that came to me from behind, from the cavernous depths of his maroon velvet armchair.

'There is a child in you, your small little self, weeping, unconsolable, waiting to be loved and comforted, waiting to be let out. Little Kranti. She is lost and bewildered and you have to help her find herself.'

I broke down at that point, my childhood rushing up to engulf me. And I wept for my tiny, faraway, suppressed self for the first time. I could see this little girl in her daisy-patterned frock. Her misery, her small hurts took over my emotions and I was hurtling back in time. But I saw her as something outside myself, as an objective reality, as if I were a spirit hovering over this rather tragic family of four, a fly on the wall, tracking their every move.

'Write down whatever you can remember,' Pierre said, 'since you find it difficult to articulate it here. If you don't find the words, sketch it in. And we can look at it together.'

'Isn't that a bit unusual, for a patient to write down things for the analyst?'

'There is no "usual" method. Whatever works is good,' he said.

◇

So here I am, finally taking the plunge. The page is not hostile the way it used to be. Is that Pierre's doing? It's even fun to say horrid things about people.

So very different from painting. When I paint, the colours move in me of their own volition, sliding sideways and crosswise, up and down, swirling dizzily, a pulsating gaseous mass verging on panic.

intangible, volatile, unstable. Painting is cathartic and dangerous but not as dangerous as writing, I think. Anyone seeing my work can only guess at the turmoil in my mind or heart. They can never know my thoughts or what caused them.

The very idea of writing paralyzes me. It needs more outright courage, a certain reckless bravado because what you put down are hard words, permanent black, that take on a life and meaning of their own and they are explicit, unlike the confused swirls of colour that can communicate only mutely, instinctively.

How far do I go? How much can I tell him? Will he hate me in the end? Call the police? Declare me mad? Have me institutionalised? Words talk. They are dangerous.

Paris, 20 November 2005

My birthday. As good a day as any to start, I suppose. I am now almost the age Aayee was when she died. Just another year to go. Living, breathing, eating, sleeping. And loving? Sexing, certainly. But loving?

Fifty-three, the moment a woman begins to fade and I dare not count the number of days – those lived or those that remain to be lived. Too many. The chronicle of a life thrown away.

This is another beginning. Or is it? Will this writing down exercise Pierre has imposed on me only add more incoherence to an already incoherent brain? Will I be able to make sense of it?

I feel the burden of remembering. So many different ways of recapturing the past. Sruti and Smriti, the two authoritative sources of Hinduism. That which is heard and that which is remembered. Sruti is revelation; Smriti tradition. They could so easily have been our names. Neutral, philosophical terms without a touch of ritual or unreason. Not quite so neutral, I see now. Revelation. That which is revealed. Would Baba have stood for it?

Instead, they gave us two names each. The first chosen by Baba, the second by Aayee, or so they said, although you could clearly see his tenacious hand, urging, nudging, guiding poor Aayee's choices, even then. Or especially then, when she was a submissive new bride and young mother.

They were lofty names too. Tai was Shanti, or Peace, named after Baba's secret goddess, his mother; the dead grandmother we never knew. Maya – Illusion or Compassion, was her middle name. I became Kranti – Revolution, and Chaya – Shade, Shadow, Reflection.

Aayee would have liked to name us after the goddesses – Saraswati, Parvati or Lakshmi, many-armed celestial creatures that embodied grace, beauty and above all, virtue, especially Saraswati, consort of Bramha, the goddess of music and the arts. But Baba was having none of that. Keep it abstract, secular. No religious nonsense, I can hear him say, picture him now, proudly introducing his two little daughters, Shanti and Kranti, Peace and Revolution. Clever!

I think it was in '68. I was just fifteen, in my first year of college. Aayee always claimed our troubles began when Baba's assistant killed the two-headed snake, the do-mooha, the bi-cephal, outside the garage. I wondered if it had a head at either end or, if, like the mythical Shesh Naag, who bears the world upon its many-splendoured, hydra-head, they were joined together at the neck, fusing into a single long body.

I saw one on television the other day. It was a writhing, glistening rope, which suddenly divided itself into separate heads with two pairs of greedy-beady eyes, and two forked, flickering tongues. Revolting.

I do not remember if Aayee fell ill after or before the snake incident. But I think it must have been after, because she walked to the side door to say goodbye to Baba as he left for the office. It was winter and everyone said the snake had curled up in the garage for warmth. I wasn't physically present when it happened. But I've heard the story so many times that I know it in the tiniest detail.

Baba threw up the rolling shutter and the coiled, two-headed snake fell behind him with a flat, heavy thwack.

Aayee shouted, 'Vijay, Vijay.'

And Thakur Sahib, Baba's minion from Meerut said, 'Don't worry, sir. I will take care.'

He was standing by to roll the shutter down once Baba had backed out the car.

Jack be nimble, Jack be quick ... as a rule, Thakur Sahib was neither. Fear it was that galvanized him and he seized hold of the long sword the mali used to level our very special Calcutta turf and cut the snake into two.

And then into two and again into two.

The head, or heads, with half the body behind them, kept moving. He slashed at it several times, chopping it into many small pieces. Then speared them one by one with the tip of the sword and flung them over the wall into the fern-filled vacant lot next door.

'My legs just straightaway turned into wool,' Aayee said later, massaging her white calves. 'It was a do-mooha, after all. You're not supposed to kill those. It brings bad luck.'

I heard the story from her when I returned from college and I went looking for the snake, intrigued by the two heads. I never found it. Crows and colonies of ants made short work of it, I suppose. I still wonder sometimes if Thakur hacked it in such a way as to vertically split the two heads apart.

Like splicing magnetic tape.

Memory plays tricks with me. I can't seem to get the dates right. Was it summer or winter when Aayee fell ill? When Baba's big boss Murthy visited? February or March probably because they took her away, a month later, on the day of my first-year college exams.

It was the time my best friend and I were jerking to the beat of Nancy Sinatra's These Boots Are Made For Walking *and Petula Clarke's*

Downtown. *The year I bought Pat Boone's* Pearly Shells, *picking it out on my Hawaiian guitar. The year I began masturbating with the guitar rod, delicately licking off the metal-tasting curd that covered it with the tip of my tongue. Alkaline, slightly salty. It tasted good. Not surprising. I was a precocious fifteen and in love with myself.*

We were living in this large corner house in Chandigarh's sector 15. A high wall separated us from the Ramakrishna Mission to the left – you could just about see the tops of the eucalyptus trees that grew in the Mission compound. Only once did I see the inmates – on Diwali night, when they shouted rude remarks at us as we lit candles on the roof. There was darkness all around, not the rooftop fairyland I expected with oil lamps glowing on far-flung terraces. Maybe they were right to have made fun of us, for, with Aayee so confused, we were lighting the candles on the wrong day – one day too early. But this was after the snake had come and gone, calamity come calling at our door; months after we were taken at the flood, our ventures lost.

To the right of the house was an empty plot, full of catkins, congress grass and clumps of devil's trumpet – datura alba, with its malevolent, evil-smelling leaves and white and purple flowers.

Next to the empty plot was the garage with its ugly rolling shutter that made a bone-shattering noise and above it, the cute two-room annexe where Baba's accountant Makhija lived with his fat, mad wife. Mr and Mrs Fat, we called them. The badminton court was laid out in the back garden, next to Aayee's potato patch.

Well, Baba's boss Murthy was on a visit and they, Sourpuss and Motherpuss, as Tai and I secretly took to calling our parents, decided to take him to the Gangotri glacier in the Himalayas. Ambitious. I don't know how far they got (Tai went with them, I stayed behind), but on the return trip Aayee started vomiting.

We didn't have a cook in those days. In a supremely egotistical compliment to our mother, we had asked her to do the cooking. 'You cook so much better than the khansama, Aayee. We are so tired of the sameness of his food', we said. So she slaved away in the kitchen.

I would find her lying on my bed, in my room near the pantry, exhausted, nauseous from the smells of cooking. Their bedroom had been given over to Murthy, who had something against staying in hotels. So there she was, piling on the good food in order to make her husband's boss happy.

She had placed a white, blue-ringed enamel basin under the bed and she would heave into it every now and then. Aayee's vomit pail, I called it. I liked the word pail. It made me think of the Swiss Alps. Cowbells and sleighbells, chocolate and milkmaids with kerchiefs tied under their chins. Travelling around with us, from house to house, city to city, hospital to nursing home, that basin was to become one of the leitmotifs of my mother's illness, of our shattered, scattered lives.

Funnily, no one seemed to care that much about how she felt. Tai and I were in college all day. Sourpuss was at work, or so he claimed. When we returned, Tai almost immediately locked herself into her room, which overlooked the empty plot and the front lawn. She even had her own separate entrance from the verandah.

Murthy left after a few days and Aayee went back to her room but her bouts of vomiting only worsened. She had stopped eating completely. It was only then that the question of a doctor was raised.

But in true nomadic fashion, we had no family doctor. It was always scorched earth policy with Baba. All those transfers, change of house, friends, school, university, like animals fleeing from ground grown too hot for comfort.

It was Aayee's architect brother Nana and his wife Saraswati Aunty who suggested calling in a Sikh gynaecologist called Mrs Kaur. I was there when she examined Aayee one morning. Aayee had grown so thin by then she could hardly sit up in bed. Mrs Kaur looked at us as if we were uncouth savages. 'This looks like hepatitis to me. Better get her to hospital fast,' was all she said. But I knew what she was thinking. How come you haven't bothered to get this poor woman medical attention? And that was how Nana uncle spoke to his pal in the Post-Graduate Institute of Medical Sciences and called the hospital for an ambulance.

It was about 11 a.m. when Aayee was loaded on to the ugly white van, more of a dog catcher's truck with iron bars than an ambulance, and taken away – she could no longer walk – but my mind is crowded with the shades of dusk as if it were twilight. Memory playing tricks again, I suppose.

They took her to the emergency room on the ground floor. Tai had disappeared – hospitals with their smell of blood and illness and formaldehyde made her sick, she said. Aayee looked horribly ill. Her face was all puffed up and I waited beside her with Saraswati Aunty while Baba got the paperwork done.

It was an interminable wait. Finally a lady doctor came and crudely lifted one of my mother's closed eyelids, shouting in Punjabi: 'Why has she been brought here? There doesn't seem to be much wrong with her.'

I could feel the anger grow in me. But what can you do when you are fifteen except look on and feel helpless? Did I understand what was happening? Did I know that the whole fabric of our life, already hanging by a thread because of our nomadic existence and the secrets that went back to my parents' early lives, was in the process of being destroyed?

Anyway, I began to understand that something was seriously wrong with my mother when she suddenly stopped answering. Refused to, I thought at first, before realizing with horror that she could no longer respond. She spoke not a word, made no movement, did not answer when spoken to. Only her eyes moved in her head – left to right, right to left, following the direction of the sound.

By the time they moved her to her room on the sixth floor, I knew without being told that my mother was in a coma. Was it that night or two nights later – time seems strangely compressed with days and nights running into one another – that they hovered around her bed until 2 a.m.?

Standing next to the bed, I watched the ballet of hands palpate her abdomen, search for lumps in groin and armpit; heard the dull thud of the rounded hammer as it tapped knees, ankles and elbows; saw the flash of a steel kidney tray. I stood there until their explorations became too intimate even for my inquisitive and shameless eyes. Then I moved to the balcony where Baba and Nana uncle stood in silence.

I can still picture them – several white-clad figures moving around my mother's high white hospital bed. The only face clearly visible is that of Dr Berry, Professor of Medicine, with his domed, shaven head and stooped shoulders. The place must have been blazing with lights – it had to be, considering they were checking her bodily functions and performing a lumbar puncture. But I see them all cloaked in shadow. As if a dark cloud had suddenly enveloped them in a menacing embrace.

They told us she wouldn't last the night and asked Baba to inform her relatives. She needed blood, Dr Berry said, and a bottle was brought up from the hospital's blood bank. It wasn't my father who replaced it, even though his blood was the universal donor type, but Nana uncle, who volunteered for his sister. Baba chickened out, queasy as ever, despite his brave words, the weasel.

6

The Angry Sentinel

That Pierre Keller. The world's number one sham and charlatan. Why did she go to that scumbag of all persons? He probably fucked her up and fucked her too in the bargain! And all this went on for nearly two years, and she told me nothing. Plotting and scheming all the while. I can't believe it.

Lost in Kranti's notebooks, hurt and furious, alarm rushing through him at the thought that Pierre Keller knew everything and could, and probably would, broadcast it to the world if he hadn't done so already, Robert-Pierre did not at first hear the faint rapping at the door.

He'd thought he'd nip by while Sophie took her usual Sunday nap and he his weekly constitutional, and the afternoon had slipped away unseen. Sophie's mother's birthday today. Mustn't be late for that. The hands of his watch showed it was almost six o'clock.

The rapping grew louder. Then the doorbell rang and a key rattled in the lock. The door swung open. Olga Savic stood there, tall, stringy, a black scarf underlining her strong, square jaw. '*Bonjour*. I came by to check. I thought I heard noises and

I wanted to make sure there were no burglars around,' she said, stepping in uninvited.

Robert-Pierre rose awkwardly, trying to shield the notebook in his hand. '*Bonjour, Madame*. Have you been keeping the place tidy? I have to thank you for it,' he said.

'I hope you don't mind. I took the keys from Madame Benoît. I couldn't bear to see the dust accumulate.'

'But I wouldn't want you to ...'

'Don't worry, it's no trouble at all, I like to clean, it takes my mind off my worries; and I love this flat, I feel she's still here sometimes,' Olga Savic interrupted, cutting off his protest.

Robert-Pierre gave in. He sat down again, gesturing towards a chair. But she remained where she was, fingering the end of her scarf.

'Would you mind if I made some coffee? I can't make it at home because Ivan isn't allowed any and I just cannot get through the evening without coffee. I could go down to the café as usual, but you look like you could use a cup too.'

He nodded assent, realizing how very tired he was, how tense and exhausted. She didn't wait for him to speak, but took the corridor to the kitchen, where he could hear her opening and closing cupboards with an easy familiarity. Unknown to him, Kranti's flat had become a refuge for her too.

She came back carrying a wooden tray upon which she had placed the larger of Kranti's two Bialetti coffee makers and a plate piled high with Viennese biscuits, cream wafers and gold-covered chocolate squares.

He did not remember Kranti ever stocking these and only once had she offered him a slice of Sachertorte, a Christmas gift from her Slav neighbour. 'She's Croatian, but she likes to pretend she's from Vienna – full of admiration for everything

Viennese. She's liked me ever since she met me in the lift and saw me carrying a copy of Schorske's book on Vienna,' Kranti had confided. 'Poor old biddy. Her husband's terribly reactionary – he's Serbian and was an electrician or something. But she's on a self-improvement trip, very conscious about going to galleries and exhibitions. So I give her all my invitations. Quite sweet, really. The son's a stunner. One of those truly handsome men one meets occasionally, and wonderfully talented. He's gay, more's the pity, but he's made a packet in Hollywood. He owns the PeterS brand of cosmetics that are all the rage, so he's really, really loaded. She was showing me the clippings. That's how they live here. The flat's his and he sends them money every month. The father loathes him, she says.'

Olga Savic suffered from varicose veins, he noted. He could see them, blue and knotted, through her stockings. The cups rattled as she put the tray on the dining table.

He saw his cup instantly, and stiffened. Why hadn't she taken out two identical ones? Did she know? Had Kranti told her? It was his, this monstrosity, his. She'd bought it for him, giggling over the garish gold and navy blue porcelain, of its chalice-like shape. He drank from it in bed after they'd made love, sitting like a tousled Roman emperor amid her fine damask sheets, before hurrying back to his practice where he'd be plagued by images of her, naked and languorous, as he struggled to listen to his patients for the rest of the afternoon.

'Ugly, isn't it? But I quite like it. It has become my special cup. It looked so alone and orphaned, I adopted it,' Olga Savic said.

He said nothing, merely watched her pour. But she must have sensed his resentment, for she suddenly looked up. 'It's yours, isn't it? I should have known. I'm sorry.'

'How could you have known?' he said, cowed by her calm.

'By the way, the jewellery pouch is on the dressing table and her other papers are in her studio, just in case you were wondering,' she said, sitting down at the dining table after handing him his cup. She downed her coffee in one straight gulp, poured herself another, then lit a cigarette and took a long, deep drag. 'I hope you don't mind,' she said in her hoarse nicotine-laden voice.

There was a tough, theatrical quality about her. She reminded him of a Czech actress he'd seen in a production of *Mother Courage and Her Children* many years ago. She would be loyal, there when you needed her. But even she had been unable to help Kranti.

'You've come here a few times already. I heard you walking about – the walls aren't all that thick. But I didn't want to disturb you.' Nervous hands smoothed the embroidered tablecloth. Care-worn fingers picked at the blue and red threads that wove in and out of its thin layers.

'Isn't this beautiful? Every object in this flat tells a story, the story of her life', Olga Savic said, stroking the fabric. 'Kranti said this was one of her most prized possessions, a gift from a poor Muslim widow whose property was burnt during the troubles. She was like that; there for anyone who needed help. I know how much she did for me during Ivan's illness – rushing out to buy vegetables, making his soup, bringing it across while I sat at the hospital. I can just imagine her saving this woman from extremists. She gave Kranti the blanket to thank her. She had nothing else left. It was all burned by the mob.'

That was not how he remembered it. Kranti had told him how she had bought it off a destitute widow in a remote drought-hit Indian village. He remembered her recounting the incident as if it were yesterday, with almost total recall. It was one of the first stories she told him about her life in India.

'A truly humbling experience,' Kranti had said. 'I must have been twenty, just out of college, poor little rich girl trying to help the world, with this movie-star image of myself distributing largesse to the starving. A couple of kilos of rice and some biscuits was all I had to give. So I went to Pathredi, which literally means the place where stones cry, fifty degrees in the shade; a place of chronic drought. And the government had this ridiculous plan called food for work, thought up by some right-wing bureaucrat who believed it was wrong to give the poor villagers something for nothing.'

That's where she had met this kid, this eleven-year-old boy, and his mother. 'He just smiled and smiled, despite everything. His father had died the year before and his uncle had taken away their fields and they had nothing to eat, so I gave them a packet of biscuits and some rice and then an hour later, this kid says his mother wants me to come to lunch. I tried saying no, but he wouldn't hear of it. I knew they were proud, so I said yes, I'd go, but on condition they kept it simple. It was a thatched shack, their house, where they cooked and ate and slept and the meal was just boiled rice and pounded red chillies served with a raw onion. No taste, just blinding heat. I got hiccups but couldn't drink their water, which was probably contaminated; but I felt less guilty because it was such a bare bones meal. I said I was glad they had kept it so simple and they smiled so sweetly, both of them. Then I told the social worker how happy I was to get to know real village people at last and how I'd eaten this dreadful meal. And she looked at me as if I was a piece of shit and said: "Congratulations, you just did them out of a week's supply of rice! Do you know what that means?" She was so scathing, she treated me like scum. She said "You're a rich city bitch who wears cotton saris as an ethnic fashion statement. A meddlesome busybody who's here on an ego trip, not because you really care." I felt as if I'd gone to sleep on a bed of roses and woken up on a dung heap. So that evening, before I left, I went to them again and told them how much I loved that little blanket and could I please buy it. They didn't want to sell it at first, they said, just take it. But finally I managed to press twenty rupees on them and they were crying when I left. Buying myself a good conscience, evidently. My first brush with real poverty...'

Thinking back, he could see the holes in the story. A twenty-year-old girl in India in the 70s, driving out alone to succour starving villagers seemed unlikely in retrospect, especially now that he knew something about the country. At that time, in his ignorance and enchantment, he had swallowed it whole.

Olga Savic cut into his thoughts. 'She told me not so long ago about these ethnic clashes when they destroyed an ancient mosque somewhere and mobs of Hindus started attacking these Muslims? And Kranti gave shelter to this poor Muslim widow who gifted her this child's blanket which Kranti used as a tablecloth. She even explained how they were too poor to buy blankets and so the women would collect their torn, threadbare saris and quilt them together. She told me the word for it in Indian, but I've forgotten it now. It was wonderful for the baby, she said, because all that washing meant the cloth was really soft and the child would not get allergies; it was good for the baby's skin. Very clever, killing two birds with one stone.'

'I thought she got it a long time ago from a famine victim in some remote village,' Robert-Pierre said. 'At least, that's what I remember her telling me.'

'Maybe she just forgot where she bought it, she got mixed up. It happens sometimes. You look tired and your coffee's gone cold. Can I give you another cup?'

'Why do you think she did it?' Robert-Pierre asked, ignoring her question, surprising himself.

'Why did she feel the need to make up stories? I don't know. Some people are like that. To make life more interesting maybe, don't you think?'

'That's not what I meant.'

'Oh. Yes, I see. I was wondering whether I should speak to you about this.' Olga Savic stood up to pull something out of her pocket. It was a piece of paper, folded many times over, tearing along the folds. Thinking it was some kind of prayer, Robert-Pierre took it reluctantly, holding it gingerly by the edge until he saw the familiar scrawl. When he looked up from reading it, Olga Savic had collapsed into a low armchair, her face in her hands.

'I don't know what to think,' she said brokenly from between her fingers. Robert-Pierre leaned across to hand her his handkerchief, a beautifully ironed snow-white square of soft cotton monogrammed in royal blue. RPP. Robert-Pierre Perrin. A Christmas gift from Sophie. 'Strictly not for use by female patients,' she'd joked, 'especially not the beautiful, exotic kind.' He'd wondered then if she knew and whether the present was a hint of some sort. Olga Savic was indeed foreign, but she was neither a patient nor by any means beautiful.

'I must have read that letter a thousand times and I still don't understand,' Olga Savic was saying. His handkerchief lay unused in her lap. There were no tears, he saw, only a slight quaver in her voice.

'She loved life so much, too much perhaps. Still, I cannot imagine her doing what she did, especially all those preparations, as if dying was a game. Do you think she was seeing a guru? Maybe she had joined a sect? But she was not like that. I was the one tempted by religion, especially after Ivan's stroke. She talked me out of it. All that genuflecting, all those Ave I was drowning in. "Try yoga, Olga. I'll give you lessons. You must learn to breathe," she told me. And then she goes and does this, this act of folly. Madness.'

'When did you receive this?' Robert-Pierre asked, pushing the folded letter back towards her across the table.

'It didn't come in the post, if that's what you're asking. I found it. On the shelf, right here in front of the mirror, just after we saw, we found ... her, you know, the body. There was my name on it. It was mine and I took it. Just before the firemen arrived. A little before you came.'

Yes, he'd seen the fire truck. The police too. And then the ambulance men, bumping into the walls with their stretcher handles. 'Some poor creature suffering from the heat,' he'd thought. Fresh from his holiday with Sophie, tanned, relaxed, with a jaunt in his step, he'd taken the lift ahead of them, one hand curled around a bottle of limoncello, the other holding aloft a large bunch of speckled lilies. Kranti's very first funeral wreath. But he didn't know it then. Until ... until he saw the open door, the fireman standing guard outside, a helmet dangling from his index finger. Until he smelt the smell that had never left him from that day to this.

'I showed it to the police one day, weeks after they kept coming back to pester me and Madame Benoît. I didn't want to tell them at first. I thought they would accuse me of stealing, taking something without permission from a dead person's house. It had my name on it. So I took it. I never thought I was doing something wrong. I don't know why I waited that long. Guilt, I suppose, and fear. But then I saw you coming here with them and I thought, maybe it would clear matters up if I showed it to them? They seemed relieved to read it, as if some great big mystery had been cleared up. I asked them what it could mean. They said they didn't know, but that if she had done something terrible, even criminal perhaps, so many years ago, in another country, it no longer mattered, did it, since she was now dead? Terribly callous, I thought. They released the body soon after. It was such a clear case of suicide, I never understood why they were holding it back.'

She didn't understand perhaps, but he did. Sitting in the hard-backed chair of the police station he was thankful he had not taken Kranti on as a patient again. 'No,' he had said in all honesty, 'I was not treating Madame de Lorel at the time of her death. I never gave her prescriptions or professional advice and she never seemed depressed to me.'

Then, just as suddenly as it had started, the questioning had come to an end. Politely, even affably, he was told the case was closed. A death certificate was issued, the body released for cremation. Robert-Pierre finally understood why and felt the tension leak out of him like air leaving a balloon. He felt like hugging and shaking Olga Savic all at once. That was how his troubles with Sophie had started. That bastard inspector had called her up. Just like that, without as much as a by your leave.

Sophie. The police were not the only ones who wanted to discuss Sophie. Kranti could barely contain her curiosity about his wife, his practice, his arrangements at home.

'What does she do?' she'd asked suddenly one day, the question catching him at his most vulnerable, in bed, spent, after a bout of unusually vigorous lovemaking. He'd put his glasses back on before saying simply: 'She teaches French literature at the Lycée Louis-Le-Grand. And she writes.'

'What does she write?'

'Books.'

'What kind of books?'

'Children's books, mainly. But she has just finished her second novel.'

'What does she write as?'

'What do you mean?'

'Does she write as Sophie Perrin?'

'No.' He'd given her a sharp look. He felt she knew all the answers already but wanted to hear him say them, a confession of sorts; under duress.

'She writes under the name of Dominique Taquet, her twin brother who died in an accident.'

'Does she know you have other relationships? Does she mind?'

'We made a pact eight years ago to lead separate lives. We agreed there was no longer any sexual attraction between us, so we released each other physically. It's a harmonious relationship. I cannot bear to live alone and I cannot stomach the thought of moving each time a relationship ends. So this suits us both fine and we look out for each other. Of course, I don't go about advertising the fact that I'm seeing someone. Nor does she. I don't know if she has someone. I hope for her sake she does.'

'How very mature and civilized,' was Kranti's only remark. He knew from her pursed mouth that he had touched a very raw nerve.

And now he had lost them both, the two women in his life.

Once, just once, had Sophie lost her calm, when she turned on him a couple of days after the police had spoken to her. 'How can you act so normally, as if nothing's happened? You knew her, bedded her, had sex with her. And now she's killed herself. Why? Don't you even want to know?' There was so much hurt and contempt in her voice, he dared not approach her. And she took refuge behind a wall of icy silence.

Perhaps he could still bring Sophie around? Exhaustion overtook him and Robert-Pierre slumped back on the sofa, closing his eyes. Before long, he was snoring gently. He did not hear Olga Savic tiptoe to the kitchen with the coffee cups, let herself out. An hour later, he was still sleeping, peacefully for the first time since Kranti's death.

The ring of the telephone awoke him. The instrument was on the table, a blue post-it sticking to its side. Disoriented, Robert-Pierre looked around him, moving his tongue inside his mouth, wiping away the trickle of saliva that had gathered at the corner of his lips. His neck was stiff, his face felt like cardboard. He stretched out his hand to pick up the phone, waiting for another ring as if to test the persistence and patience of the caller. Then he lifted it to his ear and said: '*Allô*!'

'*Oui, bon*, I thought you would be there...' It was Sophie.

'Yes. I am sorry. I should have been home long ago... Are you still angry with me?'

'What do you think? It's different, Pierre, this time. I've known a long time. I always know. Instinct, I suppose. I did not know the details, of course, until the police rang. I wanted to speak to you then, but you were so unhappy, withdrawn, silent and so trying not to show it. I thought you would tell me what really happened. So I waited.'

He had an insane desire to see her, to speak to her, pour it all out. She would be cool, matter of fact as always, distant, given the circumstances, but supportive.

'What are you wearing?' he said instead. He needed to see the colour framing her blonde head, her square haircut, the discreet diamond she wore at her neck.

'Does it matter, my Pierrot? I am wearing black trousers and Tante Annie's jet earrings with a blue jacket. I am going out for dinner. But I was trying to tell you something else. That this time, it's different. You left it too late, went too far. I need time now. I want to think about whether we can carry on as before or if we need to readjust out lives, to separate. So it's best if you don't come home tonight.' She sounded reasonable, calm, dignified as always. But he could detect the hurt in her voice, the fact that she had retreated further into herself, her habitual teasing nowhere in sight.

'But Sophie, wait. We must talk. We cannot just stop like this.'

'We will talk. But not now, Pierre. I cannot. I am taking Maman and Louis out to dinner. It's her birthday. You know that. She understands you won't be there this evening. She asked and I told her. So be kind, don't come back home tonight. Stay where you are and come tomorrow morning to pick up your clothes. Please, I insist.'

An anguished cry escaped his throat as he put down the telephone. He felt bereft. Sophie was like a mother, a sister, he'd understood that long ago. He felt protected with her around, sure she would take care of the hurts, smooth his ruffled pride when he returned, as he always did, shamefaced, to her bosom. And she never pried. He told her, however, each time, once it was over. Sketchy bits, no details. It was like going to confession, helping him get over the break-up. But this time, there was a sick feeling in his stomach. There had been a death. He was still at pains to understand why. So what explanation could he give Sophie? Kranti had managed to silence them both.

Finding nothing remotely dinner-like in the refrigerator or on the shelves, Robert-Pierre walked down to the Vietnamese delicatessen around the corner. He bought himself a plate of Cantonese fried rice, a few nem and sate sticks with a portion of roast duck, wondering where Sophie had taken her mother for her birthday.

Probably the Port Alma for some fish, close to the old lady's apartment on the Quai Kennedy. His thoughts centred on them as he warmed up his food in Kranti's microwave oven.

Sophie's father had been stiff but her mother was always welcoming, glossing over the social differences that separated them. Both Sophie's parents had been quick to recognize him for what he was – a pure product of France's republican meritocracy – and they respected his intelligence, his learning, tolerated his somewhat revolutionary left-wing politics although they were both moderate right-wingers themselves. There was an innate decency in them, he now realized, that they had quite successfully, almost effortlessly, passed on to their children.

He had taken to the casual elegance of their flat like a duck to water. His own parents were modest provincials – public servants both – and his childhood had been built upon his mother's revolutionary fervour and his father's careful rectitude as a postal employee. Their small untidy house on the outskirts of Rouen was drab, almost rustic. There were books for sure, because both his parents were readers. But there was none of the careless sophistication he found in the Taquet residence.

No paintings, no *objets d'art*, just a few faded Miro and Picasso prints on the walls. Nothing came easy in the Perrin home. As he said to Sophie one day, 'There was always a touch of self-improvement in the air. What we lacked, I think, is confidence, the natural grace and elegance, that wonderful quality that usually comes with inherited money... It was never effortless for us – always a trudge, never a sailing through.'

They were grateful too of course, for what he did for their broken daughter who blamed herself for her twin's death. After his marriage to Sophie, they had begun to treat him like a son regained.

I was young, but I was good. Steady, thought Robert-Pierre, pulling out tiny duck bones from his mouth. And I pulled her through.

Sophie had gone to pieces after the accident, falling into an anorexic, self-destructive spiral. His former professor had referred her to him. 'She needs a younger consultant she can relate to, who can understand her, take her out of herself. You're the best person I can think of.'

She'd talked to him about her dead twin, Dominique. She should have gone with him even if she had an exam the next day. He was too drunk to drive and she knew it. But she had let her brother get behind the wheel and he had never come back.

They had been two sides of the same coin, she told him, incomplete without each other. She was calm, stable, straight-haired, blond. He was mercurial, a rebel, with a wild, curly mane. She could not live without him, did not have the right to live in his absence.

Robert-Pierre had encouraged her to write and Dominique had emerged on the pages. The first stories were for children – a grumpy rabbit living alone in a house with a girl, a choir of twenty-seven mice who sang off-key, a complaining duck shot full of self-pity.

Five years ago, almost a decade into their marriage, she had published her first novel. The critics remarked on the contrast between the writer – a goody-two-shoes, a banker's daughter from the bourgeois 16th arrondissement, conformist in ideas and dress – and what she wrote. Erotic, explicit, explosive – incest and forbidden love. *Desire in the House*, she called it. 'But it's my brother's house, not my own,' she explained, telling him she was sure Dominique lived on through her. It was his spirit that wrote. Not her own.

And if Sophie was his mother or sister, he thought, slipping under the covers of Kranti's familiar antique bed, was he not, in a certain sense, her wild, lost brother? Was that why the sexual attraction had waned so swiftly to be replaced by an easy, teasing camaraderie? They were really more like brother and sister than man and wife.

But now Kranti stood between them, the proverbial 'third woman', upsetting their carefully built sand castle, stamping it out with her furious, powerful boot, showing it up for the fragile edifice it was.

He must not allow her to destroy him. His marriage was sacrosanct. Kranti had always known that. But her acceptance of it had only been a pretence, he saw. Still, her diary was not a boring catalogue of mundane details, but an extraordinary self-examination of which he hadn't suspected she was capable.

Normally he would see this as an outstanding attempt at self-analysis. But nothing was normal here. How could it be normal when she had so shamelessly deceived him? Going to Pierre Keller on purpose was an act of spite and petty meanness he could never condone.

'She is not alive,' Robert-Pierre told himself aloud. 'She can do you no harm.'

But his words did little to dispel the welling uncertainty within him. He felt sickened by what he had read so far. How could someone so duplicitous, so devious, produce such marvels of innocence, he mused, thumbing through the pictures in the red notebook. Was he dealing with a true schizophrenic, after all?

7

The Red Notebook

KRANTI AND SHANTI
A novel
BY K. GORAY DE LOREL

Poona, 1957

In a sun-drenched garden in Poona, two little girls are playing.

Thick taffeta ribbons imprison their hair in unhappy rolls atop their heads. At the back, it cascades down in long, tangled rivulets. Identical blue-and-yellow checked skirts have snagged on burrs and rosebushes, hems weighed down by muddy water are studded with leaves and tiny pebbles.

They are roughly the same height and at first glance might pass for twins. Shanti's ribbons are a clear sky blue; Kranti's a rich raspberry red. Shanti has missing milk teeth and protruding gums, which, one day, will sprout a bevy of jagged, uneven teeth. She has inherited her father's knock-knees and heavy bones.

Kranti's mouth is a stubborn line, her chocolate eyes shuttered. Already, she inhabits a private world, muttering to herself as she balances upon the line of bricks separating the phlox from the cosmos.

They are as different as fish and fowl, chalk and cheese, oranges and aubergines.

It is three o'clock on a mild winter's day. The droning of bumblebees replete with nectar and yellowed with pollen is interrupted by the distant puk-puk of a water pump and the girls' shrill, fluty voices. A coconut tree stands guard near the painted wooden gate. Too heavy for its hinges, it sags in the middle like a dropped hemline, carving semi-circular grooves in the ground on its reluctant journeys forward and back.

A marble plaque embedded in the cement gatepost says: SHANTI NIWAS. Quietly and without fuss. Below, in smaller, more modest lettering: Engg. S.G. Goray (Retd.).

The short drive from the gate to the house is lined with crotons, a somewhat dusty, welcoming army of colourful dwarfs in shades of orange, green, yellow, violet, brown, hot pink. Mixing all these colours in her paint box, Kranti comes up with a disappointing muddy-brown puddle.

Set in fat earthenware pots daubed alternately white and India Red, the gallant little soldiers have been brought to life, grafted, cloned by the engineer's never-failing green thumb. His late wife's favourite plant, they are his love and only passion.

Named after the girls' paternal grandmother, they all bear the same moniker – Shanti – but wear different number tags. Kranti practices her tables on them, multiplying Shanti Number 9 by Shanti Number 3 to arrive at Shanti Number 32. Frowning with concentration, she starts over. Shanti Number 6 multiplied by Shanti Number 3 gives Shanti Number 21. Wrong again.

The garden is somnolent, a large lazy creature soaking up the sun. Tall mango and gulmohor trees shade the back of the house, while Palanpur rambling roses and fragrant jasmine twine a forest around the verandah pillars, hiding their bare ugliness, sheltering swarms of mosquitoes and sand flies.

The girls play catch around the unused stone fountain now black with dead moss. They spin about the cement stem of the sundial, leaping nimbly over disciplined, brick-lined flowerbeds that cradle nasturtium, coxcomb, verbena and balsam. The house, built in 1943 in the heart of Brahmin-dominated Deccan Gymkhana, is a run-down hybrid, a brick and stone folly with curved verandahs and rose trellises. The drawing room sticks its triangular nose into the fragrant mogra bushes in front, providing a somewhat blinkered view of the drive and gate.

This is where Shridhar Govind Goray, better known as Babuji, broken by his wife's premature death, lives a reclusive, lonely existence, his life devoted to gardening and cricketing stories, swapped once a week at the club he visits, cane in hand, hatted, suited and booted, every Thursday evening.

Shanti has laid bare the spine of a coconut leaf. She waves it experimentally in the air. Long and dry, it makes a wicked, swishing sound. Eyes narrowed, she looks speculatively at her sister.

'I'll show them', she says half to herself, and dashes off, taking the three steps to the verandah in a single, spirited bound. Kranti knows that look. She can feel her fingers tingle with dread, her forehead dampen with perspiration.

It's the radio's dust cover. In pale blue flannel with cutouts for the bandwidths and holes for the tuning and volume knobs, it makes the ideal wimple for a nine-year-old blue-and-yellow-checked nun.

Kranti's jaw drops. She has stopped breathing.

Her head wrapped in blue flannel, Shanti is advancing on the cosmos bushes walking Mother Agnes' slow, deliberate, pigeon-toed walk. She is sucking her teeth, speaking softly, almost kindly, between each suck. Her hands dangle demurely by her side and her face wears an expression of infinite sorrow.

Mother Agnes addresses the tall flowers at the back. They are nodding at each other like excited, garrulous schoolgirls. Slowly, delicately, the coconut switch comes up to gently tap the biggest of the flaming orange heads.

'And you, Anita,' Mother Agnes says sadly. 'What is your ex-pla-na-shon, my child? Thirteen mistakes in ten lines? You know this will not do, hmmn?'

She turns her head sharply, startled by a silent sound. 'Don't giggle, Meenakshi. It is unkind to laugh at the misfortunes of others. Fifty lines! I shall not laugh at other people's troubles. Stay in until you've finished.'

Bimla is the little one in front. She had polio as a baby and uses a crutch to drag herself about the playground. 'And you, Bimla. Do not use your aff-flik-shon as an excuse to shirk work, my dear,' Mother Agnes says, her voice rising. 'Those guilty of the sin of lying shall forever burn in the fires of hell.'

There is silence. The heads have stopped nodding. 'Class, I am sorry to say that you have been very, very naughty,' Mother Agnes informs them. Her voice is shrill, like chalk on blackboard.

The switch comes down hard and without warning. It travels through the air with a whistling, hissing sound. And suddenly, cosmos heads are raining down upon the ground. Hurt, bleeding orange faces stare back at Kranti, who stands there jellified, frightened tears quickly gathering in her eyes.

All that is left of the bush are a few frayed cosmos stems. Mother Agnes spins around on her heel as she pulls off her hot, sticky, sweat-drenched wimple. She's Shanti again and the switch comes down hard one more time.

'Don't you dare tell, you stupid cry-baby,' she flings at her sister as she stomps off towards the guava trees.

Kranti has barely felt the lash. But her fingers can make out the weal on her upper arm. It is bumpy, and she is sure it's red, like when a thorny branch brushes across your flesh, leaving behind a dotted line of oozing blood.

Saru. She must find Saru. Kranti finally tracks down the maid in the small shed that once housed Baba's Lambretta and now shelters the cook's rusty bicycle. Saru is lying on her back snoring softly. Kranti snuggles up to her but the floor is hard and smells of old shoes and engine oil.

She tries scratching Saru's elbow scabs; then holding the maid's eyelashes between thumb and index, lifts her eyelid. Saru's red-veined eyeball swivels frantically from left to right and Kranti hurriedly lets go as Saru, making clackety mouth noises, yawns, then sits up.

'What's the matter now?' she asks, not as nicely as Kranti had hoped.

'Shanti has spoiled the cosmos bush and she shouted and hurt me, look.'

'Oh, that sister of yours,' sighs Saru, re-knotting her bun. 'I'll give you an extra biscuit with your Ovaltine,' she consoles, rubbing the weal, blowing on it to make it better. 'Now come and get washed, it's time to go to the park anyway. And don't let your mother catch you calling her Shanti. She's your older sister and you must say Tai, understand?'

Haribhau, the gardener, has given notice again.

From their hiding place behind the rambling roses, a dense fog of mosquitoes singing over their heads, they watch his silhouette shake its bullet head. The ruined radio cover is tucked under one arm and he holds the dead cosmos heads in his calloused gardener's palms.

'This is the fourth time these holidays. We can't even offer these flowers to God. They've trampled them underfoot. There won't be many guavas this year – they've picked them green. The pea bed's gone too. They've been jumping in it.'

The sisters smile conspiratorially in the dark, remembering the long jump competition in the freshly turned pea-bed. The soil soft and pebble-free, welcoming their bare toes, cooling the backs of their sweaty thighs.

Now they go rigid as their grandfather's querulous voice reaches them over the evening smells of rose and jasmine. 'Shanti ... Kranti ... Come here...'

Reluctantly the sisters approach his room.

Kranti can see Haribhau's hairy legs emerge from flared khaki shorts. Her eyes lock briefly with Babuji's angry grey-green stare, then quickly travel the room, taking in his white rubber slippers, the snow-capped Himalayan painting, the locked chest of drawers where, Saru says, the riches of Araby lie concealed, her grandmother's garlanded portrait with its impossibly large, dangling nose-ring, before returning to Haribhau's feet firmly planted on the coir doormat. Uncut toenails pierce the faded brown canvas of his shoes, illegally procured, as Babuji unfailingly points out, from the army supply store near Quarter Gate.

Babuji's fingers take a pinch of snuff to his nose. After a protracted, furry snort, his quavering hand fumbles for the blue napkin in his lap and a knot of tobacco-coloured snot is deposited amid its folds.

'Which of you did this?' he asks.

His normally gentle voice is harsh. Kranti can feel the pain of Shanti's pinch radiate all the way down her back. The tears start up again, as much from pain as from fear and then she is standing in a wet pool, warm liquid burning her cheeks and her dry, wind-chapped legs as it trickles to the floor.

The room is filled with the sharp smell of urine and the fight goes out of Babuji. 'Tell Saru to clean her up and ask your mother to see me,' he says, turning his face to the wall. Through the pounding in her ears, Kranti can hear an old man's weariness in his voice.

Saru is tying the bow of her favourite green-and-white frock that Baba brought back from Bombay when Aayee bursts in. She has been with Babuji and her face has that dangerous, tight-lipped look that tells Kranti a slap is on the way.

Shanti gets a box between her shoulders that sends her lurching across to Saru. She glares back unflinching at her mother. Provoked, Aayee takes two large strides and slaps the sisters hard. She is genuinely angry and does not hold back.

With Shanti making faces behind her back, Aayee pulls out their trunk from under the bed. She is dumping their clothes, books, dolls pell-mell into its bright blue painted depths.

Kranti's wailing, punctuated by painful hiccoughs, is drowned out by Shanti chanting a child's ditty:

'Would you like to hear the story of the woolly onion? What do you mean yes, would you like to hear the story of the woolly onion, what do you mean no?' On and on she goes.

Until Aayee hits her again and tells her to shut up.

A penitent Haribhau, eager to make amends, is sent off to get a rickshaw. Saru is wiping her eyes as Aayee opens her purse to pay her for two weeks' work.

Light spills out of Babuji's window, but his door remains shut as they make their way out of the verandah, through the dark and now silent garden, to the waiting rickshaw beyond.

It is in the station waiting room that Aayee begins to talk. About how sad she is to have two such badly brought up, junglee children who cannot be trusted to behave themselves as guests. About how terribly it reflects upon her, their mother. Their behaviour makes her blood thicken, evaporate even, she says.

Kranti cannot understand how that can happen. All she sees is a pot full of Aayee's blood bubbling away on the primus stove in Babuji's kitchen. The image refuses to go away, and when she shuts her eyes, her head is filled with a pretty, deep-red glow, like that of a summer sunset or the flaming gulmohor tree in Babuji's garden.

The train arrives. Kranti, who has slumped into a cavernous teakwood railway armchair, is rudely shaken awake. Aayee keeps a firm hold on their arms as their slipper-flapping trio, half running to keep up with their trunk bobbing ahead atop their coolie's head, negotiates the crowds to climb gratefully into an Intermediate Class carriage marked Ladies Only.

◈

It is Sunday and seven o'clock in the morning when their train steams into Aurangabad station. All night long, despite the closed windows, bits of coal and grit have found their way into the compartment and the soles of their feet are black as tar. Aayee has scrubbed their grubby faces with a corner of her handkerchief moistened with water and Kanta scent. 'There's no time for tea. We'll have it at home,' she says, nudging them towards a waiting tonga.

The air is cool and Kranti, her fatigue and tears forgotten, moves her body rhythmically to the merry clip-clop of the horse's shoes. The tonga sways and clatters through half-empty streets and even Aayee seems happy. Pie dogs with smiley faces run a few metres alongside the tonga, pretending to snap at the horse's legs. The tonga man, making a variety of clicking and clacking sounds, sets up a drum roll tattoo with the handle of his whip against the spokes of the wheel.

Women carrying empty water pots on their heads begin their daily trudge to wells and municipal taps as teashops blaring film music welcome their first customers. The shabby dustbowl that is Aurangabad, known for its proximity to the famous Buddhist rock caves of Ellora and Ajanta, its artificial silk mills and its indeterminate importance as a sleepy provincial town, is slowly saying hello to a new day.

They have arrived. They are home. Kranti leaps out of the tonga and rushes in, eager to fling herself into Baba's arms.

She speeds past the water tank and the straggly flower beds peopled with dusty zinnias, down the small path that runs along the garage towards the fence near the disused mosque. Not bothering with the front door, she makes her way to the back, where she can slip into the house through the servants' quarters.

Casting aside her chappals, she tiptoes towards her parents' room. Baba is probably snoring with his mouth open, and for a fleeting second, she pauses, debating whether to tickle his tummy or bury her head in it.

But once inside the door, her feet falter. There is a huge dark shape moving under the mosquito net. And it is making strange noises, as if it were hurting. On the chair, she sees a familiar yellow-flowered print dress and the white, yawning cups of a large brassiere that look like a halved, air-filled bellows. Under the chair a pair of pointy, creamy-white high-heeled shoes stand at odd angles to each other, like an angry Aayee and Baba. Aunty Cou-ee's golden lipstick has rolled out of her frock pocket and glints wantonly against the dark leg of the chair.

Kranti backs away. As silently as she has come, to stand in the courtyard feeling lost.

'Cou-ee. What are you doing?' The voice is low and gruff.

Aunty Cou-ee is leaning on the parapet looking down at her from the verandah that runs the length of the house. Only her head and upper body, now clad in the yellow dress, are visible. Elbows on parapet, hands clasped under chin. A cigarette in a long black holder protrudes from enlaced fingers. Her left eye is screwed up against the smoke that drifts out of her mouth and nostrils in lazy little curls.

Guiltily Kranti wipes her hands on her green and white frock, then runs up the steps to hug Aunty Cou-ee's legs.

'Back so soon from Grandpa's? I thought I heard a little mouse scampering about. Where's Mummy now?' Aunty Cou-ee's large hand is comfortingly heavy on her head.

The doorbell jangles and Aunty Cou-ee quickly moves to the kitchen where Kranti can hear her pouring water for tea. From her vantage point, she can see Baba, in his kurta-pyjama, hurry forward to answer the summons. She hears him murmur something about Barbara and Ayaee's sharp voice saying, 'Mrs d'Costa? But it's Sunday and only 7.30 in the morning, Vijay.'

They move towards the kitchen, Baba talking about 'office keys' and 'so much work to be finished even on a Sunday.'

Aunty Cou-ee has made tea but Aayee says she can't have it, she needs a bath first. She is angry again and orders Kranti to go to the servants' quarter and rouse Ganga.

'The children are unsettled. You should spend more time with them,' Aayee tells Baba. But she is staring straight at Aunty Cou-ee, who hurriedly looks at her watch.

'I'd better pick up the office keys and run if I'm to finish the work and get to church before eleven,' she says.

Kranti is playing by herself in the garden when Aunty Cou-ee leaves, her high heels teetering on the gravel. 'Aunty Cou-ee, will you send Yvonne over to play?'

'Not today. It's Sunday. She has to go to church.' The lipsticked mouth snaps shut. The gate follows suit. Click!

Kranti plays a desultory game of hopscotch, drawing the squares on the ground with a sturdy stick she's found by the tamarind tree. A crow caws angrily as sunlight invades her solitary game, striking her ankles, rising slowly towards her knees.

The house stands well back from the high wall that surrounds it. Painted white, it has a gabled roof, like an old-fashioned colonial bungalow, and three entrances. The girls frequently use the servants' door at the back. Aayee's nameplate – Lalita Goray, Sangeet Visharad, Classical Singing Teacher – is tacked on the small door leading directly into the living room. Black Marathi letters shyly painted on a plain brown-varnished wooden board.

Baba's nameplate is altogether grander. Written in English and engraved on brass, it is kept shiny with regular applications of lime juice and Brasso. Vijay Goray, BSc., MSc., LLB. Branch Manager, Norwich Union Assurance, with a little In-Out window. Right now, it says Out. But Baba is In. Annoyed, Kranti pushes the little button back to In. She has to stand up on tiptoe to do it.

The water in the tank glints, reflecting the sun. Kranti can see dark green weeds in its depths and suspended particles highlighted by shafts of light. Thorns float. So do twigs, marigolds and leaves. A green guava half floats, half sinks. A small stone goes right down to the bottom. Instantly. They all make ripples, even the leaf, but the stone's ripples are the biggest and fastest of all.

Kranti wanders back indoors. She finds Shanti curled up on her side on their bed, a book clutched in her left hand, the fingers of the right hand absently scratching her scalp, twirling her curls. 'Tai...' she begins.

'Go away. Can't you see I'm reading?'

The door to Baba's study is closed and she hovers outside. An argument is in progress. Baba's gravelly voice is drowned out by Aayee's shrill tones. She is going on about Mrs d'Costa. Baba calls her Barbara. They are quarrelling about Aunty Cou-ee.

'And I don't like the fact that she calls me Lalita. She has no right to,' Aayee says.

'How do you want her to call you? She's not your servant, Lalita. You are only her boss' wife,' Baba says.

Aayee says mental shock, shameless, vulgar and Christian over and over. These are words Kranti cannot understand.

She lies down on the bed next to Shanti, her back touching her sister's. The soles of her feet are thick with dirt and leave large dark smudges on the beige counterpane.

Kranti places her thumb in her mouth and closes her eyes. The two small forms make an X upon the large bed. It is eleven o'clock in the morning.

Aunty Cou-ee has sent liver in a dented aluminium box with Yvonne, who has come to play.

Like Baba and Shanti, Kranti loves Aunty Cou-ee's liver. It is chewy, hot, sweet-and-sour and never tastes bitter. Aayee does too, but secretly. All of Aunty Cou-ee's food has this lovely, spicy, forbidden, Christian taste. A mixture of vinegar and salt, ginger, sugar, cumin and red chillies. She makes things Aayee can't and Baba is loud in his praise. Kranti's mouth drools at the thought of Aunty Cou-ee's pan-fried mutton chops. Yum.

Kranti can see her mother wince as she takes the box. Gingerly. She is a silver and copper, steel and bronze person who hates enamel and aluminium.

'Only poor Christians and Muslims cook in aluminium. It's unclean. It poisons the food,' Aayee says.

When Aayee's mother Akka visits, they share a sneaky laugh about Christians – Mary-bai and Martha-bai on their way to meet Yeshu – but never in front of Baba. Because Baba is a communist, always sticking up for what he calls 'the minorities' – untouchables, Christians, Muslims and Anglo-Indians.

Akka is a widow and she goes turn by turn to stay with all her six children. She wears a strict bun and steely glasses and nine-yard saris that pass between her legs to be tucked into the waistband above her bottom. Akka fasts on Thursdays and Mondays, when she eats peanuts and sago and special things. Baba says he can't understand why Monday should be better than Tuesday or Saturday, but Akka says he wouldn't understand because he is far too educated for the likes of her.

Akka's widowed status means her saris are always white and she can't wear a red dot on her forehead or the traditional black-beaded mangalsutra around her neck. Aayee doesn't wear a red dot or a mangalsutra either. But that's because Baba is a communist and won't let her. Akka is always talking about Christians and Muslims and has forbidden the girls to share their tiffin with them. Kranti can't make out which of her friends are Christian or Muslim. Most of them have long hair and their mothers wear saris like Aayee and some of them are poor.

But Aunty Coo-ee is different. She is big and tall and manly, even taller than Baba whom she calls Boss. 'She smokes and drinks, just like a man,' Kranti has heard Aayee telling Akka. 'Sometimes even with Vijay, who keeps whiskey at the office for clients.'

Aunty Cou-ee has a bob and a fringe and wears postbox-red lipstick and Baba says she takes 'perfect dictation', especially when he is talking about Kranti's spelling mistakes at school.

Yvonne is dark, with dimples and a short bob like her mother's, toothsome and street-smart. She always wears her uniform, even after school is out. Except on Sundays, when she goes to church in white ballerina shoes and a red-belted, wide-skirted, green taffeta frock worn over rustling buckram petticoats.

'That's because her mother can't be bothered to buy her some decent clothes for daily wear,' Aayee tells Akka. 'What do you expect when all the money goes on lipsticks and high-heeled shoes? And Vijay even gave her a pay rise. He's placed her on his head from where she rules the office like a queen.'

When Aayee isn't looking, Yvonne uses Baba's toilet, delicately spreading the skirt of her pleated uniform around the commode like a queen sitting on a throne. She breaks raw tamarind with expertly thrown stones and they eat it with salt and red chilli, mercilessly pestering Ganga until she gives it to them.

But today, Aayee, who usually calls Yvonne 'poor child' and plies her with food and questions, has other plans for Aunty Cou-ee's liver.

'It's a religious fast for us today. And Kranti has a lot of homework to do.'

She sends Yvonne home and the liver with her. This is the first time Kranti has caught her mother telling a straight lie. Aayee stares through her, beyond her, and doesn't even blink.

◇

Kranti is struggling into her school shoes when she sees Aayee rush from the kitchen to the bathroom to say something to Baba, who is shaving.

Fearing she has been caught, Kranti, with one shoe on, limps into Baba's study to put back the four annas she has stolen. She is always careful to take just a little bit, usually ten or fifteen pice, enough to buy sweets, *churan*, *ber*, or to pay Amtul Mateen for letting her copy his sums.

Today she has no alternative. There are only four- and eight-anna coins on Baba's desk, and now her number is up. But her luck holds and no one comes to grasp her by the ear, turn out her pockets, prise open her fists or empty the contents of her schoolbag.

The morning torment of numbers is followed by Sister Margaret's English lesson. Kranti loves English. Because Sister Margaret is like a saint, so soft and sweet, and because she tells lovely stories about poor but good people who go to Heaven.

'Kranti', Sister Margaret's gentle voice interrupts her thoughts. 'will you read us your homework on The Story of Arjuna?'

'Yes, Sister Margaret.'

Kranti fumbles with her homework notebook, her mind racing. 'One day, a princess lost her golden ball which fell into a well in the forest. Prince Arjuna and his brothers were going that way and heard the princess crying ...'

Her notebook is so close to her face, it almost touches her nose, and her voice is barely a whisper.

Now Arjuna is shooting arrow after arrow into the well. He makes a daisy chain of arrows to form a rope. Delicately, the princess draws up the arrow-rope and takes her ball from the arrow-basket at its end.

Kranti stops dead. She folds shut her notebook, holds it tight in front of her. There is silence. They are all staring strangely.

'Is that all?' asks Sister Margaret pointedly.

The reading has lasted several minutes. Kranti has not turned a page. The monitor goes down the rows of desks to collect their homework books, but Kranti will not give hers up. Tenaciously she holds it down as Amtul Mateen struggles to wrench it from her hands.

She turns her head to escape his breath. It smells of rotting fruit, like the big market she visits with Aayee where they have to pick their way through mounds of discarded cauliflower stumps, furred, pulpy tomatoes, yellow-white widows' mops of sucked mango stones, mashed remains of earthworms, mint and coriander – trod underfoot by scores of scurrying, uncaring feet.

Kranti can feel the terrifying, wet ooze squeeze itself between her toes, rise to cover her feet. Her grip slackens. Her homework book is yanked out of her fingers. Amtul Mateen's ink-stained fingers flip the pages, come to rest on 'The Story of Arjuna', underlined in red, written in a self-consciously florid hand. Below that, nothing. Empty lines.

'Sister, there's nothing on the page!' Amtul Mateen races up to the teacher's desk, waving the captured notebook.

'Go to your place and give it back. Kranti, you may bring in your homework tomorrow,' Sister Margaret says. 'But see me after school today with your sister.'

At the end of the day, Sister Margaret hands Shanti a sealed envelope to give Aayee and Baba. Their name is written on it in perfect cursive lettering. Kranti does not know that Tai has another envelope for Aayee and Baba tucked away in her schoolbag, which she has no intention of handing over.

'You're not going to give it, Tai, are you? Please ...' Kranti asks on the way home.

'Of course I am. It's my duty to do so.' Shanti's lips are stretched across her teeth in a vain attempt to close her mouth. Her expression is stern. She looks like Mother Agnes.

Watchdog Ganga is guarding the music room door and will not let them within sniffing distance of it. Aayee's voice, mimicked by the harmonium's intrusive, repetitive braying is going round and round, faster and faster, higher and higher. The tabla's relentless metallic pounding pushes her on. The notes swirl around giddily in Kranti's head. Aayee seems perched on a merry-go-round that will not stop, forced to carry on to a dark, frightening place from where there is no return.

And underneath, seeping out from beneath the closed door is the insidious, sick-making odour of jasmine-scented incense, a forbidden smell that hints at secrets wrapped in whispered arguments in the night; silences broken by the occasional shattering of glass.

Aayee's music session has come to an end. Ganga is serving tea and biscuits. They are all sitting in a circle, tailor fashion, on the maroon-coloured *satranjee* from Sholapur that has Baba's name woven into the border.

The harmonium master has very long, curly nails on his little fingers. Kranti, ensconced in Aayee's lap, watches him pick up his cup, little finger daintily extended, like an English lady.

The incense sticks placed in front of the portraits of Aayee's music guru and her spiritual guru, Shirdi Sai Baba, have a little red glow at the tip. Streams of ash are poised precariously on the long thin sticks jutting out from the incense holder's tiny holes. Aayee has placed some of her precious parijat and green champak flowers in front of the portraits. The scent of the flowers mingles with the cheap industrial perfume of Krishna Brand Chameli Agarbatti. Kranti can feel her four o'clock Ovaltine rising in her stomach. She struggles out of Aayee's lap, sloshing tea over the harmonium's mother-of-pearl keys.

'Clumsy! That's why I don't want you in the music room. Can't you ever keep still?' Aayee pushes aside the tanpura lying on its fat brown pumpkin bottom, picks up the small towel she keeps at hand and carefully wipes the instrument. Kranti wiggles back into her mother's lap and Aayee runs her fingers absently, deliciously, through her fine, long hair. Aayee smells wonderful, of soap, talcum powder, supari and flowers, blotting out the disgusting agarbatti smell.

There is the impatient honk of a car horn. Baba is back from the office and Aayee's accompanists get up to leave. Kranti and Shanti jump up, race outside to open the garden gate. The girls are scampering around him. One after the other, he lifts them both in his arms. 'Oh, you've grown so big and heavy,' he says, pretending to be out of breath. His chin is rough with a five o'clock shadow and he playfully rubs his cheek against Kranti's smooth, round one.

They go in slowly, the girls hanging on his arms. Kranti is dispatched to get his favourite whiskey glass. An elaborate cut-glass affair from Bohemia, it once belonged to their grandmother and is the only object he took, Baba says, when he left Babuji's house for good.

'Baba, I have a letter from Sister Margaret for you and Aayee,' Shanti pipes up and produces the envelope from her schoolbag.

Baba tears it open and reads the note, a frown between his eyebrows. 'This letter is not from Sister Margaret, Shanti. This is from Mother Agnes, complaining about your behaviour. You kicked and bit another girl, then denied everything when questioned. Her parents have complained. If it weren't for our Yvonne, who saw the whole thing, we might never have known. And now you've tried to get your sister into trouble.'

'No, Baba. No...' Shanti babbles, handing over the second letter. Her face is screwed up and she is crying. Her teeth and gums stick out. She looks like a frightened, scrawny monkey.

Baba reads the second note, then flings it at Aayee. 'A fine pair of liars we are bringing up in this house,' he says, getting up.

He has caught hold of Shanti's wrist and is dragging her with him towards the music room. Kranti knows what's coming. She squirms at the sound of Tai's whimpering and moves closer to Aayee.

Like Kranti, Aayee too is trying to shut out the sounds from the music room. 'Kuka,' she says gently, 'Sister says you're very good at classwork but that you don't do your homework properly. She says your story about Arjuna was very good but that you hadn't written it down and only pretended to read it.'

'No, Baba, no ... please!' Tai's shrieks and Baba's smacks seem to come from far away. He is using Shanti's ruler.

Kranti can feel her blood freeze. Aayee's blood is frozen too, she knows, by the way her mother clutches her shoulder. Her voice is low and quiet. 'You must grow up, Kuka, pay more attention. Sister says you are not stupid, only lazy and inattentive. Tonight I want you to write the story just like you said it in class. Now promise me you will never tell lies again.'

Kranti wants to tell her how she forgot about the homework, how she was too scared to own up. But she merely nods as she catches a glimpse of her sister running into their room.

'The next time you hit someone, remember, this is how it feels,' Baba is saying as he comes back to pour himself another whiskey. 'You too, Kranti. If I hear you're telling lies again, that is what you'll get. And Lalita, don't baby her, please! Now have your dinner and sit down to study, both of you.'

There is a terrible silence in their room. Tai is crying in whispered sobs. Kranti is trying to write the story of Arjuna but cannot get beyond 'One day a princess lost her golden ball which fell into a well in the forest...' Their tables, set side by side near the window, look out on the back verandah and the inner courtyard. The night is thick and black. In the dim light of the verandah, Kranti can see a dust mouse swirl momentarily on a short gust of wind, then settle on the parapet. She opens her drawer and looks at the cowrie shell necklace from Goa that Aunty Cou-ee gave her last summer. Shanti has tried to beg, borrow, steal it at least half a dozen times. Quietly she passes it to her sister, who flings it back at her. Then Shanti rests her head on her books and cries her heart out.

◇

Kranti is at the zoo, in front of the monkey cages. There are several baby monkeys and mother and father monkeys. Kranti likes the naughtiest one best. He snatches bits of banana from his brothers and sisters, does wonderful trapeze acts and cannot be caught.

Then there is a big fight and Mama Monkey, a baby clinging to her chest, catches hold of the wicked one, smacks him hard and pushes him into a corner. He grinds his teeth and rudely chatters back at his mother from a safe distance. With bared gums and glittery eyes, he looks exactly like Shanti. Stealthily, he creeps up close to Kranti and she is jolted awake by the sound of his grinding teeth.

Next to her, under the mosquito net, Tai is gnashing and grinding away, just like the baby monkey. Outside the safe whiteness of the mosquito net is a frightening, jet black, inky sea. Kranti puts out a tentative foot, feeling for the newspaper on which Ganga places a chamber pot each night. The pot is a reconverted brass milk pail, which offers the advantage of a handle. The newspaper is a recent innovation. Kranti is untidy and Ganga is tired of rubbing vinegar into the splashes she leaves on the floor.

But tonight the newspaper is absent. So is the pail. Kranti sits half in and half out of the mosquito net, her legs hanging over the side of the bed. She is considering her options. She crawls back in, shakes Shanti's shoulder.

'Tai... Tai...' Shanti mumbles and turns over. Kranti is now shaking her hard. 'Tai!' She is panicky and near to tears. Shanti is suddenly awake and extremely angry. 'What do you want?'

Kranti is snivelling. 'I want to do soo, Tai.'

'Use your stupid bucket then.'

'Tai, it isn't there. Ganga forgot.'

Shanti slides out of bed and comes to her sister's side. Hand in hand like two little ghosts in the night, they set off towards their bathroom, on the other side of the verandah, next to the music room. Mosquitoes buzz around them and dive for the tender flesh of their calves like famished carnivores.

Kranti sitting on her haunches over the startling white Indian-style toilet, seems to take forever. Shanti uses her toes to scratch her other leg. 'Hurry up!' she says, slapping at an itinerant mosquito that has settled on her arm.

'Coming, Tai.'

The light is still on in the music room and Shanti can hear the soft babble of her parents' voices. The smell of Baba's cigarette is sharper in the stillness of the night.

'I've finished', Kranti says, hitching up her pyjamas.

'Wash your hands... Wash your hands!'

With Kranti leaving driblets of water on the floor, Shanti carefully guides her sister back to bed. Mosquitoes hover inside the net and she traps a few with a bit of vigorous hand clapping, flicking their crushed bodies to the side of the bed. Kranti is already asleep, her thumb in her mouth. With short square fingers, Shanti pulls out the thumb, brushes back her sister's baby-fine hair. 'The next time we go out, I shall walk on the side of the traffic so my little sister won't get run over,' she promises herself. Then regrets having refused the cowrie shell necklace.

She is up and fishing for Kranti's drawer key in the pocket of her uniform. Quietly she draws out the necklace; places it around her neck. She stands barefoot in the verandah, admiring her reflection in the mirror above the washbasin. A phantom face with masses of curly black hair stares back at her. Under the blue lamp that Aayee leaves on all night, the cowries glow violet and pristine.

Shanti strikes a 'dancing Shiva' pose, breaking out into the latest toda taught by her Kathak teacher.

'Chandrata pana kara, aarati prabhu ki
Naachata Shankar, Ta dhin na kiti taka thun thun

Digh dha digh digh thaiy.'

Her voice is both pure and sweet as she whirls around, the cowries clinking about her neck, her feet making sharp slapping noises on the floor.

As if in response, the voices in the music room grow louder. Shanti creeps up to the door. Then stops, listening intently.

'But Vijay, I have never told them anything. I never speak to them about God or religion. I never said anything today,' Aayee says.

'If you want to sing bhajans, do pooja, go to the temple, do that away from this house. Why has this Sai Baba picture crept back here? Did I not give it away when we moved from Poona? I do not want my children to be brought up with blind faith. '

'You may not have faith, but I do.'

'Of course you do. That's because you come from an uneducated background.'

'How can you say that? My father was vice-prime minister to the king. I couldn't study because marriage came in the way. But two of my brothers are architects.'

'Yes, and the third one is a clerk and the fourth runs a truck because he still counts on his fingers. How many times have I asked you to study? You can pass your matric privately. But, no. How do you think I feel, having an uneducated wife?'

'And how do you think I feel, after all I've been through, the mental shocks I've suffered, going about like a widow without kunku or mangalsutra? What can I say when people ask me? Kranti said someone wanted to know if we were Christians because I don't wear kunku, or a mangalsutra, because you made me cut my hair. How do you think I feel, going about looking like a widow or a Christian!'

'You should be educating our children, telling them religion does not matter, that these are superstitious, old-fashioned ideas. Be grateful you found a progressive husband. Of course you're not a widow, and you know that. So why do you pay attention to what people say? You must become a forward-looking, educated woman, stop being so backward.'

'Why did you marry me, with my backward ideas? I suppose I was just another "social case" for you. You should have found some society lady with lipstick and bobbed hair who could talk to you in English about communism and politics. But with your past, who would have you? Who would have you but me? Because no one would have me either! Like two unwilling bullocks we are yoked to the same cart. That's why you have to make do with half-caste halfway houses like Barbara d'Costa. Because no decent society lady in her right mind would want to be seen with you.'

'Stop it! Or I'll hit you.'

'Go on, hit me. It won't be the first time, will it? I'll take the children and go back to my mother's tomorrow. I'll get a job teaching music. Akka will look after them.'

'Akka, that hard-hearted, rustic woman who won't even let you call her Aayee? She won't have you. My children will be brought up here. Away from your backward family and its blind superstitions. Who paid for your lessons? Sangeet Visharad, you call yourself. Without me, you were nothing. Your tuitions cost me 20 per cent of my salary every month. But I paid because I believe in progress and education. You must stop this religious nonsense. There will be no more Sai Baba here, you understand?'

The music room door is thrown open. Shanti flattens herself against the bit of wall between the door and the washbasin.

But Baba does not even see her. His arm shoots out of the doorframe to hurl the glass-fronted, red-tilaked picture of Sai Baba. It sails across the entire length of the verandah to shatter against the kitchen wall at the opposite end.

Shanti can feel rather than hear Aayee's muffled weeping. Then the door is shut again. Quickly, she returns to bed. Not bothering to look out for mosquitoes, she slides under the sheet. Next to her, Kranti's breath is soft and regular. Shanti throws one leg over her sister's waist. She closes her eyes and places her head between Kranti's bony shoulder blades.

8

A Lacanian Pause

The bad weather has continued. Robert-Pierre looks at the sheets of water running down the grubby windows and feels depression crawl down his grimy collar like an armada of tiny beetling insects. Feeling his ill-shaven chin, he sourly examines the bleak, rain-drenched suburban landscape peopled with shabby tower blocks, identical, cramped apartments, graffiti-smeared stairwells and bald playgrounds.

From where he sits, a little to one side behind the patient's couch, he can closely observe her, catch the expressions flitting across her features. She is an angry young woman of thirty-five whose marriage is cracking up.

'... And the toast is getting burnt and here I am getting the younger one dressed while the older one fiddles with the TV with sticky hands and of course we're late for the crèche and late for school and all this while, amid the shouting and the bawling, Eric is singing away in the bathroom as if we didn't exist ...'

He knows her story intimately and is barely listening now as he allows her voice to recede to the back of his head. He can recite it back to her without drawing breath. How many times has he journeyed with her, looked into her personal hell? Someone always suffers a beating – Eric clobbers her, she clobbers the children, who vent their rage upon the dog, a garden snail, an unsuspecting spider not sanguine enough to scuttle off before small, cruel fingers tear its furry legs apart, crush its tiny chest with a satisfying crunch...

Instead, his mind is given over to his conversation with Sophie, the enormity of Kranti's betrayal, the contents of her letter to Olga Savic, what he has read of her diary and the first few chapters of her terrifying technicolour rendition of her early life. His thoughts are like a restless tongue worrying an aching tooth, going around and beneath the source of pain, looking for the little cranny that will allow closer contact.

'I don't know. Something happens then, goes snap in me. Just like that. *Je craque.* I really wanted to slap Eric for his selfishness, his stupidity. But I found myself slapping Emilie instead. Just slapping her and shaking her because everything was sticky, the sofa, the TV, the table, and I could see myself spending Saturday morning cleaning up – Eric's mates are coming over to watch the football, *n'est-ce pas*, and the house must be shining. And so I continue to slap and punch her and she's screaming away and the baby's howling and Eric grabs me from behind to say *"T'es folle ou quoi?"*. I drop the kid and lock myself in the bathroom and the tears won't stop and so he takes the children to school on his way to work and, of course, as usual I'm the bad mother, *la mère indigne* ....'

Head bowed, she has dissolved into great big gulping sobs, her harsh dyed curls moving with an inner rhythm like wriggling baby serpents. A modern-day Medea, slapping her children to get back at her husband? Disinterestedly, he watches the glistening trickle from her nose make its way into the cleft of her upper lip to lie beaded upon the crevice of her mouth. Filled with revulsion by her awkward attempt to snort it back, he wordlessly hands her a box of tissues as he stares at the chipped purple paint on her fingernails, the pointy, rivet-studded boots. A muddy landslide of irritation dams up his '*tendresse proletaire*', Sophie's ironical term for his bleeding-heart weekly volunteer sessions at a community centre.

'We'll stop there today,' he says shortly.

'But we have only just started.' She turns around to look at him, the protest gathering in her eyes.

'We have been over all this before and the session is leading us nowhere. We shall take up the matter next week.'

'But I pay for the time. I'm entitled to my forty minutes,' she says, frustration making her bold.

'It's not a question of time. We call this a Lacanian pause,' he says brusquely. 'Same time next week.'

He has crushed her with a high-sounding phrase, hiding his anger behind the voice of authority, denying her the satisfaction of reproach. He doesn't bother telling her that the very nominal fee she pays goes not to him but to the upkeep of the centre, and busies himself with the case files on the heavy steel-grey desk instead, refusing to look up as she silently pulls on her coat, fixing him with her sad, wet eyes and sighing heavily as she leaves.

He has never done this before, never brought his own problems into the consulting room and he feels out of sorts, resentful, as his thoughts race along on undisciplined, wayward tracks.

Kranti, kissing Pierre Keller as if her life depended on it. Her luminous body, pearly with sweat, willing, wanton, waiting for his embrace and Keller leaving welling purply-red love bites on her neck as she moans with pleasure. Robert-Pierre is stiff with pain and anger. And arousal. 'The bitch!' he whispers. But he knows that he does not really know. That he never ever knew. She has slipped away. And now it's really too late.

'You see, Olga, I must pay back with my life.' This is the only phrase he remembers verbatim from Kranti's letter. Her life, or what he had read of it, sounded appalling. How had she survived to become so self-controlled, urbane? Was that what had snapped all of a sudden? What could she have done that was so frightful – cheated, stolen, killed, abandoned a child? The thought has never left him. It has interrupted his tired attempts to decipher her often squiggly writing, muddle his way through dense prose.

The red book, in sharp contrast to Kranti's confessional to Keller, has a naïve, fairytale quality. But it also contains detailed drawings of different poisonous plants, their symptoms printed neatly below. Notes on prescription drugs, their uses and effects. Copious details about Strychnine, Cyanide, Laburnum, Poison Ivy. It's a terrifying litany of death. Encouraged by that scoundrel Pierre Keller, he is sure now.

This should have been explanation enough for that poor bastard, Inspector Laporte. With this in hand, he did not need a suicide note. He persecuted me for the pleasure of it. He should have persecuted Keller instead.

But horrified as he is by these details, it is the black notebook that intrigues him more. Was any of that real? Was that how she truly lived?

He tries to concentrate on the task at hand. The best time to collect his things would be in a couple of hours, before Sophie's return from school. It would be unwise to seek a meeting just yet. He cancels his afternoon sessions, then heads back home.

The flat is quiet, muted. Robert-Pierre drifts from room to room, looking intently at the classic Louis XVI chairs in faded browny-pink velvet, the waxed, creaking floorboards, the silver candlesticks, the brass fire screen, as if visiting for the first time. The austere formalism of the salon is in startling contrast to Kranti's riot of rich, oriental colour. Lingering in Sophie's bedroom, he drinks in the smell of lavender that hangs about a pile of freshly ironed clothes and wonders about his double life. In his study, his eyes rest on the small bronze goddess Kranti gave him last Christmas, breaking her piggy bank to buy it, he knew.

'I should have given it to you in time for Laxmi poojan,' she'd said, explaining the role of the goddess as consort, as shakti, as the giver of boons. 'Then you could have prayed for health, longevity, sexual prowess and lots and lots of lovely lolly...! You can still do it, of course, it's never too late. Or try next year.'

She had talked about Indian female morphology – the narrow, pinched-in waist, large, high, rounded breasts, prominent nipples, generous hips, flaring thighs and always, always the sensuous pad of stomach, the flesh dipping gently into the navel.

'Not like your western mannequins, flat as boards, or Titian's heavy-boned, ample beauties,' she'd said, feverishly turning the pages of a book on Indian sculpture. 'Our goddesses were fine-boned, narrow-waisted, demure in face, but oh so oomphy!'

It's true, he thinks, caressing Laxmi's lush contours. He wonders if Sophie has remarked upon the steady collection of Indian objects in his study – the Nathdwara miniatures, the catalogues of Indian art exhibitions, the silver paan boxes, an intricately worked nutcracker, a cloth hand fan; if she has noticed the recent disappearance of the ivory negress from

Senegal. Nothing escaped her, he knew. As usual, she was keeping a discreet silence.

Robert-Pierre steps into his closet, fingers his suits and ties hanging in neat rows above an equally orderly line of polished shoes. Piling half a dozen shirts, ties, pocket kerchiefs and a couple of suits on his bed, he proceeds to pack them methodically into a black leather suitcase.

On the way out, he leaves his house keys to let Sophie know he has honoured her wish. It is also a way of making sure she will be there to let him in when he calls to say he has forgotten something.

At Kranti's, he makes room for his clothes, pushing her dresses to one side. Nothing would have pleased her more than to have him move in with her. She had hinted as much a year into their relationship, but he had never allowed her to articulate that wish, making it plain that his real place lay next to his wife. As his clothes nestle against hers, he wonders if she can see him here, if she knows. He is going to have to get rid of her clothes one day, a decision he has put off these past weeks.

A bag of groceries and a covered dish await him on the dining table. A veal casserole, more like Hungarian goulash, his nostrils tell him. The bag holds milk, butter, eggs, tomatoes, coffee and a packet of pre-washed salad. Next to the bag is a note with a short message: *Bonne chance*! Call me if you need something or just knock. We never go out! – Olga.

They were supposed to dine out tonight. He wonders what Sophie will wear, what she wishes him to do. Alain and Yasmina are her friends more than his, so he does the decent thing and cries off. Just a temporary separation, he tells Alain, nothing to worry about. She'll explain. He can count on Sophie to put them off without any sort of explanation. What is there to explain anyway? Alain is her family lawyer. He hopes she is not starting proceedings for a permanent separation. That would be unbearable.

He has shaved, bathed, eaten, napped and, sitting on one of the red velvet sofas, switched on the television. A repeat of the weekend game between Paris Saint-Germain and Marseille at the Parc des Princes, a bloody match with hysterical, baying fans. He loves football and would normally relish the game. But a strange restlessness grips him. Perhaps it's the fact that the match is a replay, not live. He hovers moodily at the window, looking out at the same roundabout, the Sofitel hotel, familiar landmarks now that bring him no respite. Finally, with a mug of coffee at his elbow, he settles down at Kranti's desk, once again restlessly turning the pages of her notebooks.

9

The Black Notebook

22 November 2005

In the end there is a beginning. Or so I would like to believe. I think I shall come back to these pages every time I make a fresh beginning. Let us see then, how many endings there are and how many beginnings...

24 November 2005

It is ten to eleven p.m. I always come to these pages too late. But as R says about his work, Discipline is the Key. One must have the discipline to apply it though. Keeping R at bay and writing everyday must become the two main objectives over the next couple of months.

Baba's birthday today. I miss him. In spite of all the bad things, I can feel my heart go heavy and my eyes well up. Do I really believe all those ghastly, monstrous things I've spewn onto these pages? I've called him a weasel. He was a wonderful father to us when we were small and I think that is what endures – the grip of those early memories of happiness, of utter bliss.

I make him out to be a tyrant, a cruel, selfish S.O.B. Is that what he was, or is that what he became? Did alcoholism and sex addiction make him that way? He had that power; that gorgeous smile, that quick wetting of the eyes when someone told him a cruel or moving story. They say dictators love little children and are kind to dogs. Well, Baba was a bit like that, crying at the most soggy, sentimental stories, quick to emote. Hated dogs, though! But his underlying self-indulgence, his utter and complete devotion to himself and to hedonistic pleasure was unbudgeable. Hard sheet rock.

What got us hooked? He was intelligent, good-looking and well-read, until he got lazy and sodden with drink, that is.

The problem was that the three of us, the women of the house, Aayee, Tai and I (and by then Tai and I were no longer wonderstruck little girls but fully-grown and highly critical young women), had seen through him. We knew him for the fraud that he was. But we loved him nevertheless. And we fought over him. Bitterly.

Looking back, I have never ever loved anyone so totally, so truthfully, so absolutely as I have my father nor hated anyone as much. He was bold, wild, clever, wonderful and playful, defying all the strict, conformist norms laid down for Indian fathers.

For a long, long time, we adored him, both Tai and I, and he remained in my eyes a miraculously gifted, generous, just and kind person – a perfect father, who punished only when we had done wrong. Until I turned fifteen and woke up to reality and the coiled-up snake tumbled out of our garage and life fell apart.

They pulled her through that terrifying black night. But she, the essential Aayee, was no longer there. She had gone for good, vanished somewhere along the way, on her return from death. In her lucid spells later, she said she experienced strange sensations as if there had been, for a small moment, the possibility of escape to some other, happier resting place.

She had a tube going up her nose, needles stuck into veins in both arms – glucose in one, saline through the other, pumped simultaneously.

Blood dribbled in through a small plastic tube inserted into an incision on her ankle. This little tube became a permanent fixture over the months – a direct access to her body; a convenient opening to squirt in medication, to draw endless vials of blood for tests and more tests.

Baba was jocular. 'Oh, she's on nasal feeding,' he said. 'They've pushed in a couple of eggs this morning along with milk and orange juice. And, of course, the medicine. Very convenient, this nasal feeding. No stains, no spills, no slip between cup and lip, ha ha.'

How did I react? How did Tai react? For the first week or two, Tai refused to go there. Blood, she shied away from it. I'm not sure I understood what it meant to lose one's mother. I behaved as if everything was absolutely normal and my best friend was a great help. But now, thinking back, I know this utter selfishness had by then become part of our family ethos.

We were all, by that I mean Baba, Tai and I, so incredibly selfish, so very egotistical, that we did not really give a toss about poor Aayee. She could have lain there until kingdom come for all we cared. Or perhaps I'm too harsh, perhaps we were, quite simply, in denial.

One day, Baba came home from work to find me dancing to one of the popular numbers – probably Summer Wine *or* Delilah, *bought at Banga's rhythm corner in Chandigarh. My room, sandwiched between the pantry and the bathroom I shared with Tai, was little more than a passage, a sad little room with a worn grey drugget carpet, a chipped wooden table and chair, a string bed and a built-in cupboard that smelt of wet cement.*

So Baba came back from work at about noon one day to find me swinging away to the strains of some far-away ballad and blew me up. Did I not feel this was inappropriate? How could I dance when my mother lay dying?

Guiltily, I yanked back the stylus. 'Of course he is right,' I thought at first. 'How could I?' and rearranged my features into a suitable expression of mournfulness. But my mind was neither sad nor still. Instead, it seethed with anger. A kind of mindless, uncomprehending fury that remained unspoken for all that.

And yet, it never entered my mind to ask: 'And what about you? How can you come home to swill gin and take long afternoon naps while your wife lies dying? What are you up to when you're neither home nor at the office, or when you fail to show up at the hospital on sultry summer afternoons?' I didn't. Impossible for me to harbour such thoughts about the person I loved above all else in the world. Impossible too, because though all the signs were there, I stoutly refused to admit he could do anything wrong. Blind loyalty, I guess. Or blind love, maybe.

He never stopped moaning about how hard he worked and how much he did for two ungrateful kids and a nagging wife whose hospital bills he was now paying. And I was truly contrite. I commiserated. Wholeheartedly. Suspecting, but resisting all knowledge of his visits to late night cabaret shows where the dancing girls were little more than bottom-wiggling, chest-thrusting whores. I was sublimely unaware of how he preyed upon hapless under-educated lower-middle-class women who applied for jobs and got them only to discover their real work lay not with insurance claims but with their boss's thingammy on his office couch.

How could I have guessed that his Sunday morning beer-swilling buddy sessions with assessors and garage owners were in fact a front for a veritable factory manufacturing false insurance claims that defrauded the company of hundreds of thousands of rupees?

Perhaps it was convenient not to know, not to ask. His cushy job coupled with insurance fiddles made sure Baba always had thick wads of money in his pocket. And it was those crisp hundred-rupee notes nonchalantly peeled off in front of as large an audience as possible that got me Pat Boone's Pearly Shells, *Tom Jones'* Delilah, *the latest*

Beatles albums and a surprise present in the form of a Hawaiian guitar with a shiny, chrome-plated guitar rod that I later learnt to put to good use.

A Hawaiian guitar does not lend itself to rockin' n 'rollin'. It's a stodgy instrument that you play sitting down, working the strings with a plastic plectrum while dragging the rod across the frets to produce a wailing, plaintive sound. The rod prolongs the sound, making one note run into the next – very unsexy.

I was furious, of course. I wanted a Spanish guitar, one you could play standing up like a real pop idol. And I had sulked over this handsome gift bought without my consent or approval.

But then I would have sulked over most anything. My surliness had everything to do with a blooming adolescent crisis. I had just discovered, via a porn novel smuggled into college by one of the older girls, the lewd mechanics of sex, and it had set my juices flowing. I wanted desperately to meet boys but was terrified of being called fast and, unlike some of my classmates, wasn't lucky enough to have an older brother who would introduce me to all his dashing friends (they were actually gawky, pimply youths of the type I would later learn to abhor, but no matter).

So most nights I wrung myself dry, clamping my vaginal muscles tight around my puny guitar rod, my mind inflamed by a mixture of raw sex and romance in the shape of studio close-ups of effeminate Hindi film stars – the term Bollywood had yet to make its appearance – whose faces bore a leery resemblance to my father's, and what I imagined to be rogering of the most lowly kind. But try as I could, I found it impossible to imagine my parents at it, especially now with Aayee looking like a famine victim.

Every afternoon, after college, I would go to the hospital to sit beside my mother. I either cycled there or took a bus to the university in sector 14 and walked across to the hospital in sector 12. Sector 13 didn't figure anywhere on the map. But I knew it existed. It was the cremation ground.

Aayee came out of coma – emerged? Surfaced? Was it sudden or gradual? Did she wake up like Rip Van Winkle to find a changed world or did she, like Sleeping Beauty, merely blink?

There were terrible physical changes in her. She dribbled constantly, for one, and we ended up placing hand towels on her chest, like a baby's bib. And then came the babbling and the bed-wetting. Her hands began to shake and twist, turning round and round in erratic, circular movements – involuntary motor articulation, they called it – as if operated by a jerky, invisible robot.

What had happened to her? She chattered; nonsense most of the time. Her shoulders moved awkwardly. Forget walking, she could neither sit nor stand without support. My proud, erect mother had become bent, stiff, gaunt and flat-chested. Her medical papers were dotted with question marks. Post-encephalitis features? Parkinsonia? They just could not say.

The one 'P' that never made it to the written report, however, was 'P' for poisoning.

What I did not know then but learnt later was that the doctors suspected Baba of trying to poison her. 'They told us to go over the house from top to bottom and bring them any tablet, liquid, syrup, powders, whatever we could find. But your father was too clever, he must have hidden whatever he had used,' Saraswati Aunty told me many years later, on a rainy monsoon afternoon in her lonely widow's flat near the Banganga pond in Bombay.

I scoffed at her then, but I find myself wondering at times. It's true their arguments had reached their zenith just before Aayee fell ill. They would quarrel violently, often into the early hours of the morning. Baba was frequently drunk and abusive and she would accuse him of bedding his secretaries at the office, of winking at the maid, the cook, the washerwoman's twelve-year-old daughter. I was so in love with my father I refused to believe any of it and for a long time remained convinced my mother was a selfish nag, a killjoy, a wet blanket. And then, as time went on and her behaviour became aberrant and erratic, I became convinced she had gone just plain cuckoo.

Often, the words that sallied forth from her mouth would have made a sailor blush. A whore's brat, a bugger, a pimp and sodomiser, bhosadicha, randicha, mawali, haramkhor, used turn by turn in infinite permutations and combinations. But poisoning her? My mind couldn't quite grasp that.

It was at the hospital in Chandigarh that Tai and I began to learn of past secrets, when one of the nurses asked us: 'Isn't this a second marriage for both your parents?'

'No...' we stuttered, looking at each other in confusion.

'Don't ask them anything. They probably haven't been told,' her colleague cautioned.

But Tai got it out of Aayee when she was in one of her babbly phases. Slyly, she suggested she knew all about Aayee's first husband. Aayee didn't seem surprised. She didn't even want to know how Tai knew, let alone deny it. It was as if a long-held taboo had been breached, a wall of silence pulled down, and once she got started, she didn't seem to be able to stop.

'He was an impotent gandu,' she said. 'They married me off to this man who was not a man at all. And my own brother did it! What brother would do that to his sister – marry her off to his own buggering lover!' she raged, cursing her eldest brother Raghunath, who had arranged the match. 'I was sixteen and beautiful. I wanted to dance and sing and Akka had already received offers from talent scouts from V. Shantaram's film studios. I could have been an actress; I could have had a career. Instead, I became a virgin widow. Can you imagine that? At sixteen? Untouched and a widow? But I don't

blame that bastard gandu as much as I blame that filthy brother of mine. I was innocent, but not that innocent. I knew what happened between men and women behind closed doors. I had seen dogs do it. My husband couldn't even bring himself to sit by my side. But the sounds that came from the bedroom when Raghunath was visiting his younger sister would make a prostitute turn red with shame.' Aayee literally hurled the words at us.

We both instinctively disliked Raghunath Uncle. Like all her male siblings, he was tall, and had once been good-looking with boyish charm and a Hollywoodian crooked grin popular in the 40s. But when I knew him, the bloom had faded, the charm evaporated, to leave a grim individual, insufferably preachy and stingy to the point of miserliness. He had risen through the bureaucratic ranks to become Assistant Sales Tax Commissioner for Bombay and wore his honesty for all to see, like a chestful of war medals.

'I could have been very rich if I'd wanted, much richer than your father,' he'd tell us. 'I've been offered thousands of rupees but I've never taken a single bribe. Which is why you people drive about in your fancy cars while we live on a government official's salary in this cramped flat.'

The 'we' included my grandmother. He had sacrificed his life and happiness so his younger siblings could go abroad for foreign degrees, marry well, lead good lives, he said. We were always told of how he had financed the British education of two of his brothers, and never married in order to look after his old mother. But Aayee knew better.

For all his boasts of simple living and high thinking, I could sense, even as a child, that Raghunath Uncle was an unhappy man. A man with a heavy past who had a big iron safe of guilty memories locked up inside him. My mother's presence was a constant reproach; my father's flagrant virility a thorn in his side; our very existence a jeering reminder of his own empty loins.

It has taken me thirty years to piece together the full story.

January 2006

Christmas has come and gone, the New Year is here, and I am still struggling.

I keep trying to write 'I' but find myself writing 'R' instead. There must be a Freudian slip somewhere.

I think it is over. He won't tell me. But there isn't very much to say. We run out of breath, of words, of tales to tell. I feel like calling him to say: It's over, isn't it? To prompt him to protest that it is not, that I am being absurd. But I am under no illusion. For R, I am just an exotic plaything and a broken one at that. If I'm beautiful and creative, he will be at my feet. If I am not, he will away, take wing.

My designing is nothing; at least nothing that I care about, just commercial stuff. Which fashion designer produces art with a capital A unless it's a Chanel, an Alaïa, a St Laurent or a Courrèges? It pays the rent and I must eat, but it's hardly the way to R's heart. He barely looks at my sketches. And when he does, I feel he's looking sideways, ashamed. Is that why our worlds remain so separate? After all those Turners, Tintorettos, Titians and Carpaccios we've seen, after Klimt and Beckmann, Dali, Freud, Picasso, do I dare show him my canvases? He'll only laugh that gentle laugh and call me his 'pauvre canard'.

I haven't seen Pierre for so long. It's simple. Nothing to show him. I must heed his advice: putting it all down, getting it outside of myself, where I can truly examine this disease that is eating into me – sick, slimy, like some worm-ridden, maggoty growth.

Spitting it out is the only exit. Or is there really no exit? There are some terrible truths there, and harsh though they be, they must be told. I fear these ruminations of mine are nothing but artful dodging, avoidance tactics to keep from facing the real issue. And the real issue is their story;our story; my story.

It would not be wrong to say my world fell apart. I was fifteen. But it would also be wrong to say that everything dropped upon our heads ike Hiroshima or Nagasaki, just like that, in one blind nanosecond when all hell broke loose. The signs had been there and coming. But f their constant bickering, the ever-so-frequent transfers, change of house, school, friends, university had been hell, Aayee's illness was heller than hell.

How did we cope? Well, to start with, we got a cook, a clumsy Bihari called Ram Singh, who served us runny, underdone mutton curries and thick, shapeless chapattis. The other servants came and went at will. The floors became grey around the corners, dust piled inch-thick on the unused plates in the pantry, and there were always mountains of clothes waiting to be washed and ironed.

Only the gardener did his job, whistling popular Hindi tunes as he tinkered with Aayee's favourite rosebushes or set up a trellis for the sweet peas. She loved her garden and he looked after it, as if holding it in trust. He dug up Aayee's potatoes, brought in carrots, lettuce, radish, French beans, aubergines, lady's fingers, tomatoes and pumpkins. The pantry overflowed with the abundance from her garden. I stubbed my toe on a particularly large pumpkin. The kitchen reeked of onions gone bad.

We did not see the seasons roll by. Tai and I did nothing around the house. Baba was hardly ever there. We met occasionally – fleetingly over breakfast, desultorily over dinner. Anyone could have come in and stripped the place clean.

It was then that I first began to paint. Baba had given me an easel, my first proper canvas and a set of oil colours for my birthday – a low-key, mournful affair with Aayee still in hospital.

Squeezing out a gash of bright flame orange to outline a flower, filling it in with shades of purple, hot pink. No pencils, no drawing, just pure paint, raw and glistening on the canvas. What emerged was Babuji's old Poona house, the driveway lined with crotons in their Shanti garden pots. A touch here, a dab there, shiny wet, fully alive, my childhood miraculously recaptured.

I could have swooned with pleasure. I was always good at drawing, but it won me no accolades (that's all very well, Kranti, but art doesn't get you any marks, they'd say, you cannot look forward to a profession, a career).

During Aayee's illness, painting afforded some relief, became a lifelong anchor. Aayee's brother, Nana Uncle, who was the principal of the architecture college, encouraged me. 'Stop trying to be merely decorative, you have good strokes, strong emotion in you, let it out,' he scolded. It was he who brought me prints of Old Masters from his college library, introduced me to Da Vinci, Vermeer, Rembrandt, Goya, Titian, Tintoretto, Velasquez and the others, taking me through the pointillists, the impressionists, the surrealists and the fauves, the secessionists, the cubists; talked to me about Ravi Varma, Jamini Roy, the Bengal School, revealed the naïve wonder of Alpana and the classical beauty of traditional Indian motifs, laying the foundations I would build upon later. Within his overblown, heavy-jowled, balding hulk, I discovered a sensitive, poetic heart.

With Aayee away the house had lost its soul, a presence, her presence, and it didn't even register with us. I remember the first time she came home. It was winter and the flowers were in full bloom. Her black roses gave out a divine scent. She wore a pale grey salwar kameez – Baba had decreed that saris were too cumbersome, awkward, bulky, difficult, and the more practical Punjabi suit, with elasticized salwars for easy pulling down had become de rigueur, her hospital uniform. I had been instructed to get the local tailor to stitch six of them and had made a tidy profit on the charges.

Her hair was short, without a shade of grey. She was weak and frail but beautiful, leaning heavily on Baba and me, as we helped her out of the car. But she did not want to go in. She wanted to linger in the garden, smell the flowers, take stock of the seedling beds. 'It's been eight months since I felt the sun upon my back, the ground beneath my feet,' she said, before going in.

Aayee would be home for a couple of days and she would seem all right. Then the vomiting would start again; and with it, the churning of the wrists and hands, the hallucinations, the black rages. After a few days of that, in a state of extreme dehydration, off she'd go to hospital once more.

And that was when she would begin to talk. Telling us about the thousand humiliations Babuji and Baba's brothers and their wives had heaped upon her. She wasn't quite the high Brahmins they were; a meat-eating Saraswat, not part of their grey-eyed, brown-haired, superior Chitpavan Brahmin clan. Gecko-white and buck teeth is how Aayee would describe her older, educated sisters-in-law. But secretly I knew she longed for their grey-green eyes and mousey brown hair, for the raw-edged boniness that seemed part of the female Chitpavan physique.

I once found her begging Baba to let her sing a bhajan to Shiva. She was trying to get hold of his feet in order to beg better; he was trying to restrain her. 'Please, Vijay, let me sing just one bhajan, just one bhajan please...' 'Yes, yes,' he kept saying, having finally understood, I suppose, the damage his crusade against religion or any form of worship had wrought. But she was somewhere else, in her own never-never land, incapable of hearing him, her pleas an unending, plaintive wail.

Many years earlier, when we were in Meerut, a filthy provincial city that Baba had temporarily made his headquarters, he had convinced Aayee to cut her hair short and perm it. Now the perm had gone and her hair framed her face in soft, short waves. Very nice, I thought. But he had other ideas.

'Why don't you go to the hairdresser's for another perm?' he suggested one day. 'Kranti can take you down to the Chinese hairdresser around the corner. It'll be a good outing for you.'

The dolt. Did he not know that a perm meant sitting up in a chair for forty-five minutes waiting for those ghastly ammonia-drenched curls to form? I tried to dissuade her. But my poor suggestible mother – even in that state, she wanted to please him, sexually attract him. Maybe she just wanted to look pretty again – her idea of prettiness, which meant his *idea of prettiness: tight corkscrew curls all over her head, like a sari-clad English memsahib.*

We had to take a cycle rickshaw from the house to the corner lane, where the Chinese girls from Calcutta operated their salon. Baba had not sent the car. 'It's so close, you'll manage,' he said.

I had phoned to book an appointment, roughly sketched in the details, that she was ill, would need to rest. Aayee's face, jerking shoulders and stiff movements alarmed the girl. 'Sure you want this done? Strong chemicals. Take mo' than one hour. No stop in middle,' she warned.

'Aayee, why don't you just get a trim and we'll go home?'

But she was adamant. A perm was what she wanted and a perm it was going to be. Why did I not put my foot down, intervene, to say no, you're too weak, you won't be able to bear it? Too chicken? Too afraid? Brought up in the old way and taught not to contradict one's parents? Or indifferent, callus, uncaring?

With the curlers upon her head, Aayee's face looked more skull-like than ever. They placed cushions around her, then made her lie back with her head over the sink. The stink of ammonia filled the room. The Chinese girl kept dousing the curlers with the ammonia fixer, jiggling them roughly to make the liquid penetrate the tightly wound hair. Aayee's head was pushed around this way and that like a disembodied toy skull. Low moans escaped her lips. She struggled to sit up, but the Chinese girl pushed her back down, placing a wet hand on her forehead to pin her head to the sink. 'Not now. Curls not done yet,' she said.

'Kranti... Kranti! Take me home please.' I could barely make out the words; her voice was so low and hoarse. The Chinese girl looked at me with ill-concealed irritation. 'Can't stop now. Curls have to fix. Stop now very bad, hair terrible, curls no stay.'

Aayee lay there pawing the air, her dead mutton eyes wide open, pleading silently. Ashamed, embarrassed, exasperated, I flounced all the way to the market in the afternoon heat to hail a rickshaw, blinded by angry tears and the golden glare of the flower-laden laburnum trees that lined the road.

Sweat snaked through my hair, giving my scalp an insane itch. But there was no question of scratching oneself in public. So I strode on, looking like a thundercloud, spoiling for a fight, waiting to pounce on the first person that dared cross my path. The rickshaw puller, poor man, got it in the neck.

The curls looked all right for the first two days. Then Aayee said she wanted to wash her hair. Her scalp smelt funny, she complained. It did too – ammonia mixed with sweat deposits and sebaceous secretions, a heady combination, ha ha!

So we went through the hair-wash ritual, a tad more complicated than the bath ritual that we had by now perfected. She was so weak, you couldn't put her in the bathtub. So we would place her on a low stool in the bathroom with a bucket and a mug of ready mixed hot water.

I would remove her salwar, sliding it off her bony white legs with skin so cracked it looked like famine-parched land, while Baba would sit her up and take off the kameez in one smooth, practiced gesture. Then, a heave-ho, sideways, to push her onto the large bath towel spread on the bed next to her. By now she was already out of breath, so we would wait a few moments for her to breathe easier.

Then Baba carried her to the stool while I whipped off the towel. Quickly, with him propping her up from behind, I would pour a couple of mugfuls of water over her head and shoulders, then soap her down with a small square towel.

The first time we bathed her, he soaped the upper part of her body. Then handed me the towel to get it done down there. 'Tithe kar' – do it there, he said. Her pubis felt rough and scratchy to my touch and I was invaded by shame. That day, I looked at my mother for the first time in many years. Really looked at her, I mean. She was a body withered before its time, bony, fleshless, sexless almost. Her shoulders jerked, her elbows stuck out; the skin was stretched tight across her hips.

For a long time, even before she took ill, our mother had stopped being anything but cook, housekeeper, servant-in-charge. I looked again for Aayee, my caring, simple, homespun mother who had fed me mouthfuls of daal-rice on the verandah of Babuji's house in Poona. I tried to find the gentle spirit that had patted me to sleep, offered her children coloured, sweetened curd when they refused to drink milk; I searched that face for the proud yet vulnerable beauty who had stood so tall, walked so straight, sung so sweet. She was gone.

I had bought a bottle of Sunsilk egg shampoo and I poured a couple of generous capfuls on her hair, working up a fine lather. Some of it trickled into her eyes, and she began to whimper and shake her head from side to side like a wet dog. There wasn't enough water in the bucket to get the soap out. And I had to mix a second bucket under Baba's disapproving, angry stare. By the time it was over Baba and I were drenched with Aayee tottering on the stool, crying quietly her mewls fainter than those of a newborn kitten.

He carried her dripping to the bed, laid her on the towel. I turned her over on her stomach to dry her hair and comb out the knots. My hands touched something sticky. There was a large, bright red patch beneath her face.

'Baba,' I screamed, turning her over. Blood was gushing out of her nose like a quick red mountain stream, running down the craters of her face, drenching the towel, sheet and mattress. It was pouring out thicker and faster than the slimy ketchup I had seen in Hindi films, and her face, neck and chest, her newly washed hair was now smeared with the stuff.

I knew exactly what needed to be done. Hadn't I just finished a St John Ambulance Brigade First Aid Course?

'Sit the patient up in a chair, or on the side of the bed, with his face leaning slightly forward. Pinch the soft part of the nose for about ten minutes. Loosen clothing around the neck and make the patient breathe through the mouth. Do not allow him to sniff or blow his nose for a few hours.'

Those were the instructions. But they did not tell you how to deal with a yelling, semi-hysterical bully of a father and a patient so weak she couldn't hold her head up.

I tried pushing Aayee into a sitting position but it was hopeless; she kept toppling over. Baba had pulled out all the clean towels from the linen cupboard and they lay in a pile at our feet, the top ones as bright a red as holi gulal, the lower ones a rusty India red, the colour of Babuji's Shanti garden pots. Baba kept pushing her head back, insisting that was the right thing to do.

'Never, never push a patient's head back, he could choke on the blood,' the teacher had warned.

'Don't do that, Baba,' I heard myself scream. 'It's in my book, I'll show you.'

But I never made it to the door, fainting on the dirty beige carpet that covered the floor. When I came around, my bottom hurt and Baba towered over me, calling me a stupid, inefficient fool.

Aayee looked like Pinocchio. Her muzzle clamped by a red plastic clothespin, she seemed to be thumbing her nose at both of us. He had managed to sit her up, propping her against the headboard with a cliff of pillows. Her eyes were closed; blood still trickled from her hair onto the pillow and a drop hung at the tip of her chin. A skin-and-bone bedraggled Kali, *eyes half closed, mouth slack, a clothespin at the end of her nose. In her hand she held the bloodied half of a raw onion. Baba had tried to make her smell it, resorting to grandmothers' remedies when all else failed.*

'Get up now. We have to clean her again,' he growled. This time we did not take her to the bathroom but sponged her down on the bed, wiping away the blood as best we could, ignoring the crust of dried blood on her scalp.

Only a week later, when her head was finally washed and combed, did we see the extent of the damage inflicted by the abortive trip to the hairdresser's. Her hair stood on end, dry and lifeless, halfway between a curl and a crinkle, like a halo of dirty brown candy floss. If, before she had looked delicate and fragile, pretty despite her extreme thinness, she now looked like a survivor from a concentration camp, an apparition risen from the grave, enough to spook an unsuspecting ghost.

◇

I came home one day to find Tai closeted with Aayee in her room. Aayee seemed to be improving and although she remained weak, her jerky movements had stopped. I knew something was up when I saw my sister turn her head guiltily away from me.

Aayee had begun muttering. I could make out curses, female ones this time. And then, with superhuman, maniacal strength, she was up, lurching out of her room towards the kitchen. The screen door banged shut behind her. I rushed after her to find her heading away from the back verandah, towards the two-room annexe where Baba's accountant Makhija lived with his wife. Mr and Mrs Fat, we called them.

She knocked. Mrs Fat opened the door. But her smile of welcome lasted only a few seconds. Aayee was upon her like a fury, her hands grabbing hold of Mrs Fat's face and hair in a vain attempt to scratch her eyes out.

I grabbed her from behind, trying to pinion her arms, but she shook me off with terrific force. 'Kuthe hotis tu randey?' she screamed at Leela Makhija. Randey in Marathi, randi in Hindi, both have the same root – raand. Whore. It was not lost on Mrs Fat who let out a loud 'Hai Ram'!

I understood Tai's guilty look. She had told Aayee about our cook Ram Singh's attempt to kiss her one evening when Aayee was in hospital. Baba was away on one of his ruts, while I lay blasting my ears with the Stones. 'I left my daughters in your care. Where were you, bitch, when they needed you?' Aayee was asking Mrs Fat, shaking her by the shoulder.

It was one of my dressed-up days and I had pinched Aayee's favourite Lucknowi cotton sari, a pale lilac number with chikan shadow work embroidery. I struggled to separate Aayee and Mrs Fat, while trying simultaneously to keep the pallu on my shoulder and avoid stepping on the pleats. Aayee suddenly went limp in my arms and we both toppled over, our heads narrowly missing the cement ledge of the steps. Mrs Fat slammed shut her door and we could hear her howling inside like a wolf on a moonlight night.

I looked up to see a small gaggle of people enjoying the spectacle from the road. A couple of rickshaw pullers had stopped mid-tug to gape while the urchins who helped the corner bicycle repair fellow were standing on the parapet wall, telling anyone who cared to listen: 'Aarey, bola tha na? Yeh Madrasi log to sub paagal hain.' *Not only were we 'Madrasis' from down south (we weren't), we were now also barking mad.*

Aayee had quite simply blacked out. Tai and I carried her dead weight in stages, first to the cracked leather couch in the back verandah, then to her bedroom, with a small halt on the dining-room carpet. She came back slowly, muttering gutturally. Her hands were moving in familiar patterns. We had lost her again.

The phone was on the blink. Ram Singh had disappeared. Leaving Tai with Aayee, I biked to the phone booth in the market, pedalling like the devil himself, holding up the pleats of my crumpled lilac sari with one hand, looking every inch the lunatic I was now reputed to be. Bumping headlong over potholes, the wind rushing in my face, my hair streaming wild behind me, I remember thinking of Achilles the Fleet of Foot or Mercury, little wings fluttering nervously around his thong-bound ankles.

To Baba's credit, he hoofed it back within twenty minutes of my phone call, Makhija in tow. Mrs Fat would not open the door. Makhija had to break it down. They took the evening train out, she looking vacantly around her, occasionally emitting a small, sharp yelp like an animal in pain. She'd been given electric shock treatment after the loss of their baby three years ago. He was taking her back to the asylum in Ranchi, he said, since there was no other way he could cope.

A silence hung around the house as if we'd all gone into collective mourning. Baba sent two of his office peons to hunt down Ram Singh. Aayee slept, helped along by generous capfuls of Largactyl, her hands continuing their bump and grind routine.

It was night by the time they ran him down at the paanwala's stall in the market. Baba sat waiting on the leather sofa in the back verandah, whiskey glass in hand. The sofa's matted coir stuffing peeped out from between his trouser-clad legs like an obscene pubic thatch. Lights blazed in the Makhijas' empty flat, but nobody bothered to trot across to switch them off. Tai sat reading in a basket garden chair beside Baba, but I could tell she was tense, looking every now and then at the Favre Leuba watch they had given her for her seventeenth birthday. You could hear the peons' abuse and Ram Singh's frightened squeals as they walked up the garden path.

His head bound in a muffler as if to hide from the world, Ram Singh looked small and shrunken between the two peons who held his arms. Like a terrified rabbit, he looked this way and that, his eyes, unnaturally bright, resting briefly on Tai's face before dropping to Baba's shoes, for which he tried to make an unsuccessful dive. He was blubbering seriously now. 'Sahib, hamar koyi galati nahi, Sahib...'

Baba placed his whiskey glass carefully on the floor beside the sofa. Casually, he glanced at his watch, then began undoing his shoelace. Ram Singh redoubled his entreaties, his voice hoarse with fear. 'Khamosh!' *Baba's voice rang out cold and angry, reducing the servant to snivelling silence.*

Despite his hanky-panky with the ladies, his lying and his cheating, Baba never swore. 'I'm a wordsmith, so why would I use dross to fashion my gems?' he told me once. 'People swear because they cannot find the right words to express their anger or frustration. A gentleman never swears.'

The gentleman in question had one shoe off and was now working on the second one. I looked at Tai's face. Hair drawn back, eyes blazing contempt. She had her sulphurous Sophia Loren look, lips parted as usual, showing her oversized teeth. Her mouth looked fleshy and succulent – rafflesian ... like the putrid petals of a carnivorous plant.

A shoe in each hand, Baba advanced towards Ram Singh, who tried to tuck his head into the crook of his shoulder. But Baba was not aiming for his head. 'I'll teach you to touch my property,' he said, bringing the shoe down hard on the servant's groin and then, as his screams echoed around the back verandah, Ram Singh was no longer pretending to be in pain.

I don't know when I turned and fled. But there I was in the dark living room, my back against a wall, screaming, 'No, no, no, don't hit please, don't, please, please...' Scalding tears ran down my face, my wails echoing those of the terrified servant.

And then my mind went back to a night in Delhi some years earlier. I was about twelve and ignorant, stupid rather, the tomboy who knew nothing about sex. I awoke feeling suffocated by a heavy weight on top of my body. Tai was lying on me, sucking furiously at my mouth, which felt all swollen and funny, inflamed. And then, shame, oh shame, my body pulsed with an electrical charge. I kissed her back. I was frightened and excited. In the half-light, she looked strange and menacing, her hair wild and loose about her face. She wore a blue sprigged nightgown which had ridden up to her shoulders. She was trying to tease my pubescent nipples with her fingers, but ended up hurting me instead. Suddenly disgusted, with her saliva accumulating in my mouth, I turned away to spit on the floor. She got up and left without a word.

The night after, my shame and disgust forgotten and an unfamiliar eagerness inhabiting my body, I was waiting for her, my ears straining for her footstep, on the balcony, her tap at my window pane. This time she took me by the hand and led me to her room which, like mine, had an oversized wooden writing table, salvaged from Baba's office when he decided to throw out his massive old colonial furniture in favour of ugly grey desks in tubular steel, courtesy Godrej.

'If you do what I tell you to, I'll give you eight annas,' she said. Eight annas meant two bottles of Coke. My sis knew exactly which buttons to push every time she wished to get me. Coke was my one enduring weakness, my true passion. I would go to any lengths, lie, steal, cheat to get hold of that wondrous fizzy brew. I nodded and she stripped off my buttercup yellow nightie, pulled down my knickers, pushed me towards her mammoth desk, gesturing me to climb on. Perched on that table, cowering and awkward, I did not recognize the sister who gazed at me from the bed.

'Now, randi,' she commanded in a strange, gruff voice, 'Open your legs and show me what you've got in there. Go on, lift up your leg and show me the pink inside.' She had a rapacious, greedy look, an expression I had never seen before. 'Now push your finger in. Push it in and out, harder, in and out, you bitch.'

As I stood precariously balanced on one foot, my girlish vagina on display, acutely uncomfortable and suffused with shame, she came up to the desk and began running her hands up and down my thighs, slapping them hard. 'Come on, open up more, you raand,' she said, throwing a couple of coins at me. One of them hit me hard on the knee, sending a shooting pain through the bone. Shame turned to anger as I leapt off the table to punch her in the stomach, finally managing to replace her cruel laughter with tears of real pain. 'Keep your stupid money,' I panted, pulling on my nightgown. 'You're a bad, bad, wicked girl.'

On my return from school the next afternoon, Tai and I avoided each other. Then, after dinner, when we bid our parents goodnight and the door leading to their side of the house was closed, she came by, leaning her body against the doorjamb. 'If you say anything, I'll tell them about the money you steal from Baba's trousers, about the fake signatures on your sick leave notes. I'll tell them how you skip school to see Hindi movies.' She didn't have to say it. I wouldn't have snitched, anyway. But she made doubly sure I got the message.

With my back to the wall in the dark living room, Ram Singh's screams, pretend or real, reverberating through the house, I was pouring out my grief at that old hurt, weeping for lost innocence, for the terrible twisted creature Tai had become. Ram Singh had responded to her come hither signals. Was he really all that much to blame? I was lamenting our corruption, what we had done to ourselves, what our father had done to us.

For a very long time after that nocturnal encounter, I thought of Tai as someone unwashed, unclean, with sweaty hands and sour, smelly armpits. I could no longer call her Tai but took to calling her by her name and found myself furiously wiping my cheeks every time she tried to kiss me.

As I write, I feel some sympathy for Tai, who was physically acting out the way she imagined Baba behaved with his prostitutes. Her pendulum has swung the opposite way since, her early fascination with ugly, violent sex replaced with a repressed sexuality and a hypocritical, middle-class morality. Her new persona is that of an ace prude, upright scholar, good mother and fat, belligerent wife. Maybe that's why she does not want me around, I might just pollute her precious daughters. I remind her a tad too much of her crudely vulgar adolescence.

I brought up our 'seduction scene' with her once long ago. Today, even the faintest suggestion that something like that ever happened would be met with a horrified denial. But just that once, she agreed to discuss it, thinking out aloud about how Baba's behaviour had affected her.

'I don't remember any of this happening at all, Kranti', she said when I tried to confront her. 'I have absolutely no recollection of it. But it could have happened. I was weird, you see. Sexually warped because of Baba. I would eavesdrop on their conversations, I knew everything about how Baba went to brothels with his office buddies. He'd come home to tell Aayee how he'd seen naked women lined up in a room, how he'd screwed them senseless. I think it hurt her and gave her a sexual rush at the same time. Of course, implicit in his remarks was the assertion that he went there because she wasn't good enough. That is why she was so fascinated by Guru Dutt's film Sahib Bibi aur Ghulam. *She compared herself to the landowner's wife who acts like a whore to stop her husband visiting the brothel every night. I would crouch outside their door in the corridor, listening to the sounds of their sexual antics. He was a real old pervert, our father. He needed to tell her, that's how he got his thrills. It was like showing her blue films, like face-to-face phone sex. He drove her crazy.'*

And Tai was right because crazy is what Aayee did become.

A little after the Ram Singh episode, our grandfather died in his sleep, in much the same manner in which he had lived, quietly and without fuss. Baba received a copy of the will. He had been left nothing except a paltry couple of thousand rupees, less than a month's salary, just about enough for a few bottles of smuggled scotch whiskey, and Aayee wept with disappointment.

The house in Poona, where we had played as children, had been promised her, she said. But after due consideration, Babuji had decided to cut off his wastrel middle son despite the care and service lavished upon him by the no-good's dutiful wife.

I think Aayee took that as a personal slap in the face. Baba had always been horrid to Babuji, stealing from him during his student days, mocking his extreme frugality, his clockwork regularity when it came to meals, his secret worship of the Hindu gods he kept locked up in a drawer, afraid of his communist son's caustic barbs. But Aayee had always been the model daughter-in-law, looking after his health, making his favourite food, listening patiently to oft-repeated stories about his cricketing and shikar exploits. He had promised her the house, told her so in as many words. It was reserved for her, he'd said, for her, the good daughter-in-law who'd managed to tame his wayward son.

So Aayee cracked up in a way we'd never seen before. I found her lying stretched out on her stomach in the back verandah, doing obeisance to a bhendi *bush, where she thought our dead grandfather's spirit had taken refuge. She had sprinkled the plant with turmeric and vermillion and was muttering some prayers.*

'What are you doing, Aayee? You can't lie there like that. Come on, get up and come inside,' I said irritably, grasping her arm to try to get her up.

'Shh... don't talk so loudly. Babuji doesn't like noise.'

'What Babuji? There's no one there, Aayee, now get up.' I yanked her up rudely and led her, still muttering, to her bed.

After that it only got worse with Aayee wandering around the house in the middle of the night, pouring water over herself and us, purifying the house so Babuji's troubled spirit might find peace.

Convinced she had done something to displease the old man before he died, she was doing penance to wipe out her sins. She imagined Babuji's hungry, restless soul hovering around, waiting to pounce upon her daughters. She would hold our wrists in a vicelike grip, refusing to let us go to college. The only way we could get away was by drugging her. I tripled the dose of Largactyl and with Aayee asleep, Tai and I would sneak off to college.

Terrified by these scenes of madness, the servants left one by one. We became known in the locality as a family that practiced black magic. Our unsavoury reputation kept us safe. The door unlocked, a sleeping corpse inside, we could have been robbed a million times over. Nothing like that ever happened. And then, unable to cope with the lack of servants, with a mad wife and two lazy, resentful daughters, Baba decided to move us back to Poona.

10

Venetian Colours

Robert-Pierre's mobile is beeping him a reminder. Confirm Venice hotel booking, the smiling icon says. He stabs at a key to silence the buzzer.

He has been trying hard not to think of Kranti and her notebooks, of their cruel, ugly contents, of her life before he knew her. But he is haunted by images of what she has lived through. That awful sister. Is she the same conventional middle-class woman whose picture is pinned up in the study, the person he spoke to just the other day?

He finds himself scrutinizing that face, searching for a clue. She could have been attractive once, despite the protruding teeth. From what he has read of Kranti's notebooks, she appears to be a hugely damaged person, twisted by an unhappy childhood. Her aggressiveness over the telephone no longer surprises him; it only confirms the picture that emerges from Kranti's account.

He feels an unaccustomed conflict brewing in him, pity, guilt and anger chasing one another. Kranti's betrayal with Pierre

Keller hurts the most. It's hard to understand and difficult to forgive.

The little girls' story is an account of her early childhood. What made her want to fictionalize it, and why is she so nostalgic about those years which were evidently far from idyllic? She has given herself a childish innocence, a purity, as if to make herself stand out like a lotus on a dung heap. The contrast between the two notebooks intrigues him. One is harsh, straight from the shoulder, blunt, honest. The other is seen through a child's innocent eyes. He has been living with a complex, multifaceted individual given to lies and dissimulation. As his clinical brain takes over, he has an uncontrollable desire to get to the bottom of Kranti Goray de Lorel, to know her from within.

In the two weeks since he left home, he has known a wrenching loneliness he didn't know existed. He's desperate to recapture the old tenor of his life, get back to a steady, even keel. And he has begun strategizing, plotting how best to engineer his return.

He misses home, misses Sophie, her cool humour, her brisk, no-nonsense ways, their complicity, private jokes and unspoken communication. And he longs for the clean patrician lines, the spare emptiness of his home with its Breugel and Hubert Robert, its slim cherry-wood bookcases, immaculate, waxed floors. Kranti's flat, crowded with heavy gilt mirrors, wall hangings and carpets, its flurry of silver boxes and waxy plants, he finds suffocating. Except for the odd painting or artefact, the flat is full of kitch – too much colour, too much clutter. Like an over-rich Indian curry, he thinks, all right for a day or two. But now I want my grilled fish and salad, basta!

What am I doing here, living like an outcast? I should be home, where I truly belong. A month is all I need, he thinks, the blood rushing anew in his veins at the thought of a fresh chase, even if it is to re-conquer his own wife. During which time, he plans to fête her and make her laugh. It'll be like an old-fashioned courtship. Christmas together! The thought cheers him.

Beep! The mobile goes again, shriller this time, and he silences it anew. It will probably pop up once more, closer to her birthday which, he realizes with a pang, is now almost exactly a month away. Kranti would have turned fifty-three, or was it four, the same age at which her mother died.

Their last dinner in Venice, a year ago, is still with him. Somewhat exaggeratedly, he imagines her, iridescent, in spun, coppery gold. It is her birthday and she's wearing her mother's wedding sari, a decades-old diaphanous silk, tearing vertically along the folds, which she keeps preserved in layers of tissue paper.

Together they make a self-consciously elegant pair, looking intently into each other's eyes, smiling, holding hands. They are sipping Bellinis at Harry's Bar, waiting for their table, talking about how they would like to die. Or, more precisely, how they would want their bodies disposed of.

She talks of a book by the Chinese novelist Ma Jian, in which an enterprising provincial turns an art school ceramics furnace into a private crematorium. 'That's the new China, ruthless, money-making, capitalist. One yuan for playing a revolutionary song to accompany the body, eight yuan if you want a banned piece of decadent, reactionary music such as Chopin or the Rolling Stones. And, of course, the dead person's mandatory new clothes have been secretly passed on from one corpse to the next. Sensible recycling!'

Every fifteen minutes or so, the restaurant's world famous barman with his saturnine face and shock of grey hair winks pointedly at Kranti and pushes back the hands of the clock by a quarter of an hour so that its face always shows a few minutes before nine and she smiles back, complicit in the joke that's wearing a bit thin.

Their booking was for 9 p.m. It is now past ten o'clock and he is on his third Bellini, but Kranti doesn't seem to mind, bending low over the bar, cunningly allowing her sari to slip in order to show off her décolleté where a large pearl, suspended from a gold chain, nestles between her breasts like a glowing teardrop.

His mind goes back over every detail of that evening, of their entire stay, softening sharp edges, giving it a numinous quality, like a film shot through a soft filter.

Even though they are talking about death, there is nothing morbid about their conversation. That morning, they visited the cemetery at San Michele, going from tomb to tomb discussing styles, statues and inscriptions, wondering how much it cost to have and maintain a family crypt and whether concessions were still available.

'I think the Hindu way of cremating the body is much healthier,' Kranti argued. 'Death becomes real because you see the body burn in front of you. Not like you guys, shutting it up in a box and burying it away forever. You can never get over your loss that way, because you continue to see the flesh-and-blood person lying serene and calm in death. That image never leaves you – it's difficult to imagine the worms, the flesh falling off the bones, the hair that continues to grow. With us, one strike of the match and bingo, all you've got left is a couple of teeth and a heap of ashes. So you come to terms with death very quickly. You shrug your shoulders and move on. None of this slow mourning that Western psychology makes such a to-do about!'

Robert-Pierre wants a plain granite slab with an inscription from Robespierre or Saint-Just. He will be laid, he says, in a moment of inattention, in Sophie's family crypt in Montparnasse cemetery.

He winces, remembering the awkward pause that followed the mention of his wife's name. The magic broken, Kranti quiet, withdrawn. Even now, he can feel his old irritation return. She never actually said anything about Sophie, but he could sense her resentment, tightly reined in, bubbling beneath the surface. She wanted a more permanent relationship, he knew, public recognition. More than anything else, she wanted Sophie to know and accept her as an integral part of his, of their lives – a long distance *ménage à trois*. But some things are just not possible, he'd told her. And for the first time, he sensed their relationship fraying. He felt pressurized and resentful while harbouring a vague sense of guilt.

Their visits to Venice had become a birthday tradition. Room 209 at the Gritti Palace, its balcony in the upper left-hand corner of the renaissance façade overlooking the Grand Canal, with the church of the Salute diagonally across.

She revelled in the beauty of their room with its high, carved wooden ceiling painted sienna, indigo and gold, the marble-topped tables, the bombé cupboard with inlaid marquetry that she said looked like a squat, fat man, the huge high bed with its crisp linen sheets.

They had developed their own little rituals – waking up in each other's arms to the sound of lapping water and the shouts of gondoliers, then ginger tea with honey and milk before breakfast. She brewed the tea herself, ceremoniously opening the ancient tea chest in highly polished Chinese lacquer that she lugged around on all her travels, pounding fresh ginger in the wooden pestle and mortar, boiling water in the small electric kettle that fit snugly beside the fragile teapot and cups in translucent Japanese bone china. Newspapers over breakfast, followed by an excursion on foot – a ramble through the *ghetto ebraico*, a morning spent at the Dalmatian Brotherhood gazing, forever awestruck, at the beauty of the Carpaccios, wading out in thigh-high gumboots when *aqua alta* inundated the city and forced her to lift her skirts.

How many times had he smiled at her delight in twirling truffle-smothered linguine around her fork, watched as she placed the tightly wound ball precisely upon her tongue, closing her eyes in wanton surrender as the tuber's aromas flooded her senses? He'd taught her a great deal; they'd shared fine wines, music, paintings and books, but not Italian cooking. Where had she learned to roll pasta like that?

'I lived in Italy. I was taught,' she said, giving away as little as possible.

It was on their first trip to Venice that he sensed she had a more than passing acquaintance with Italy. 'I worked in a design studio in Gallarate, near Como. That's where most of your Italian silk ties and scarves come from. I lived in Milan and commuted. I still do commissions for them. It was okay. But I prefer Paris.'

He knew there was more of course, probably a man. Surely a man. Someone had taken those nude shots of hers on the black beaches of Stromboli. Who? But it was too early in their relationship for him to ask. And then, a year later, when he did bring up the mystery Italian lover, she said: 'It's all over now. It was fun while it lasted, but it didn't work out. We've remained good friends. We talk over the phone occasionally and he visits sometimes. But that's all. And we don't share a bedroom when he comes, if that's what you're brooding about!' But no name, no description, nothing about who he was and what he did.

He was amused by her secrecy, her childish attempts to make a mystery of her past, thinking she merely wanted to appear interesting. 'Well, I shan't play the game and Madame can stew in her own juice,' he'd thought, admiring his own control, his mastery of the situation.

It was in Venice that she recounted her first meeting with Guillaume's parents at the Cercle Militaire in Paris. 'I had no idea how I should dress. Should I wear a sari or Western clothes? How did they imagine me – as a sophisticated townee or a poor, uneducated village belle? I pondered that for a while and then made the worst possible choice – western wear, which meant a cheap pleated grey woollen skirt from Monoprix – that's all I could afford then – a pinkey-lilac tucked-in blouse and a grey silk scarf. Me, can you imagine, me, with my love for colour, looking like a little grey Indian mouse? I looked hideous and sallow, bumbling, gauche, with my hair in a ponytail – a genuine Third World immigrant in that ornate, gilded, very formal setting. Worse, we were forty-five minutes late for dinner and the kitchens were closing. So the first thing my prospective ma-in-law said to me in that haughty patronizing drawl she adopts with shopgirls and other members of the lower orders was: '*Mademoiselle, aimez-vous les betteraves?*' I didn't know *betteraves* meant beetroot. So I politely said one of two words I knew in French '*Oui, Madame*' (the other being *merci!*) and suddenly, I was face to face with a plate piled high with the stuff. I swallowed it, of course, but oh, was it beastly! I've loathed beetroot ever since. Her words made me think of Françoise Sagan's *Aimez-vous Brahms* but when I mentioned it as a conversation gambit, I got nothing but uncomprehending, frosty stares in return. They didn't approve of Sagan, of course, thought her decadent, immoral and left wing, while I adored her. That's how it was, right from the start.'

A chateau in Auvergne, a flat in Paris near the Trocadero, a house by the seaside, another in the mountains, and the sons all generals and priests. God and country, anti-abortion, right-wing politics. 'They're that kind of family, the Lorels. Except Guillaume, of course, who was quite Third World for a while and remains a centrist, an MP to boot, and going places by the sound of it. But they were good to me. Always kind, always considerate. Their only demand was the religious wedding, to which I gave in with sly grace, getting my own back by turning the ceremony upside down.' She gave an embarrassed laugh.

'There were some funny moments with them – like finding my father-in-law on his knees before the TV set receiving the Pope's Easter blessing – that really knocked me for a six – or travelling to the Vendée to lay a wreath on the tomb of the collaborationist Maréchal Pétain of Vichy fame. But otherwise, life was pretty cheerless – formal, governed by rules and responsibilities of a *noblesse oblige* kind. You had to be down for breakfast fully dressed. No question of dawdling around the house in your dressing gown! We visited the family's retired retainers in their grimy cottages on the estate, received the *curé* and other boring local notables for Sunday lunch or tea and went to mass in the village church. I really couldn't bear any of it. They saw me as a part of my country's elite, but heathen nevertheless, and far less fortunate when compared to them.

'From my Brahmin's superior vantage point, I saw them as sabre-rattling army types – socially my equals, intellectually my inferiors. They were part of the old French nobility, tracing their ancestry back to the Crusades. I liked that bit, I quite fancied the aristocracy and, for the first couple of years, I enjoyed being a countess. That was one of my reasons for marrying Guillaume in the first place, that and a desire to escape India, one broken marriage and an unfaithful former lover with whom I was still desperately in love. Of course, at that time, Guillaume was more approachable, full of the Third World concerns I shared, not the ghastly stuffed shirt he became later, and initially, he loved me to distraction. But he became cold, undemonstrative, wrapped up in his work – politics, lobbying, stuff like that, which I considered futile. In a peculiar way, intellectually at least, I was far more sophisticated than any of them, even Guillaume. I just got bored with all that *noblesse oblige* stuff, I guess. I started taking lovers. So we split.'

Robert-Pierre remembers laughing with her as she regaled him with stories of cheap wine served in shining crystal decanters at the Lorel table. Of watery, deep-frozen fish dished out on Fridays and *Bouchée à la reine* filled with a grey mushroom sauce that made her stomach turn. 'You should see the penny pinching that goes on in these so-called grand houses. Bulk-frozen food passed off as fresh. Sauces out of packets, even pastry unfrozen and reheated. The only thing my mother-in-law cooked well was vegetable soup (didn't cost her much, since all the produce came from the *potager*) and roasts. But there too, the meat was cut ultra thin and two slices was the most it was considered polite to eat. I remember my constant frustration, wanting to dig into a good hunk of meat but never getting the chance!'

The memories have brought a smile to his face, pushed his anxieties aside. For a split second he has forgotten Kranti's death. But she is gone. For good, leaving him a poisoned legacy. And with a stab of guilt, his mind gallops forward to Sophie.

When he called her that morning she was civil but cool. 'I'm dashing off to the rue Daguerre to do some shopping. There's nothing in the house and if I don't buy Maria a new mop and vacuum cleaner bags, she'll start grumbling again.'

'Can I come with you? I could lug the basket.'

'Since when have you enjoyed carrying shopping, Pierre, even on a Saturday? When I last asked you to do it, you said I was snatching your week-end lie-in.' Her voice is impersonal but there is a smile lurking there. Except, he can't tell if it's gentle or tinged with acid.

Life has fallen into a pattern in which he is a most unwilling participant. Olga Savic pops her head around the corner almost every evening when he returns from work, but they carefully avoid talking about Kranti. She tells him about Peter and Ivan, seeks advice on how to deal with Ivan's anger with his son. Ivan hates everything about Peter, she says. His homosexuality, his lifestyle, the way he sits, talks, eats. But most of all, Ivan resents his financial dependence on someone he considers beneath contempt. Olga Savic talks, much in the manner in which she poured her worries into Kranti's sympathetic ear, and Robert-Pierre listens. It amounts to giving her free professional advice but for once, he does not mind. Olga usually brings him something for supper and occasionally they play a hand of scopa, a 40-card Sicilian game Kranti had taught them both.

He has tried going out with friends a couple of times but with Sophie conspicuously absent, the occasions have been strained. So now he has taken to filling his empty evenings by catching up on some essential professional reading, ploughing through accumulated submissions for the magazine he edits. A part of him welcomes this monastic existence. It is his way of offering penance, seeking forgiveness, expiation.

But another side to him chafes at what he sees as an imposition, an enforced exile. He hates Kranti's queen sized bed, where his feet stick out. It never seemed to matter before. And he is irritated by the clutter in her bathroom – all those jars of cream and shampoo, bottles of perfume and assorted beauty products that must have cost a fortune. He has a sudden, furious urge to sweep everything out, restore the flat to what he imagines to be its original roomy state.

The thought of Kranti's manuscripts fills him with dread. But inexorably, as night draws, he is lured back by the red and black covers, struggling with Kranti's untidy prose until an uneasy sleep claims him once more.

11

The Red Notebook

KRANTI AND SHANTI

Kranti sits up bolt upright in bed. A man's hoarse voice speaking into a megaphone reaches her from a distance. In a trice, she is out of the house, running barefoot into the garden. Aayee finds her at the gate, watching the flag-bedecked three-wheeler tempo go slowly past. The national tricolour fixed to its side flutters in the cool, early morning breeze. A megaphone fitted onto its luggage carrier blares out a message.

The sky is overcast and a branch from a neem tree has fallen in the previous night's storm, spilling its tender green berries on the dark ribbon of wet tarmac. The procession is going at a snail's pace, the three-wheeler followed by another equally run-down car and several curious street urchins. 'Brothers and sisters,' says the man sitting next to the driver, a huge steel microphone stuck to his mouth. 'This morning at four o'clock, our respected education minister Maulana Abul Kalam Azad passed away. All government offices and schools will remain closed.' Then he repeats the same message in Marathi and Hindi. Kranti is almost six. It is August 1958.

She slips her soft child's hand into her mother's palm. Silently they wait until the procession is out of sight, then, as if one, they move hand in hand, for a turn in the garden. The grass is soft and mossy underfoot, still wet with rain, and Aayee feels a surge of love for this child, so vulnerable, so strange and lonely, and yet so trusting. 'You come straight back in if it begins to rain again,' she calls out, going back into the house.

Aayee and Baba are talking and they don't hear Kranti creep in.

'We can send them to one of the neighbours while you finish that bit.' Aayee sounds worried.

'There's no need for that. They'll have to know some day. We can't just uproot them like that. We must give them time to get used to the idea. The sooner we tell them, the better,' says Baba.

'I'll get them home for lunch and get them ready by three o'clock,' Aayee says.

Baba has not gone to the office. He is dressed in his best suit and looks like a film star. Aayee has arranged plates of cream crackers and Bourbon biscuits in the living room and Ganga has cleaned the silver kept-for-special-occasions tea set. The girls are wearing their Diwali clothes. Kranti's ankle length parkar and matching polke is black with tiny red and green parrots; Shanti is in spangled blue and gold. Aayee and Baba want them to make a good impression on the visitors. Aayee whispers, 'BB', which is Goray family-speak for Best Behaviour.

Three men arrive at four o'clock bearing boxes of Parry's sweets for the girls. They are Baba's bosses from Bombay and have been sent down specially to try and make Baba change his mind. They remain closeted away for a long time with Baba in his study. Then they all come out, to drink a cup of tea before the visitors leave. 'I am so happy it was done with good grace,' Aayee tells Mr Prabhu.

'Your husband is a very intelligent man, Mrs Goray,' Mr Prabhu says. 'We were not able to convince him to stay on, but you know he can come back to us any time. Thank you for the tea, it was first class.'

That evening Aayee and Baba tell the girls that they will be moving house to go to a faraway place called Lucknow where Baba went to school as a boy.

'Baba came first in a test to go to Singapore, but the chairman's son was sent instead. So Baba has left,' Aayee says. 'Resigned from his job, because it's not fair, and he has got a better job now. So we will move to Lucknow and you will go to a new school and must learn Hindi.'

Baba wants to pack up and leave immediately. 'Everything can be arranged within a week,' he says.

But Aayee is reluctant. It's better to wait out the notice period in his contract, she says. 'It will be difficult for the children to start a new school in the middle of term, especially for Kranti. Let's at least wait until they finish the school year in December.'

She is afraid of going to Lucknow, a place where she knows no one and doesn't speak the language, afraid of abandoning her music school and pupils.

Baba has a few suggestions, but they do not please Aayee. In the end, he produces the ace he's been hiding up his sleeve.

'Bombay wants me to open the new office within six weeks. I shall have to send Barbara ahead to purchase the furniture, set up the office.'

'Mrs d'Costa? You never told me she was going. You can't do this to me, Vijay, I won't have it.'

'What am I doing? The head office hired her. She never told me she had applied. Her family is from the north. She grew up in those parts and wants to go back. She is an efficient worker and will make an invaluable assistant. I can't object to her appointment. You can stay on with the children, if you like. I can go up ahead and make the arrangements, start up the office. You can join me later.'

'When is she going, Vijay?'

'They are leaving next month. Her husband's found a job in a cousin's motor workshop. She says Yvonne's admission won't be a problem. It never is for Catholic children, is it?'

'Why didn't you tell me this before? You're hiding things from me as usual.'

'What's there to hide? Nothing to hide. I couldn't tell you before. I just found out myself.'

'Then we'll leave when they leave, Vijay.'

'Yes, I suppose we could do that. You know, of course, I have to make an advance trip to hire an office, a house, find servants, fix up the girls' school admission?'

'I know, Vijay, I know.' And Aayee gives in, as he knows she will.

◈

That was two months ago, and now they're really off. It's October and school is out for Dussera, so they cannot even say a final goodbye. The furniture has gone, taken away in a big truck to be auctioned, and the house is empty with clean patches on the walls in the place of paintings and photographs and a long streak of dirt where their bed once stood.

Kranti walks through the house. 'Goodbye,' she whispers in each room and her voice bounces back to her, off walls suddenly grown strangely taller. Her mind is a jumble of questions and she is unable to concentrate on the last game of hopscotch under the tamarind tree in the slanting light of sunset. The sky is already streaked scarlet and the shadow that runs ahead of her is that of a long, thin stick figure, the kind Sister Margaret draws on the blackboard during science lessons.

The train pulls them along strange, sere landscapes, some brown, some red, others almost black. Kranti sits glued to the window, fascinated by the telegraph lines as they dance up and down to the rhythm of the wheels. They rumble across wide riverbeds strewn with rocks and pebbles, chug past sleepy villages, wave to people waiting at railway crossings.

At first they travel west on a narrow meter-gauge line up to Manmad, a large junction where they will board the legendary Amritsar Express that goes almost all the way to the border with Pakistan. At another major hub, Jhansi, their compartment will be de-coupled to bifurcate east towards Lucknow while the Express carries on north.

The monsoon has failed and, even in October, it is unbearably hot. An irritating fly keeps returning to the corner of Kranti's mouth. Baba has maps and a detailed railway timetable and he reads out unfamiliar names of the places they will pass. Bhusawal, Khandwa, Hoshangbad, Bina, Babina, Itarsi.

'At Manmad, which is right here on the map, we shall have a midnight feast. I have already ordered biscuits and Ovaltine for you,' he tells the excited girls. 'Bed tea in Bhusawal, breakfast at Khandwa and lunch in Itarsi, but maybe drinks first, in Jalgaon, and if you are very good and there is no fighting or quarrelling, you might even get an orange drink,' he says.

'I want a drink at Bina,' shouts Kranti.

'And I want a drink at Babina,' declares Shanti.

'Well, we'll have to choose, one or the other. We'll toss a coin,' Baba says, pulling out a four-anna piece from his pocket.

Shanti is quick. 'Heads for me.'

'Heads for me too.' Kranti's mouth is clamped shut, but her lower lip wobbles treacherously.

'Baba, I said heads first. She always wants what I want.'

'Quiet, you two. This time Kranti will have the choice because she's younger. The next time, it will be for Tai to choose,' he says, irritably putting away the coin.

The carriage windows are closed. Aayee, who is nursing a head cold and has raw, red nostrils does not want them open. Small noisy ceiling fans churn up the hot, dry air. They are installed in a first class carriage with four berths, a tin basin containing a large block of ice placed at the centre, their very own bathroom with a shower, and a door they can close to shut out the outside world.

Baba has slipped his soda bottles under the ice while Aayee has placed round steel tins of food on top of the slab. Baba hates this fuss. They could very well order food from the railway catering service, he says. But Aayee disagrees. 'Kranti has a weak stomach,' she says. 'I don't want that child to get diarrhoea on the train. It's never simple with her. Loose motions bring on fever and you know how quickly she gets delirious.'

'It's like being in our own little house, na, Aayee?' says Shanti. But Aayee is silent, as she has been all these days, barely replying, not smiling.

Helped by the servants, Aayee has spent the past few weeks packing everything into trunks and crates, wrapping the glassware carefully in old saris, towels and newspapers. Baba has painted their name on every single piece of luggage: V.S.

Goray, B.Sc. M.Sc., L.L.B., Aurangabad to Lucknow – thirty-one pieces in all, baskets, bedrolls, holdalls, trunks, large and small wooden packing cases.

'We're going to have wonderful new furniture and a lovely car, separate beds for my two little birds, you'll see,' laughs Baba, burying his head in Kranti's stomach, making her scream and kick her legs to escape the tickling.

Baba has already made a trip to Lucknow. He has hired a house, taken an office and fixed up the girls' school. His new deputy, a Mr Chaturvedi, will be meeting them at the station. With their new car.

They chug steadily northwards, the tired diesel locomotive shrieking into the night. Kranti awakens with a jerk as the train pulls into a station in the early morning haze. There is the sound of a window going up and the regular, nasal chant of 'Chai garam...'

'Kuka, come down and taste this. You'll never get such tea anywhere else. It's kulhad chai,' Baba says, handing Kranti a small earthenware pot full of a dusky steaming liquid. He is right. The tea has a rich, loamy smell like parched earth after the first monsoon shower. Sitting on Baba's lap, sipping her tea, Kranti closes her eyes. Baba is stroking her head and hair, his breath like kisses at the back of her neck. She would like time to stand still. Right now. And never move again. Dreamily, between sips, she pats her father's cheeks.

And then she feels it. A funny movement, followed by a wet stickiness at the back of her pyjamas she knows doesn't come from her. Not this time. She can feel Baba gently lifting her off his lap, setting her down on the floor. She turns back to look at him as he gets up. The front of his blue pyjama is wet, the stain standing out dark and patchy like the rainfall area on the map he showed them yesterday.

'Shh...' Baba places a finger on his lips and gestures towards Aayee's sleeping form. 'Sometimes big people do it too. You won't tell, will you?' he bends down to whisper. And leaves her solemnly shaking her head, the wet stickiness on the back of her pyjamas drying up to feel like the crackly starch Ganga puts in Baba's white office shirts.

Poor Baba. Now she knows why Aayee is always shouting at him and pulling long faces. She imagines herself telling Aayee in a soft grown-up voice: 'You can't always stop it in time, you know. Look what happened to Baba, that's what happens to me too. I don't mean to wet my chaddi. It just happens, Aayee.' But the Aayee in her mind is stony, not listening, not seeing, not even acknowledging her words, a little bit like the Aayee now asleep in front of her.

It's a new world. The hard consonants of Marathi give way to a softer burr. The cadences are different, the women less angular, more buxom and rounded.

At Jhansi junction, where there is a long wait, their bogie is detached and joined to another train going eastwards. Baba tells them the story of the queen of Jhansi, Maharani Laxmibai, who fought the British bravely, cutting down nasty English soldiers from horseback, her six-month-old baby strapped to her back. They learn their very first poem in Hindi:

Bundele Harbolon se yeh humne suni kahani thi,

Khoob ladi mardani, woh to Jhansi wali Rani thi...

The words are unfamiliar, the sound of Hindi sweet and delicate, quite unlike the harshness of their native tongue. 'You must be brave like her, Kuka,' Baba says.

'Can I also ride a horse and have a sword?'

'Those days were different. There were no cars then and people rode on horseback. You must learn to drive a car.

You can even fly aeroplanes. You don't need a sword to fight nowadays. This is modern India, where girls grow up to be as strong as boys. You can fight with your brain. But for that you must study hard and do well in your exams. Now I'm going to see if our luggage has been loaded,' Baba says, swinging off the top step onto the platform.

They are at the door of the carriage, watching him stride off down the platform, when Tai giggles. 'I've got a secret, a secret and you don't know it,' she sings.

'Oh tell, Tai, please tell.'

'What'll you give me?'

'What do you want?'

'Your dolly. I'll give you mine in exchange.'

'No.'

'Then I shan't tell. I know the secret. But I shan't tell.'

Kranti weakens. But she cannot quite quell the sharp stab of guilt as she kisses her favourite doll goodbye before placing her in Tai's outstretched hand. Tai gestures her to leave the compartment. Not here, not in front of Aayee, she signals.

They huddle in the corridor. 'Aunty Cou-ee, Yvonne and Uncle Vincent – they're all going to Lucknow with us. Baba has gone to fetch Aunty Cou-ee. But don't say it aloud because Aayee won't like it,' warns Shanti.

'It's not true. You're only making it up to get my dolly. I'm going to ask Aayee...' But Tai has grabbed hold of her hand.

'Shut up, you stupid idiot. She'll get really angry if you ask her. She doesn't want them to come, but I know they are coming. I heard Aayee and Baba fighting about it. They're on the train. In a third-class compartment. And Baba's gone to meet them.'

'Hello sweety, where's Aayee?' says Baba heartily, climbing back into the carriage.

'Inside, where else?' mumbles Shanti sourly, looking up from her book at Aunty Cou-ee, who was standing on the platform wearing a travel-rumpled cotton skirt and a red sleeveless blouse. Her upper arms look sturdy, like thick beige pillars, and there are dark sweat patches around her armpits but the lipstick is in place as always and her hair falls in shiny waves around her face.

They squeeze past Shanti, bent over her book on a steel trunk in the corridor, to enter the compartment where Kranti is playing a game of snap with Aayee. Screaming with delight, Kranti hurls herself at Aunty Cou-ee, throwing a quick guilty look at her mother, who is staring out of the window with studied indifference.

'Cou-ee, Cou-ee, how's my little mouse, my sweet baby,' says Aunty Cou-ee, tickling her in the ribs, leaving a dark red imprint upon Kranti's plump cheek.

'You're going with us, I'm so HAPPY. Is Yvonne there, can we play with her?' Kranti is jumping up and down.

'Darling, we're not rich, like your daddy here. So Yvonne is in our carriage on the other side of the train. But the train stops here for two hours. Maybe you and Shanti can go there? And then we can't all crowd here, can we?' she says, looking at Baba.

Aayee whips her head around, her face a cold mask. 'No, Vijay. I won't let the girls go like that. It's too dangerous, I don't think it's safe.'

'Nonsense, Lalita. They're cooped up here, they need someone to play with. They'll be quite safe.'

'If it's like that, I'd much rather go with them.'

'It's carriage number 22,' Aunty Cou-ee says.

Without a word, Aayee grabs Kranti roughly by the hand. Carefully they make their way to carriage number 22 to join Yvonne and her father.

Yvonne's carriage is beyond the platform, and they find themselves walking on the rough gravel that lines the tracks. The compartment is packed to capacity with people squatting on the floor. Aayee and Kranti pick their way between baskets, bedrolls, bodies, shoes and bare feet, between smells of curry, pickle, urine and shit.

Vincent and Yvonne both have window seats, but the places next to them are filled by what Aayee usually describes as 'terribly poor, unwashed people who give you ringworm.' The woman next to Uncle Vincent has her blouse open, with a baby sucking at one breast. The other one is barely covered and Kranti, her eyes big as dinner plates, finds herself mentally comparing them with Ganga's brown melons. Flies are buzzing around the baby's head and the woman shoos them away with a languid wave of her hand. Her husband snores loudly on her other shoulder, his open mouth showing a large paan-stained tongue and discoloured teeth.

Vincent is a small, wiry man with permanent mechanic's black under the fingernails. 'Good afternoon, ma'am, so good of you to come. You need not have taken the trouble. How're you doing, Kranti baby,' he says, his eyes full of shame, as his hands try to clear the mess around him.

'Ma said you might be coming. How nice,' Yvonne says, brushing back her bangs with the back of her hand. She is sitting in a pool of peanut shells and her hands and mouth are stained with orange juice, the discarded peel and pips lying by her feet on the floor.

Aayee is standing there unsure of what to do next. Vincent hurriedly scoops up the peanut shells and throws them out of the window. From his pocket he pulls out a checked cotton handkerchief, dabs it with water from a small enamel mug and wipes Yvonne's hands and mouth.

'Aye, thoda lady ke waste jagah do. Hamara ek aur seat hai idhar,' he tells the young man who has occupied Aunty Cou-ee's seat next to Yvonne. *'Aur tum apna paon upar leyo,'* he tells the feet dangling from the upper berth that are reluctantly pulled up by their owners.

'Please, ma'am, sit down,' he says gently, indicating the now empty seat. 'Baby Kranti, you come here on my lap.'

Curious eyes are looking at Aayee and Kranti. People have imperceptibly gathered around them, as if for a show.

Aayee is gracious but declines Uncle Vincent's offer of tea. 'Do you know where you'll be staying?' she asks.

'For the time being we will stay with Barbara's cousin, Eric. His missus has gone home for a baby. They've been calling us over for quite some time. So lucky about Barbara's job. You and your husband have been so good to us and to Yvonne. Thank you, ma'am.'

Aayee asks him polite questions about Lucknow, Yvonne's school, their staying arrangements while the girls try to play jacks with a small rubber ball and four round stones. But the ball regularly bounces off the small tablet fixed below the window and they abandon it to observe the goings on outside.

'Oh look, *Pyaasa*,' squeals Kranti pointing to the huge cinema hoarding that lines the busy street by the railway track.

'That's just a rubbish Indian film,' says Yvonne. 'We saw *The Guns of Navarone*. That was really good.'

'No, it's not rubbish. My Baba says it's a very good film, all about rich people and poor people, and the songs are lovely, I heard them on Binaca Geet Mala.'

'We only hear the English service of Radio Ceylon and my Mum says Hindi films are all rubbish.'

'What does your mummy know? My Baba is very clever and he's her boss. And your father's only a car mechanic. You all are poor and stupid and that's why you're going third class.'

Yvonne's eyes are swimming with tears. 'Dad, tell her it's not true,' she says.

In the embarrassed silence that follows, Aayee gets up, shaking out her sari. 'We should be getting back, the train leaves in ten minutes. Kranti, say sorry to Yvonne for making her cry.'

'But Aayee, she said *Pyasa* was a bad film and Baba said it was good.'

'Just say sorry, Kranti. That's all.'

They stumble out of the compartment to the gravel beneath, walking back to compartment number 6. As they approach, they catch a glimpse of Baba and Aunty Cou-ee looking at each other and clinking glasses. The amber liquid in their tumblers is whiskey. Baba beams, young and boyish and happy. His dimples flash. And Aunty Cou-ee, looking a bit like Ava Gardner against the dark green upholstery of the Railways, throws back her head to laugh, showing white teeth and the firm column of her neck.

She gets up with a swish of skirts, gives Aaaye a hug and trips off down the platform.

'Baba, why are Aunty Cou-ee and Yvonne and Uncle Vincent going third class? Why can't they come here? It was so dirty, Baba, and so hot, and so much noise. Are they really that poor? They're less poor than Ganga, no?'

'Ganga is a servant. Aunty Cou-ee is not, she's a steno-typist. But Baba, how come they are poor if her grandfather was an Englishman?' asks Shanti.

'The English disliked us because we were not white, like them. They treated their own Indian children like slaves. You are lucky to be growing up in a free India, although freedom has not brought us equality. It has not removed caste or poverty. People like Mahatma Gandhi asked the upper caste rich to show respect to the poor; they were their trustees, he said. But when has anyone rich given up his money? It's only when the means of production are controlled by the worker, when the profit motive has been removed, that India will make progress. But for that, we need a communist revolution.'

'Vijay, don't talk to them of politics,' Aayee remonstrates, 'They're too young. They don't understand what you're saying.'

'You don't either, do you? But one is never too young to start learning these things,' Baba counters. 'And of course they understand. I make things simple.' And he does make it sound like a happy world where everyone will have everything they want and there'll be no poor people. Except Baba can't get away from phrases like 'dictatorship of the proletariat' or 'withering away of the state' and while Tai nods eagerly, Kranti, who doesn't understand any of these things, mentally recites the new poem she has learnt about *Patjhad*, the season when leaves wither and fall.

Kranti feels lost and left out when Baba talks like this. When he and Tai discuss the Communist Party, Marx, Lenin, someone called Albert Einstein, and all those books Tai reads. Tai wants to be a scientist when she grows up, but cannot decide if she will study plain physics or nuclear physics.

Tai wins all the prizes at school, including the one for Earnest Endeavour, and Kranti's class teacher Mrs Menon often says with a coffee-scented sigh: 'That sister of yours is doing beautifully. Why are you so far behind?' But Kranti cannot fathom her sighs.

'Shanti's got a remarkable mind, so quick to grasp ideas,' Baba says to Aayee. 'I'm more worried about Kranti. You must pay more attention to her homework and baby her less, Lalita,' he says.

Kranti is plump and placid, pretty but stupid, and sometimes sly. Shanti is clever, tough, pushy, impulsive, but also generous and terribly sensitive, especially about her looks. Large jagged teeth make her lower lip protrude, exposing its pink fleshy underside and when she laughs, her hand automatically creeps up to cover her mouth. Someday, orthodontic treatment will improve her teeth, but Shanti will never stop believing in her ugliness, just as Kranti, emerging from her chrysalis, will see herself as a dumb, sluggish caterpillar, never a beautiful butterfly about to take wing.

Faced with a common enemy, Shanti is fiercely protective of Kranti and like any pair of sisters they dream, fight, play, invent games, cry and make up. But unlike normal sisters, they also hate each other with a ferocious intensity that will remain with them throughout their adult lives. The vein of hatred is as deep as the well of unconditional love they bear their father, so that jealousy and relentless one-up-manship will dog their footsteps long after both Aayee and Baba have turned to ashes.

But now, as the train chugs into Lucknow Central station, they are about to embark on a new life. Lucknow is the first of over a dozen large and small Indian cities they will inhabit over the course of the next fifteen years, changing homes and schools, at a dizzying rate.

But all that lies ahead. At the point at which we are, Mr Chaturvedi and his short, veiled wife are waiting on the platform holding fat ropes of roses, marigold and jasmine in their hands. A black and white photo clicked that day shows Aayee, Baba, Kranti and Shanti standing stiff and immobile, their decapitated heads floating above the massive silver-threaded garlands wrapped around their necks.

12

Hidden Sorrows

Telling his mother of their break-up was the hardest bit. Robert-Pierre tried to make light of it, but without success.

'Sophie says you won't be coming for lunch on Sunday. It seems you're no longer living together. She gave me this number.'

'It's only temporary, Maman, just a misunderstanding. I'm staying at a friend's flat for the moment.'

'That's not the impression I got. Anyway, who's this friend? How come he's got a convenient flat to loan you on short notice like that? Or are you staying with a woman? Is that why you've moved out?'

Brusque, direct, uncomfortably close to the bone, she makes him squirm, like the little boy of yore.

'I'll tell you about it, Maman, but not on the telephone like this. Shall I drive out to see you this Sunday?'

'Why don't you pick me up at Montparnasse? Then we can go to La Coupole next door. I haven't been there since Papa died. It's my treat. *C'est moi qui t'invite.* I can catch the 11.30 and we can be there by a quarter to one, before it gets too crowded.'

He wants to say no, but can't. Impossible to tell her he can't take her to La Coupole. He has used it shamelessly, lunching with his mistress, dining with his wife, until it has become his private canteen. It would be inappropriate to be seen there with his mother as well.

'We'll see, Maman. That sounds good, but perhaps you might want to go someplace new that we haven't tried before? La Coupole isn't what it was. They've begun to sing Happy Birthday with candles on a fake cake. Quite American.'

But his mother is not one to be put off easily and come Sunday, he is pacing the platform, waiting for her train from Fontainbleau. She emerges from a first-class carriage wearing a classic navy suit with a printed silk blouse and a smart short coat. Retirement suits her. She is devoted to her garden and there's a healthy bloom in her cheeks. She loves the fact that she now pays half the fare and can travel First Class, an unaffordable luxury before. He notes how carefully she has dressed for her day in the capital, with matching shoes and handbag, hair tinted and lacquered, and feels a twinge of discomfort, bordering on embarassment, at this provincial giveaway.

When he and Sophie visit her in the old stone cottage she inhabits, everything appears just right, the much-wiped plastic tablecloth with its large yellow sunflowers, the overblown roses in their chipped porcelain milk jug 'too good to be thrown away', the sap-stained wicker baskets containing pitted apples from the garden, sorted according to size and age, napkins that never seem to match, the wholesome peasant fare she cooks. But here, dolled up for her outing, she seems out of place and he finds himself mentally comparing her to Sophie's casually elegant mother with her slim slacks and St. Laurent spencer jackets.

Completely unaware of the thoughts going around in her son's head, Madame Perrin has launched into a diatribe against her local plumber, who has stood her up three times in a row. 'The problem is, the job's too small – just a leaky tap. Now, if the boiler needed changing or if your father were here, he'd come like a shot. The truth is, I don't offer him a glass of Calva like Papa used to, and he can't get started until he's tanked up to the gills. You're going to have to come over and change it for me, Robert.'

She has always called him that, whereas Sophie, without any sign of hostility, has doggedly stuck to Pierre. 'Robert makes you sound like a dictionary. I much prefer the softer, sweeter Pierre,' she said.

The relationship between the two women has never been warm or completely easy. They are devoted to each other out of a sense of duty and kinship but Sophie's distance and irony, her cool self-assurance have put off Françoise Perrin from the day they met. They are both teachers. But there the similarity ends. Françoise Perrin was a small-town primary schoolteacher. Sophie teaches French to school leavers at one of the capital's most prestigious Lycées.

The daughter of a market gardener, Françoise struggled to educate herself while helping out after school, weeding, watering, fruit picking, occasionally accompanying her parents to country markets. A firm believer in the French Republican school system, she has been a reader and a militant all her life, voting communist, devouring history, philosophy and literature, naming her only child after her revolutionary hero. But she has never lost her strong country roots, nor been attracted by the artificial lights of Paris that her son finds so seductive.

Françoise is passionate where Sophie is 'mannered' and although she continues to be somewhat intimidated by her daughter-in-law's sophistication, Mrs Perrin is convinced she is the better, more genuine person of the two. Her assessment of her daughter-in-law, although laudatory, always carries with it a tinge of contempt.

Since his marriage to Sophie, Robert-Pierre has been oscillating between these two opposing muses. Françoise, not her late husband Jean, was the dominating force behind their small but fiercely united family. She cheered the student uprising of 1968, lighting the revolutionary flame in her son and egging him on when he became a political firebrand at the *Ecole de médecine* in Paris. His choice of private practice over institutional work disappointed her, as did his choice of Sophie for a bride. 'A bourgeoise from stylish schools,' she said to her husband, but tried to hide her misgivings, and although the stiffness in their relationship never went away, even after Jean's death, she developed a genuine affection for her daughter-in-law. 'We are different,' she concluded and left it at that.

They are at La Coupole. She has had her way and he, inevitably, has been recognized. With a conspiratorial smirk, the *maître de* leads them to their table in the vast restaurant. '*Monsieur, Madame, par ici, s'il vous plaît* ...' in a tone a shade too deferential. Oblivious to the undercurrent, she gives him a regal nod. Then proceeds to order unseasonal hothouse asparagus, which she eats with relish, dousing the tips liberally with sauce hollandaise before tucking her napkin into her neckline in anticipation of her seafood platter.

Robert-Pierre is off his food. It has been almost a month since he was turfed out and he had had no success with Sophie at all. She has declined several invitations to lunch. He has not hazarded dinner, and all attempts to engineer a chance meeting through the few sympathetic friends he has left have failed. The only person who could perhaps convince Sophie to forgive and forget is his mother. But for that he will first have to bring her around.

Françoise has finished the last of her crêpe. Pushing her plate away with a regretful sigh, she says, 'Now tell me what is going on. Why are both you and Sophie so upset? It's not like you to have an impaired appetite.'

'Well, Maman, the flat where I'm staying is actually mine now. It was left to me by the person who died.'

'*Mon Dieu*!' Her eyebrows shoot into her hairline. 'Who was?'

'Kranti ... that was her name. She was Indian. I was seeing her on and off for the past five years...'

'Five years is a long time, Robert, half a decade. So what happened, was she ill? Is that why you were treating her?'

'I was not treating her, Maman, I had an affair with her.'

'For five years? That's like having a bigamous marriage, a second family!'

'Not really. She was very independent, both financially and otherwise and, of course, out of respect for Sophie, I never met her in public except for a few discreet trips outside Paris.'

'I would hardly call that respecting Sophie. Did she know? Obviously she knows now,' she remarked.

'Well, she knows because the police told her.'

'The police? Why would the police be involved? No wonder Sophie is so upset. What did you expect? Roses?'

'It's not what you think. She committed suicide,' he says, going on the defensive, suddenly unable to continue. 'You'd better come back to the flat with me.'

At Kranti's, Francoise Perrin looks appreciatively around her. 'This is a beautiful flat, very unsual. Was she an artist, your friend?'

'Well, almost. She was a designer, a good one. She did attempt some serious work and she was trying to become a writer, but I think she realized she would not make the grade, either as an artist or a writer.'

'Is that why she killed herself, or was it because of some mental illness?'

Every psychiatrist needs a mother confessor, thinks Robert-Pierre as he takes the plunge. 'I don't know, Maman. I don't know at all! It was so strange, almost staged. Everything prepared in advance, like a play, as if she was on stage, playing out a role. But there was no sign, no warning.'

He knew Kranti was not always happy, he tells his mother, but then, who in this world does not harbour some hidden chagrin? She was always so controlled, so sure of herself, except perhaps in sleep. Very secretive about her childhood in India which was, from all accounts – her writings mainly – terribly traumatic.

He sees the look of expectation on Françoise's face and sees he is getting nowhere. His mother is waiting for him to tell her, really tell her.

Sitting on the carpet, his head on her knee, he tells her all. How they met, what they did. Kranti's jealousy, his own impatience. The tears come at last and he sobs out his anger and self-recrimination.

'She planned it all, Maman. Planned it so it would hurt. She wanted to punish me because of my relationship with Sophie. She could not understand how I could love her and have a happy marriage at the same time. She wanted me to choose.

I couldn't do that. I told her so. She was so resentful of our holidays together, it took all the joy away.'

'Well, five years is a long time in any woman's life. Can you blame her if she began to harbour expectations about some sort of permanence?'

'She kept on bringing up the question of my holidays with Sophie, although I went away with her for several long weekends each year. She just wanted more all the time!'

'I'm not sure I blame her, Robert, especially if she lived alone and had no family or friends.'

'It was such a well-planned, deliberate act. She had thought of every detail. She even left a suicide note for the neighbour, about something terrible she had done in her past. The police did not show me the medical report, but there must have been an autopsy. It was they who told Sophie. I was so nervous, being under suspicion, I never dared ask. But going through Kranti's papers, I found detailed notes on datura, a common poison used in India.'

'I know all about datura. I grew up on a farm, remember?'

'Yes, and I learnt all about stramonium, which is the active element, when I was in medical school. She used massive quantities of it. But I think she was very disturbed. I'm going through her diaries right now and there are things in there she never spoke about. It's dreadful, frightening at times. No stability, a life dictated by the fickleness and whimsy of obviously maladjusted parents. She was seeking permanence. She just could not accept the fact that I refused to leave Sophie or even tell her about our relationship. And then she was seeing Pierre Keller, that little shit. I'm sure he pushed her, egged her on.'

'You can't blame him, Robert. How would you like it if someone said you drove your patients to suicide?'

'You don't know him. He's an unscrupulous bastard.'

'Are you implying that Pierre Keller manipulated her, deliberately pushed her over the precipice? It's a very serious charge that someone in your position should not be making. You're prejudiced. It is absurd to think anyone of Pierre Keller's reputation would set out to do something like that.'

'I don't know. She was seeing him and writing this confession about her family for him. It's grim reading, Maman.'

'Yes, but I can't believe this affaire of yours went on for five years. And all this time, you managed to keep it from Sophie? I know you both have an understanding of sorts, that you lead more or less separate lives. But Sophie loves you. Arrangement or not, open marriage or not, she is quite naturally upset, especially since this woman died in such terrible circumstances. She gave me no details, only said something about a police enquiry which, by the way, she found acutely humiliating. She talked about someone dying and that you had moved out. I thought it had to do with a patient of yours. I didn't know you were that way involved. Then there's the question of the inheritance...'

Her voice trails off and they sit quietly, listening to the patter of rain against the windows as darkness steals into the room, and the street lamps blink on one by one.

Robert-Pierre gives her hand a squeeze but does not get an answering one in return. He gets up to switch on the lights, draw the curtains, make coffee. When he returns with the tray, she is still sitting somewhat primly on the sofa where he has left her. To her, this is Kranti's home, not his, and the owner's absence makes her uneasy. 'You cannot accept any of this,' she says at last. 'It must go to her family.'

But Robert-Pierre already has an idea of what he is going to do with the flat and the money. The spare bedroom would become his *pied à terre*. He could use Kranti's living room as the reception area, cordon off her studio for his editorial meetings and convert her bedroom into his office for private consultations. Most of the furniture could be retained along with the paintings and the best artefacts. Some of the money could be pumped into the magazine and he could even institute a competition, with a respectable sum endowed in her name as the prize for the best article. He could form a trust. The Kranti Goray Trust. He would have to get rid of the other stuff, of course – the linen, the clothes and books, her art materials and archives.

'I hope you aren't planning to keep any of this? Given its location and size, this flat is worth over a million at least?' asks Françoise, looking about her. 'Robert!' She exclaims seeing the shuttered look on his face. 'You can't do that. It wouldn't be right. Especially since you say she killed herself in order to punish you. In which case, weighing you down with her property is an even greater punishment. It makes you beholden to her forever, even after she's gone! It gives her a power over you she never had during your time together. And then, if you sincerely wish to mend fences with Sophie, you must make a clean break with the past, with all this. You must not keep any of it,' she says, looking around.

He says nothing, weighing all she has said.

She takes this for his habitual obstinacy, the obdurate, grasping quality that she has long regarded as the fatal flaw in his character, a profound self-centeredness, like a bottomless well.

'There is no point in my speaking to Sophie if you are not prepared to deal with the past. Perhaps you should stay here a bit longer, give it more time,' she says.

He remains silent. She is sympathetic but firm, biting down the rush of love and protectiveness that well up at her beloved son's obvious distress. 'Well, I'd better be leaving if I'm to catch the last direct train to Fontainbleau,' she says, consulting her small gold watch.

They wait for the lift on the landing and as it lurches to a stop, Robert-Pierre steps forward to open it. But before he can touch the handle, the door is flung open and out steps Olga Savic, accompanied by a tall young man. Robert-Pierre has never seen anyone this handsome in the flesh before. He looks so much like Alain Delon. In fact, he's better looking than Delon ever was in his youth, he thinks, taking in the tall broad frame, the dark Byronic locks and deep blue eyes.

'*Bonsoir Docteur*, how are you? Allow me to introduce my son, Peter.' Mrs Savic looks wildly happy, brimming with pride and joy.

'*Bonsoir* Peter, Robert-Pierre Perrin. It's good to meet you at last. When did you arrive? Your mother talks all the time about you. Olga, may I present my mother, Françoise? She is just returning to Fontainebleau. I'm sorry, we have to rush off or else she'll miss her train, but we'll catch up if you're staying a while.'

'Two weeks at least, I hope. Unless a fight with my dad drives me out like it did the last time,' says Peter, smiling.

'What a divinely good-looking young man. He reminds me of Delon in those early films with Romy Schneider, when they were so much in love, you could see it coming out of their pores. How beautifully dressed and so polite,' Francoise Perrin gushes as they leave the building. 'It must be difficult to possess that kind of beauty and stay normal.'

'How strange, I too thought he looks like Delon. There is a striking resemblence. But you're right, Maman, it isn't always easy for people with such good looks. He's gay as a coot. Lives in Hollywood and is much in demand, making up all the top stars. He's got a cosmetic company and houses galore and it's his money that keeps them in style here. Can't stand his father, who objects to his homosexuality. His mother worries about him, fears he'll be clobbered to death or die of AIDS. Which might well happen one day.'

'Robert, how can you talk like that, it's so cynical.'

'Oh Maman, if you heard and saw half the things I do, you'd turn cynical too, I assure you. I have some very difficult patients at the moment – anorexic teenagers bent on destroying themselves, playing stupid and dangerous power games. And now I'm discovering dreadful things about someone I thought I knew and loved and who, I presumed, loved me. Perhaps I was mistaken. You don't do things like that to people you love. She didn't really care about me. All she cared about was how it looked, the *mise en scène*! This was her way of taking revenge. I wonder what life really meant to her, after all. Perhaps Olga Savic is right, perhaps it was all just a macabre game.'

13

The Black Notebook

Paris

April 2006

Am feeling lovesick and unhappy. R again. It is difficult not to pick up the phone and call. But I know I shall get that artificial recorded voice and I refuse to put up with it any more.

I have stuck notes on all the extensions – Do not call R. I hope that helps. Is this love or infatuation? Does it matter? It seems real enough. The desire, the frustration, the pain and the joy. The act of love. I feel radiant when he is here, a powerful current of energy flows into me. Should I deny all this, lose it all for foolish, childish pride? Is it childish pride or a deep instinct – in him to dominate and in me to resist?

I try not to think of his wife. I know he loves her, cannot leave her. Nor do I want him to. I just want to know her and for her to know me. No, much more, to accept me. The wife and the mistress slavishly serving the same master, even becoming friends in the process, the Indian concept of sautan. In a sense, that's what I am, the sautan, the 'kept' woman, but does she know it? And if she did, would she be able to acknowledge it publicly? Just goes to show how Indian I am, have remained, despite the Western veneer.

6 April 2006

Back at my table again. Unbelievable procrastination. Being separated from R makes me fractious, querulous, incapable of concentration. Imaginary conversations swirl around in my head. I promise myself I shall not

7 May 2006

I shall not what? Interrupted mid-sentence? Or frozen in my thoughts? A month has gone by and I have not properly returned to these pages.

Pierre and I hardly talk. He reads through whatever I give him, whenever I give it. He takes his time and I wait in trepidation, as he reads slowly and deliberately. Our sessions have become irregular, dependent on my travels and work, on what I have been able to pen down. And the pickings are meagre, I have to admit.

I know I shall not be able to stop until I have told him all. But why then is it so difficult to persevere? My will falters at every step and yet, like a weak-kneed, lily-livered alcoholic I return, shamefaced and unsure, on tottering legs to my true mistress. What is this dynamic of attraction and repulsion, nay, need, which makes me come back to the charge time and again? What I write is fragmented, like myself. Bits and pieces scattered over time. Is it because of this that I despair?

I get the frightful and frightening feeling that I am entirely alone. Defenceless, like an abandoned child. I carry that child in me – fearful, weeping, looking around apprehensively with large wounded eyes, unable to find those anchors of security that should rightfully be mine. Pierre said there is a tug of war between fear and desire and the dice seemed loaded in favour of fear. 'Who is watching over your shoulder as you write?' he asked me. I and myself, I answered. And another. Of course, another. Who else?

He holds me captive, my absent father. You are me, he says, so you must live my life, emulate my every word and deed, gesture, smile. You should be quick to tears and selfish to the core. You must charm and captivate, beguile and fascinate. You must bind others to you with invisible thongs of attraction. For without them, without the admiration you see in their eyes, you are nothing, just as I was nothing. I lived through others, through a looking glass, darkly, and now, because you are me, so must you.

His grip will not slacken even now that he is dead. In the nightmare to which I awake most nights, I feel like a tiny beetle, pinned under the weight of a huge heavy rock. Is he the rock that crushes me the beetle? Or am I both, beetle and rock – submissive lover-daughter carrying the unbearable load of my invisible father sitting upon my chest?

Am upset with R today. He is so elusive, like a fish slipping through my fingers. In fact, I'm angry and frustrated with myself and using R as a whipping boy. He can't make time to see me. I feel he is avoiding me. That's absurd, I know. He has his work, after all.

12 June 2006

Still annoyed with myself. Wasted a lot of time these past weeks. R appears to know what he wants. I am floundering.

Dinner with R last night. La Coupole. Oysters and Gewurztraminner. Wore my wig and looked ravishing. He said young. Felt sexy. Found myself hanging on to his lips. Literally. With mine. Couldn't let him go.

◇

What happened was an accident. I know that. Although there's no knowing if it would have happened anyway, some other way, some other day.

May. Just before the monsoon broke. It was unbearably hot and muggy. May, the marriage season. We were in Bombay for the wedding of my cousin Vasudha. Aayee was happy for once because her entire clan was there. Chatting to her brothers and cousins, re-living her childhood in Kolhapur, she was animated, with colour in her cheeks for the first time in months. By now we had moved to Poona, where I was attending university and where the ghosts from my father's past were to come back to haunt me.

My aunt had hired a marriage hall – a large, reconverted suburban house in Mahim – and everyone congregated there, sitting on mattresses laid out in a row along the walls, lolling around on bolsters while tucking into tea and batata vada, singing songs, exchanging gossip. Noon and night, we were spoilt by professional cooks who produced delicious 'marriage food', sweet-hot curries made from ripe mango, jackfruit and pineapple, fresh tamarind pickle, sour and tangy, that left a trail of heat upon the tongue, sizzling orange jalebis dripping syrup, washed down with tak, liquefied and seasoned curd – and a yoghurt-based sweet called Srikhand that set in your stomach like a tubful of new cement.

After which, of course, you were expected to retire for a post-lunch siesta before the next round of eating began. For those with a sweet tooth, there were boxes of wafer-thin, fragrant Mahimi halwa, rich yellow motichoor laddoos, anarsas crusted with poppy seed and crescent-shaped karanjis filled with sugar and grated coconut. Spicy chivda and crackling chukli to crunch in between lunch and tea. There was as much paan as we wished to eat and we joyfully went about with mouths stained a lascivious red. Nobody appeared to mind the fact that there were only six bathrooms for about a hundred people and that the smell from the latrines had begun to invade the large hall reserved for the main festivities.

Little groups had formed. Those who were my aunt's direct relatives tended to stick together while those from her husband's side had their own cliques going. Maushi, Aayee's sister, was the only one looking harried, conferring with cooks, making sure none of her husband's crabbity female relations were given grounds for complaint.

Tai was lying behind a pile of rolled-up mattresses, her nose stuck in a book, which made Akka turn to Aayee: 'You're lucky she wants to study. At least she'll get a job as a teacher somewhere. With such dark skin and those elephant teeth, who will marry her?' She was always cruel, my grandmother, ever since I could remember. She passed it off as plain-speaking honesty, but I know there was intention to hurt. Akka was also getting back at Baba, a son-in-law she had never wanted but had perforce to accept because no one else would marry her widowed daughter. Unwillingly, she'd had to acknowledge him as her daughter's saviour, a fact she'd never been able to digest.

Aayee flushed. There was an embarrassed silence and then one of her cousins said diplomatically, 'Akka Saheb, these days marriage isn't everything. Girls are becoming ministers and managers and Shanti is lucky to have so much encouragement from her father.' Akka glowered at him, furious, but held her tongue.

Akka saw Tai as an extension of Baba. She was fearless and spoke her mind, occasionally mocking our grandmother for her fasts and taboos. I was much more in what Akka called 'our mould'. I resembled them physically; I was slim, sharp-featured, accommodating and not at all studious. In short, I was a good, normal, marriageable girl while Tai, Akka felt, belonged to the intellectually superior Goray clan. Since she dared not attack Baba directly, my poor sister became a convenient target.

But such tiny barbs apart, we were part of a big, noisy, garrulous marriage party. We gossiped, played endless card games, sang syrupy Marathi bhavgeet and Hindi film songs, in voices that were loud, and off-key, over-emphasizing the delicate Hindi words in our harsh Maharashtrian accents.

Except Tai, who hated the empty-headed, boring inanity of the whole exercise, and Baba, who was always a little out of it as far as Aayee's family was concerned. There was his communism for one, the fact that he made them feel uncomfortable about their religious beliefs, lecturing them about their superstitions, pooh-poohing their rituals, managing to place all of them at a disadvantage, including my lawyer and architect uncles who, despite their degrees, did not possess the intellectual tools to fend him off. And then there was his prison record, his philandering past (we didn't know about all that then, but they did). They disapproved of him, found him morally corrupt. They had to show him respect because he was married to my mother (the girl's side always ends up eating crow somehow), so they paid him compliments to his face and ran him down behind his back and the poor slob mostly failed to see through any of that.

After the first day of 'Hello, how are you?' they tended to avoid him and Baba took to hanging out with us young cousins. He laughed and joked with us and they all thought Tai and I were lucky to have him for a father, especially when compared to their own stuffy, conservative progenitors.

I loved dressing up and Aayee for once had allowed me free use of her most precious saris – she didn't want her sister, who had married a wealthy lawyer, to think we had nothing to put on our backs! I had worn her saris before, but never in public. My thinness usually made me look like a stick wrapped up in five metres of cloth. I had no contours to speak of. But that day in May, knotting my blouse choli-style, high above my navel, I realized I had finally grown a pair of perfectly acceptable breasts – small but smooth, round, nutmeg-tipped, and that below the column of my waist, my hips flared out gently, in soft womanly curves.

In a heavy emerald-green Paithani sari, my hair pulled back in an old-fashioned chignon, eyes darkened with mascara and eyebrow pencil, with Aayee's gold jewellery glinting at my ears and throat, I looked much older than seventeen. My skin was smooth if dark, my features clean cut, my eyes velvety and alluring. I was immensely pleased with myself, aware that people were looking at me speculatively, as if seeing me for the first time. In a self-conscious gesture, my hand kept patting my hair, fiddling with my sari pallu, keeping it in place over my new-found breasts.

'Stop behaving like a strumpet. You look like a cheap film star,' Tai told me sourly, not least because her sari clung to her middle in a lumpy heap. But she was right. I was over made-up and walking with a new, hip-swinging gait that said: 'Look at me, oh look at me.' But did I care? Unlike Tai, I was madly happy at that wedding and having a grand time.

The ceremony itself was be held in a mandapa, a large square demarcated by four young banana trees held upright in copper pots filled with sand. A purple-red banana flower, like a mottled, fully erect penis, hung off one of the branches, an obvious symbol of fertility without which no Hindu wedding was complete – that and the ubiquitous coconut. The muhurta was for 11:06, the most auspicious moment as declared by the groom's astrologers. My aunt's chap had suggested a later time but she had to bow to pressure from the 'superior' side. After all, my cousin Vasudha was immensely fat and despite a sizeable dowry, it had not been exactly easy to find a suitable boy.

I was amidst a gaggle of people standing around the mandapa, having grabbed one of the best places from which to pelt the couple with fistfuls of uncooked rice once they were declared man and wife. The bride and groom had just been brought in and Vasudha was trying hard to look coy while peering at the guests from behind the curtain of flowers that covered her face. Logs of wood made a pyramid in the havan, the sacred fire, around which the couple would pronounce their vows. It was elevenish and infernally hot. We were all sweating under our heavy silks, hair plastered to our heads, dark patches forming under armpits, rivers of salty liquid flowing freely down necks and backs.

To escape the heat, I had positioned myself next to an enormous whirring electric fan that churned up the hot air, tugging awkwardly at my pallu to prevent it from blowing off my shoulder. There was a commotion as the priests approached, carrying glowing embers to start the sacred fire. I heard Baba call out a warning as I craned my neck to see better. But it was too late. A moment's inattention and my pallu floated off my shoulder to land on the pot of glowing embers. My father's arm, which had shot out protectively to push me back, was lying across my bosom, his hand cupping my breast in it's low-cut choli. Above the screams of 'Fire!' my gaze locked with his and it seemed an eternity before he wrenched his eyes away. Maybe that's just my overheated imagination. For, in fact, on seeing the flames, a surge of sheer terror shot through me and with a barely audible cry of 'Aayee', I fainted.

My father saved my life to become the hero of the day. With astounding presence of mind, he stripped the burning fabric from my body, stamping on it repeatedly to put out the flames. By the time he had pulled the sari off me, however, the flames had touched my waist, the gold-threaded silk leaving second-degree burns on my skin. Baba had hideous burns on the soles of his feet. Despite the accident, the ceremony had to go ahead at the exact time decreed by the astrologers and so two events, one highly dramatic, the other colourful yet solemn, took place side by side.

A doctor was called in and he bandaged Baba's feet, put Burnol on the patches on my waist, covering them with lint and soft white gauze. I was in shock, he said, and would quite possibly run a fever. I remember drinking tea, wearing only my blouse and petticoat, half-reclining on a mattress in one corner of the large room while the priests held up a ceremonial curtain, the antarpat, between the bride and the groom, chanting the Mangalashtaka as relatives and friends showered the newlyweds with rice and rose petals.

Aayee had lost interest in the proceedings. She was in the grip of a cold, white anger and would have hit me had there not been so many people present. 'Who told you to stand so close to the fan? Aren't you ashamed of yourself, making such a show? What face am I going to show now, wrecking such an important occasion? Cover yourself properly,' she hissed, throwing me a filthy white sheet pulled off a nearby mattress.

The ceremony was barely over and already tongues were wagging. There was a huge show of sympathy towards me, but I noticed some of the women who came to commiserate did so with malice in their eyes. Decked out in my borrowed plumes, I had become an unwelcome competitor in the marriage market. Apparently Aayee had already received a couple of proposals before the incident took place and these had now been quietly withdrawn. The rumour ran that I suffered from a 'very strong, evil Saturn in the marriage house'. Anybody who married me was surely doomed. Why, hadn't my very presence there threatened to turn Vasudha's marriage into a tragedy? The whole mandapa could have gone up in flames.

It was the fault of the groom's astrologer, who had got it all wrong, especially the time of the muhurat, my aunt would say later, the day Vasudha came home with a broken arm and a huge black eye. As for their pronouncements about my marriage, they weren't very wrong, as it turned out. Perhaps I should have paid more heed before riding out into the sunset with all those men – MGGR and all others in between.

14

A Letter from Chennai

A blue envelope with foreign stamps is lying on the carpet. Robert-Pierre picks it up, flips it back and forth. It is addressed to him in writing very similar to Kranti's, only much better formed, without her flamboyant flourishes. The postmark tells him it was sent from Chennai almost a fortnight ago.

Written on a sheet of ruled paper torn from a school notebook, it begins with a simple '*Hello*'.

Robert-Pierre does not like surprises but he has been half-dreading, half-expecting this. I do have a name, dammit! How rude can you get? I knew she wouldn't give up, he seethes. The sight of the letter has set his teeth on edge.

'This is to inform you that I shall be travelling to Paris to recover my sister's ashes. You will understand that since the purchase of the ticket has proved extremely dear, I would like to stay in my sister's flat during the duration of my visit. Also since I do not speak French and this is my first experience outside India, I would be grateful if you could meet my flight at the airport. Otherwise there would be a problem with the key, etc.

I shall be arriving on 5 November by the Air India flight that lands at Charles de Gaulle airport at 11.30 a.m. I hope this letter will reach you without delay so that you have enough time to make the necessary arrangements for my stay.

I would like to make an inventory of all of Kranti's belongings, so if there are papers or jewellery in a bank locker, could you kindly make sure they are withdrawn and kept in the flat? I would like to sort everything out in a positive spirit and it would be best if I were to be the sole occupant during my stay.

Please do let me know by telephone on 914428576361 or by fax at our neighbour's house where the number is 9144267572920. I cannot telephone you since we do not have STD facility and the nearest public phone booth is quite far away.

Sincerely yours,

Shanti Aiyer (née Goray)

The gall of it. Well, she can stay here if she likes, but he is certainly not moving. And, of course, there is no question of allowing her to 'make an inventory' or any such thing. She isn't even the legal heir, just an unpleasant relative, albeit a close one, and here she is bossing him about long distance as if he were her skivvy. He sends off a laconic, barely polite fax in acknowledgement and does not receive a response.

Come the day, however, he finds himself driving to Roissy airport, spending an irritable hour on the *périphérique* listening to France Culture radio discussing the future of Halley's comet, followed by their usual 11 a.m. programme on psychology. The dulcet tones of Pierre Keller waxing eloquent about the difficulty of handling patients from distant, foreign lands only serve to heighten his bad temper. 'He could just as well have said "alien" cultures,' mutters Robert-Pierre, wondering if Keller is in any way referring to Kranti. And then, to his utter disbelief, he does, although obliquely.

'I had this very talented, absolutely remarkable Asian patient, you see, who I could not really help,' Keller is saying, empathy dripping from his voice like honey. 'Because even if our primal emotions, our impulses are the same, they are conditioned and triggered by cultural specifities. And I tried very hard, but in the end I could not really help this particular patient. Our worlds were very far apart and what this person said to me sometimes made little sense although, in a literal way, it was perfectly coherent. Perhaps patients like this one need help from someone from the same cultural milieu, who can place their fears and anxieties in context. That is certainly a problem for non-Western foreigners living here.'

Robert-Pierre notes how cleverly Keller skates on thin ice, never revealing the sex or exact origin of the patient. But he is talking of Kranti, he is sure. 'Bastard!' he shouts, pushing down on the horn, willing the car ahead of him to move forward.

He has not made much headway with Sophie. She is pleasant on the telephone but avoids any discussion of his return, and they have met just once, in their old neighbourhood café, over an orange pressé, when she pleaded for more time. Perhaps Maman is right, maybe I should refuse this inheritance, give it away. But the thought of the property going to the sister repulses him. Anyone but that one, he thinks. But if I tell Sophie I no longer have the flat, that I've turned that page for good, given it away, she might reconsider. It would mean giving away over a million euros, though. Maybe I could transfer it all to the magazine, to the Trust.

When he finally gets to the airport, almost an hour late, there is no sign of Shanti Aiyer. The plane landed fifteen minutes ahead of schedule and the passengers streaming out of the exit gate are mostly black – the Nairobi flight that's listed after AI 137 from Bombay. He hangs around nervously for fifteen minutes. He should have left earlier; he should not have come at all. Why couldn't she take a taxi like any normal person? Cursing roundly, he drives back to the city.

There is no one waiting for him in the street outside Kranti's building and no one on the landing either. Perhaps she missed her flight? Perhaps the letter was full of lies and she never intended to come in the first place? Bah! He had cancelled an appointment for nothing. As he opens the appartment door, he hears voices and his olfactory buds swing into action: the smell is alien, strong, but not unpleasant.

Madame Savic is plying the stranger with tea and chocolate. Shanti Aiyer is evidently very cold despite the heating in the flat. She is huddled deep into a large green-and-white-flecked woollen coat and he can see bits of the crushed brown and pink silk sari that makes a puddle around her legs. Her feet are clad in thick beige socks and black open-toed sandals. Hardly suitable for early November with its distinct nip.

The two women are acting out a strange pantomime. It is evident Olga Savic cannot speak any English except 'yes' and a decidedly French '*non*'. But her hands and the non-stop, incomprehensible gibberish that flows from her mouth more than make up for that. The stranger is definitely Kranti's sister – he recognizes her from the photograph, just several sizes larger, the cheekbones lost under cushions of flesh. She is looking at Mrs Savic with an expresion that is helpless, bewildered and, Robert-Pierre notes with satisfaction, somewhat alarmed.

Shanti Aiyer jumps up as he approaches. 'You must be Robert-Pierre,' she says, joining her hands in an Indian greeting.

'Welcome,' he says, extending his hand, which she chooses to ignore. 'I go to airport. Little late. But your plane arrives early. You are gone. I am sorry.' He too states the obvious.

'I waited but saw no one who seemed to be expecting me. So I took a taxi. I can't believe the expense! Five thousand rupees for just forty kilometres! Totally beyond my means and I'm sure the driver cheated me! But here I am at last. If you don't mind I must call my husband immediately to tell him I have arrived safely. He tends to worry.'

Robert-Pierre gestures to the telephone and a minute later, Mrs Aiyer is deep in conversation in a language that sounds harsh with ringing consonants and peculiar twists of the tongue. All he can make out are the words '5000 rupees', uttered repeatedly in angry disbelief. The husband's name seems to be Raja or maybe that's just the word for husband in whatever language she's speaking.

'I have put her suitcase in the corridor. It's heavy. I wonder what she has in it, bricks?' Mrs Savic says in a hoarse whisper. 'Maybe we should show her to her room. She was here on the steps, waiting. Madame Benoit brought her upstairs and I let her in. She says the taxi over-charged. I'm not sure he did, but she is upset.'

Between them, they lead Shanti Aiyer to the spare bedroom that also doubles up as Kranti's studio. 'Is this where I am supposed to sleep?' she says, gesturing towards the sofa bed, Kranti's easel and stacked canvases. 'What about the proper bedroom, my sister's bedroom?'

'Well, I stay here too. This is my home now. There is third bedroom but it is full; impossible to sleep with all her art materials. So you stay here, I stay in other room,' Robert-Pierre says firmly.

To their utter consternation Mrs Aiyer hits her forehead with her palm and begins to cry quietly. She sinks into the sofa-bed, utterly desolate.

'We need Peter,' Mrs Savic declares, turns on her heel and hurries out. Robert-Pierre leaves the weeping woman to shut himself in his room. 'What did I ever do to deserve this?' he mutters.

A few minutes later, Mrs Savic is back with Peter in tow. He strides into the studio and without a word engulfs Shanti Aiyer in his arms, murmuring, 'You poor thing. You must be shellshocked. My mother and I will look after you. Don't worry, you're with friends. We'll make up the bed and you'll see it's very comfortable. There's lots of space. Just think, you're surrounded by your beloved sister's paintings. What more could you ask?'

He rocks her back and forth and Shanti Aiyer weeps harder, clinging to his hand, before drying her eyes and finally giving him a watery smile.

'It's so good to hear English,' she sniffs, 'even if it's with an American accent!'

He smiles. 'Listen. Robert will sleep in the other room because he has nowhere else to go, but don't let that bother you. And you can call us whenever you like, we're right next door. You could have stayed in our flat except that my father is recovering from a stroke and needs all the quiet he can get. We loved your sister, Shanti, and you are more than welcome here. She was really special. My mother found ... her. We were the only family she had in Paris. So don't hesitate. I suggest you have a bath and change. It's almost time for lunch. Then you can have a nap, and later this evening, we can all get together and talk and I shall be your official interpreter.'

With his easy charm and bedside manner he has deflated the indignant Mrs Aiyer, dissolved the tension. She gives him an uncertain smile, takes his hand again. 'Thank you,' she says. 'You are so good. In Marathi we say *Devmanus* meaning a god in human form. If my son had survived he would have been just like you.'

He stiffens, then pats her shoulder gently, propelling her towards the bathroom. 'Take a long hot shower or better still, a bath. It will warm you up. And don't wear your coat in the house or you'll feel very cold when you step out. Now you unpack, have a bath and I shall get lunch ready.'

'I'm a vegetarian,' she says, some of her earlier belligerence creeping back into her voice.

'No problem, so am I,' he replies.

They all lunch together at the dining table. It's a tense affair. Peter has cooked for everyone – omlettes for Robert-Pierre and his mother, a salad with mozarella on the side for Shanti and himself. A crusty baguette and a large cheese platter.

'Oh, but this stinks!' Mrs Aiyer says pushing the cheese away.

'Yes it does rather. But you get to like the smell, even love it. In LA where I live, I have a wonderful baker and cheese man who keeps the ripest Munster and Epoisse aside for me. No Brie or Camembert. I like my cheeses strong, washed down with some really good wine. That's how I get my proteins and calcium. How do you get yours, just dal and yoghurt, huh?' Peter asks.

'Yes, all kinds of dals, sprouts and yoghurt,' Mrs Aiyer says eagerly. 'I could cook for you, if you like. I have brought all my spices and dals with me.'

'Your sister was a wonderful cook and she gave me several lessons and recipes. So now my partner Emile and I cook Indian food quite regularly. Maman quite likes it, except for the fact that it's vegetarian and she's a real carnivore, like Robert here. But my father has never taken to foreign food. He is a goulash and soup person, as my mother will confirm.'

'I find it difficult to deal with meat. I married young and my family is strictly vegetarian Brahmin. I just can't get used to the thought of eating the flesh of dead animals.'

'We are not barbarians here, and you will make some adjustments too, I'm sure, *non*?' Robert-Pierre asks.

It's more of a statement than a question. She obviously cannot be allowed to dictate terms this way. 'I sometimes cook a steak. Maybe you will try. Very good in this cold weather,' he says, and sees her wince. 'Of course, I will not cook same time as when you want to use kitchen,' he offers.

'Oh, I thought I could cook for everyone. But, of course, I cannot touch meat,' she says, obviously put out.

'Why don't you use the kitchen when Robert is out of the house, during the day? Then he can do his bit in the evening when he wants and you can warm up your dishes in the microwave,' soothes Peter.

'I don't know how to use a microwave. I've only seen one on the television,' she says nervously.

'I'll show you. It's very simple and it heats up food within minutes. Very convenient, you'll see. You'll want to take one back with you! Now, would you like to try a sip of white wine?'

Mrs Aiyer shakes her head. She appears to be dozing off. Peter gets up to lead her back to her room. 'Come, don't bother with the rest. We'll load up the dishwasher. You need to rest. You haven't slept at all and you're probably jet-lagged, especially if this is the first time you've travelled. You can arrange your things later. And don't think about the taxi fare,' he says, placing a hundred euro note on her bedside table.

'But I can't take money from you and, in any case, this is too much. I only paid sixty euros,' she protests. 'And then too I could have taken the bus, but I was afraid of getting lost. I should have listened to Raja, my husband, and let him come instead of me, or not come at all. What am I doing here?' She begins to cry again.

'What you need is sleep and a strong cup of coffee when you wake up,' Peter says, gently shutting the door. Oh boy, this is going to be rough, he thinks.

They have a huddled conference in the living room. '*La pauvre*,' says Olga, 'she seems completely lost. I would be if I had to go to India or even to Los Angeles.'

'I could have sent her the ashes by special delivery. She didn't have to travel all this way. She didn't have the money for Kranti's funeral, but now she's suddenly found it and she's here!'

'We all know it's not about the ashes. She has come about the property. That much is evident. The point is, what does she plan to do? I can help her to adjust, but I cannot go around with her. Ivan needs me too much. Perhaps you can take her around, Peter?' Olga suggests.

'I don't know. She's very highly strung and upset. Who wouldn't be in her shoes? But sorry as I feel for her, I'd be betraying Kranti if I took her under my wing. This lady has never been very kind to her sister, has she, Maman? Kranti told me once she'd been insulted and asked not to visit because of what the neighbours would say.'

'Oh, but Kranti also liked to lace things up a bit. It wasn't all that straightforward with her. You know that. You are an only child, Peter. You cannot imagine how complicated and hard sibling relationships are. Just look at me and Magda. The way she talks about me – as if I were her enemy, not her sister.'

'That's not the point, Maman. The question, is what does Robert here do with her?'

'Do? I plan to do nothing at all. I would much rather she wasn't here. And at some point, I shall make that plain. But not today. Tonight I shall give her the spare key. She can come and go as she likes, cook the food she wants. She can take the ashes back home with her, I have nothing to say about that at all. Let her take the initiative, speak her mind. Then I shall tell her exactly what I think.'

15

The Red Notebook

KRANTI AND SHANTI

Their new house once belonged to a nawab, Baba says, who squandered his family fortune on gambling and nautch girls.

The decaying mansion is set in an unkempt garden with tall trees and masses of red, magenta and orange bougainvillea. Its blue, green, silver and gold-painted interior bears testimony to the nawab's extravagant tastes and lifestyle. Aayee wrinkles up her nose and says it's 'gaudy'. Neither is she pleased with the fact that Baba has decided to make it an 'office cum residence', with his staff crowded into the front of the building and the family occupying the rear.

Aayee says the wave-like blue and white tiled mosaics that cover the enormous high-ceilinged dining room with whirring electric fans dangling from ten-foot-long metal rods make her dizzy. Kranti says it looks like the sea.

One day a boat will paddle within these walls, but for the moment, the nawab's former baithak has become the main typing pool, and Aunty Cou-ee rules over her kingdom from a small, glass-fronted plywood cabin erected in one corner. She has been promoted to administrative assistant and sharply scolds the nervous, untried typists who pound out insurance policies all day, correcting their stencils with a pink fluorescent liquid that Kranti steals to wear as nail paint.

Aayee, who wishes to have nothing to do with the office, pretends it doesn't exist. She insists upon a separate walled-in entrance for the office staff in order to avoid ever having to clap eyes on Barbara d'Costa. And once the partition goes up, the two women are destined never to meet again. She no longer allows Yvonne to visit, but does not mind Kranti going over to play at Aunty Coo-ee's after school.

Uncle Vincent has joined his wife's cousin, Eric, in his garage business and the d'Costas now share his lime-washed cottage surrounded by neem and peepul trees and the carcasses of old cars. Loud hammering comes from the shed that serves as office, workshop and garage.

At Baba's insistence, Aayee joins the Stella Maris College of Music, later to become Bhatkhande University, and works towards her Sangeet Praveen degree. Kranti sees her cycling off to college every morning, her books and lunchbox nestling in the wicker basket attached to the handlebars. This is Pandit Nehru's India and everything seems possible. The war with China is still to come and there is great talk of Peace, Five-Year Plans, Socialism, Literacy and Public Welfare. Aayee and Baba both appear to believe in this, particularly Baba, who, despite being a communist, has unreserved admiration for Panditji.

'What intellect, what style!' he exclaims, discussing Nehru's *Autobiography* or his *Discovery of India* with Tai. Secretly, he wishes he could have written such letters to his daughters from prison. Except, when Baba was in prison, he was not married and had not even met Aayee. He tells the girls of his days in Yeravda jail 'with Achyut Rao Patwardhan and other freedom fighters', about the patriotic songs they sang to keep up each others' morale and the secret notes that were passed around in the prison yard during the exercise hour. Baba, of course, was the bravest and cleverest of them all, often singled out for extra punishment because he was so defiant of the guards.

Relative calm has descended upon the Goray household and although Kranti is doing no better at school, she is coming to grips with Hindi and is tentatively making friends. Until the day she sees Aunty Cou-ee looking all puffed up and round like a football, wearing a maternity dress in her favourite yellow. 'My mum's going to have a baby,' says Yvonne nonchalantly. 'But my dad's not happy and they're fighting like cats all the time. She'll be dropping it in a few weeks. I hope I'll have a baby brother, so nice to play with.'

That night at dinner Kranti, who has just returned from Yvonne's, announces: 'Aayee, Aunty Cou-ee is all fat and round with a baby inside and Yvonne says Uncle Vincent isn't happy and they fight all the time.'

From the moment it leaves her mouth, Kranti knows she has said the wrong thing. A long silence drops over them like an oppressive curtain not allowing them to speak or breathe.

Aayee scrapes back her chair and leaves the room, banging shut the door. Then Baba pours himself another whiskey and goes into his office on the other side of the partition that divides the house and they hear the door bang as he too shuts himself in.

The monsoon has arrived early and it has been raining non-stop for the past four days. Large, heavy drops that hit the skin like pellets and set up a ceaseless drumming on the roof, the trees, even the parched lawn. Aayee finds that the roof of their fancy nawab's office-cum-residence is full of holes and there is a drip-drop concert as buckets, pots, pans and tubs receive their share of the steady downpour. The garden is sodden, the plants bowed down, helpless beneath the onslaught. The rain refuses to let up and the blue-and-gold walls of the dining room film over with a fine green moss while wet clothes sit heavily on the line, hastily strung up inside the house, dank-smelling, unable to shake off the moisture that weighs them down. Fat purple earthworms crawl in the bathrooms and the air is filled with the eggy, vomity smell of rotting vegetation.

There is disturbing news on the radio. The waters of the Gomti are rising. They have crossed the danger mark and the Monkey Bridge risks being washed away. Baba has decided not to send them to school and after giving everyone at the office the day off, he packs Aayee and the girls along with suitcases of clothing, schoolbooks, provisions and food parcels into his claret-red Austin of England car and drives them to the house of his friend Rehman, who owns an enormous Victorian-style sandstone pile called The Burlington Hotel, where they try to settle into a gloomy suite of rooms on the first floor, with heavy, black furniture and low-wattage bulbs that emit a dim, bleary light.

The day they arrive, the sky is low and dark with gigantic black cumulo-nimbus clouds. Kranti cannot sleep all night. Flashes of electric blue lightning throw the dark furniture into frightening relief while ear-shattering cracks of thunder drive her under the pillows. The wind has risen to gale force. She can hear the rain's wind-whipped, jumpy heartbeat, the clanging of tin roofs ripped from their moorings as they are blown off into the night, faraway doors banging open-shut-open-shut. The morning reveals the full extent of the devastation. A tall Ashoka tree lies drunkenly on its side and the garden looks as if someone carefully dropped a tonne of garbage from a helicopter circling overhead. Rags and plastic sheeting are caught in tree branches. The ground is littered with assorted detritus – bits of corrugated tin, twigs and paper, branches torn off trees by the angry wind, even an entire shop sign from Suresh Cloth Stores, Suppliers of Fine Hosiery. But the rain does not stop; puddles become fast-flowing baby rivers.

And then comes the news everyone has been expecting and dreading. The Gomti has burst its banks, the Monkey Bridge swept away. The only way they can return home is by boat. Kranti peeps over the balustrade to look at the rising water. The hotel's garden and driveway have disappeared, the water is just inches below, lapping at the first-floor verandah where she stands, and all she can see are the tops of trees and the Burlington's splendid Victorian folly jaggedly mirrored in a turbulent muddy brown sea.

People are floating in the swirling mass, clutching at twigs rushing past, desperately lunging at debris as the water carries them forward. Cows, buffaloes, handcarts, even an occasional car, float past her astonished eyes, borne swiftly by the current. The roar of the water is immense and frightening. Kranti is transfixed.

It will be ten days before the waters recede and they can go back to school, which is now much farther away. Ten days during which they will remain holed up, dining by candlelight, subsisting on dal-rice khichidi and Parle Gluco buiscuits dipped in Ostermilk. Kerosene, sugar and vegetables have disappeared from the market. There is no fresh milk, no radio, no newspaper, and rumour is all they can feed on: babies dying from hunger, thousands carried away by the waters, a cholera outbreak in the old city.

What was only a temporary arrangement has perforce become permanent. Baba's Austin of England is dead, drowned, its engine flooded. Aayee goes over to the house in a rickshaw, crossing the river by boat, and comes back looking pinched and weepy. Their house is caked with mud and slush. Waterlogged gunny sacks of rice have sprouted mushrooms. Bloated doors and windows refuse to open and once opened, refuse to close. Her radio, her new sofas, the newar beds are now fit only for the rubbish heap. Thieves plying country boats have made off with her crockery and kitchen equipment. Nothing can be saved. Nothing at all.

And yet, when they finally return to school, little appears to have changed. There is a prayer meeting for Anjana Massey and her family, killed when the leprosy mission her father ran was flattened by a mudslide. But other than water marks along the walls, there is no discernable evidence of damage to the school. The nuns have had the prescience to move desks, chairs, blackboards, registers, cupboards and the school safe to the third-floor terrace, covering it all with lengths of tarpaulin. The flood becomes part of their lessons in geography and maths. Five hundred and fifty-three corpses (mostly slum dwellers) recovered; another hundred and eighty persons feared drowned, thousands made homeless.

Kranti has not seen Yvonne at school for over a week. Ignoring Tai's warnings and their rickshaw puller's pleading that he will get into trouble with her parents, she hops off at a point close to the d'Costas' garage home.

Silence and an air of neglect greet her. A child's mud-choked watering can lies abandoned on the path. The neem trees are denuded and the garden looks angry and ruffled, as if giant fingers tickled it sick. No hammering emanates from the workshop or the paint shed. An eerie quiet has gripped the garage. A car stands forlorn to one side, its bonnet open, its front door sagging, its floor a scummy pool. A frog sits on the seat, ready to drive off.

Kranti lets out a silent 'Oh' and her hand goes up to her mouth in disbelief. A peepul tree has fallen on the roof of the cottage, almost halving it in two. Its roots show gnarled and twisting while its leaves and branches form a canopy overhead, one languorous and still-leafy branch dangling, like a fractured, useless arm, by the door. By some miracle, the house itself is still standing. It is a scene of desolate and indescribable beauty, a Turner landscape in sub-tropical technicolour.

Kranti wants to turn back and run, but curiosity drives her forward, makes her knock timidly at the door, opened almost instantaneously by Yvonne. There is something different about her friend. She is no longer wearing her school uniform but a shabby frock with gaping holes in the back where the buttons once were. Nor is she smiling her familiar toothsome, street-smart smile. Wordlessly, Yvonne turns to go back inside and Kranti follows, her child's instinct telling her she is now a mourner, entering a house of death.

The furniture has been pushed in a jumble against one wall, while an assortment of battered pots and basins in enamel and aluminium, Kranti notes, have been placed in a row beneath the gaping hole that lets in streaks of dirty grey afternoon light. She looks around for her favourite wooden sign, showing a long-haired, bearded Jesus with arms outstretched, blessing a smoke-puffing cottage with the words 'Bless this House and Us, O Lord' painted upon a rainbow, and is relieved to see it's still there, albeit slightly askew, on the wall above Aunty Cou-ee's head. She is on a string bed, sitting propped up against a wooden board, her legs spread wide. She looks dull, sick and thin, like a deflated balloon, not at all puffed up, her hair falling about her face, and Kranti wonders what happened to the baby that was blowing up in her.

'So, how is my mouse?' she says to Kranti with a wan smile. 'And how are your daddy and mummy, everything all right?' Her voice comes from far away as if the person or the thing that unpuffed her also ran away with her voice. With shaking fingers, Aunty Cou-ee lights a cigarette and inhales so deeply, she begins to cough. 'You say hello to your daddy for me,' she says between spurts of coughing. 'And to your mummy. You tell her she has nothing to fear from me. Nothing at all.' Her eyes are suddenly filled with a peculiar, unpleasant glitter, with something nearing accusation, bright, brittle and malicious. Kranti feels she has been slapped.

She has not said a word and she goes out silently, Yvonne beside her. At the gate they pause, briefly holding hands. 'She fell down in the garden bringing in the washing, and my Pa couldn't get a doctor because of the rain and all. The water was up to here,' she points to her waist. 'He died, my baby brother. What to do?' Yvonne shows her the tiny mound, bearing a crooked wooden crucifix. They are two commiserating, bewildered children, holding each other for comfort. Wordlessly Kranti turns her feet back towards home as the silence grows and grows inside her. She has been touched by destitution and raw grief and it has struck her dumb.

They are waiting for her with stern faces, Aayee with a

worried frown, Baba a ruler by his side. Aunty Cou-ee said to say 'Hello'. But Kranti cannot get it out.

'Where were you? Why did you go without permission?' Baba asks.

Silence. Head hung in shame, eyes staring at her muddy shoes.

'Kuka, tell Baba where you went and why. We were so worried. Why did you get down from the rickshaw?' Aayee's gentle voice cuts in.

But Kranti's voice is locked up inside her like a genie in his bottle. Baba gives her six smacks with the ruler. Two each for Rudeness, Defiance and Disobedience. For the first time in her life, she does not cry, does not go snivelling for consolation to Aayee. She is sent to bed straight after dinner. She will speak again in a couple of days, but never again as easily or carelessly. She will gauge and judge, measure each word slowly and carefully.

It is during the children's meal with a silent Kranti and a chattering Tai that Uncle Vincent comes to visit. He usually comes only on Christmas Day to greet the Boss' family, in the company of his wife and daughter, looking uncomfortable and slicked down, as if recently pulled from under a laundryman's press, carrying 'Xmas cake and home-made marzipan'. But tonight he is wearing his mechanic's oil-stained overalls and doesn't even acknowledge Aayee or the girls as he and Baba step out into the verandah. There are raised voices and a lot of shouting and swearing. Baba comes back, slamming the door behind him, as Kranti slinks off to bed, her silence unnoticed.

'What does he think, that he can just come here and threaten me like this?' asks Baba, belligerently reaching for his whiskey.

'But Vijay, you should have offered something, some token. After all, it appears they have lost everything.'

'So did we. We lost everything. But are we complaining?'

'No,' mutters Aayee, 'we can't complain because, thanks to your position, we received hefty compensation, far in excess of what we lost' – but under her breath, because she knows better than to remonstrate with him when he has that whiskey glitter in his eye.

'In any case, what can a fellow like him do to me, I can squash him in two seconds, just like that, like a fly.'

But Uncle Vincent is a lean and hungry man, and as we all know, such men are dangerous. Having lost his livelihood, his unborn (bastard?) child and the Ava Gardner that once lived inside his wife, he is indeed determined to do something. Baba has not made any provision for Wounded Pride.

The letters sent to Baba's headquarters in Bombay are accompanied by bills stained with engine grease. They give tangible proof of how Baba has masterminded a scheme to systematically defraud the company of thousands of rupees in fake accident claims.

It will end very quickly, this chapter in their lives. Within a week, Bombay has sent a certain Mr Tyagi from the company's administrative machinery to trawl through the accounts. But if Baba has made no provision for Wounded Pride, he has made plenty for Departmental Audit Enquiries. He has papers that will make things very awkward for his bosses in Bombay. For if Baba has committed Little Fraud, they have committed Big Fraud and, of course, Baba is now ready to pull the plug.

It's true what Baba says, a fellow like Uncle Vincent, a mere motor mechanic, not even a full-fledged garage owner – what can he do after all? So Baba gets a promotion as Manager of the Delhi Region, because, as the bosses say, he has a magic formula for bringing in business and ultimately, that's what counts, doesn't it? And under those circumstances, who can blame him for helping himself to a little bit of the moolah, we all do it, don't we?

So Aayee is back at her packing cases and the girls are paying whirlwind visits to Wonders Tailors in Hazratganj, Rasta Shoes in Nishat Ganj and Ghulam Rasool, Travel Good Specialists, in the Chowk area, getting kitted out for boarding school in the hills. It's such a chic school. Naturally, since Baba's a big manager now.

It all happens in the twinkling of an eye. Shanti's sky blue trunk and Kranti's raspberry pink one, their names printed on the top and side, find themselves on the luggage rack of Baba's spanking new Ambassador Mark II as it snakes uphill towards Musoorie to deposit them at the doors of the Convent of the Sacred Heart. Kranti is almost ten, Shanti twelve.

This then will be the pattern of their lives over the next ten years. A new school, a new home, a new town as Baba moves from job to job, place to place, becoming, with each passing year, a little coarser, a trifle more dissolute. Although he will remain a handsome man, his good looks will turn florid, as will his taste for poetry. He will dump Auden and Yeats for flowery Urdu compositions from his own pen, theatrically declaimed before an admiring band of freeloaders with a yen for whiskey.

Shanti will become religious, strident, rooted, the antithesis of her father, even as Aayee goes quieter by the year, haunted by recurring nightmares in which Baba is led away handcuffed by the police, shuffling miserably on shackled legs. Until one day, Aayee refuses to leave her bed at all, becoming sere, shrunken in body and spirit, an invalid before her time. Her fears and insecurities she will pass on, whether through dream or osmosis, to her younger, more fragile daughter, the one brought up to believe she is a stupid, sluggish caterpillar. Until the day the young lady becomes aware of the effect she has upon men – young, old, middle-aged, squat, fat, tall, tiny, dark, fair, black, brown, blond. All men. Including her father. Especially her father. At which point, she will shrug off her chrysalis, open her multi-hued wings and swirl off into the great wide world, turning the tables on one and all.

16

A Portly Woman with a Vermillion Dot

Darkness is falling around her like a soft, cushioning blanket as Shanti picks her way amid the uneven paving stones that line the towpath. In her ample green coat, blue sari, tightly wrapped embroidered shawl and fluorescent sports shoes borrowed from her sister's cupboard, she looks like a daft bag lady, the large vermillion dot a blood-red stigmata on her forehead. An ambling, whale-like creature, so strange in the ordered landscape, she gets curious stares from a pair of tramps warming themselves beside a makeshift fire.

It was bright and sunny when she left, but that was over two hours ago, and she seems to be going round in circles although she has stubbornly stuck to the riverbank. Did she cross two bridges or three? Is she headed north or south? Has she come this way before? She cannot remember seeing these navy blue tugs moored near the river's edge. *Isadora, Nova, Arabella, Mars, Oceania, Reine de la Seine, Kiss Me James* are some of the names she has memorized. But she cannot make them out in the fading light.

She looks around her fearfully every couple of minutes to make sure no predator is following her. With all the vile stories of theft and pickpocketing coming out of Paris, she has taken care to leave her passport and valuables behind. Her hands feel strangely naked without their heavy gold bangles and although she's cold and her nose is running, she has an irrestible urge to walk on, to get some air into her lungs.

She has peered into so many boats and barges, admiring their crimson-studded holly bushes, winter perennials and pretty lace curtains, her head is so filled with images that she feels completely lost, unable to remember if she is on the Right Bank or the Left.

Panic begins to grip her and she fumbles in her bag for her map and the telephone card Peter has given her. But then she catches sight of the *Canaïma 1888*, a burgundy-painted sloop, now just a dark shape looming on the inky river, and looking up, in the distance, she recognizes the tower of the Sofitel hotel. Relief floods through her. She is facing south after all. She must cross the bridge and turn left to get back home.

The magnificence of Kranti's flat, from the marble cupid in the foyer to the paintings on the walls and the silver objects placed artlessly around the rooms has increased her sense of smallness. She feels like an unsophisticated hick suddenly thrown into a world of glitz and glamour, of unuttered, secret codes. But then Kranti always had that horrible, uncanny ability to make her feel both shabby and inadequate. Even now, when she's no longer there.

I have done so little in my life. Travelled to relatives' homes and back, that's all. It was so different when we lived with Aayee and Baba. How much my world has shrunk. Now it's just Raja and the girls. And Girish, who continues to live in me.

These people don't know Kranti like I do. They have never seen the cold manipulative side of her. How she would twist Baba round her little finger, how contemptuous she was of poor Aayee. They defend her, think the world of her because she has always managed to hide her real motives behind that smooth, charming facade. Sleeping around to get her way, using sex, preying on people's weaknesses; how she used and cuckolded poor Guillaume, who was so madly in love with her, and all those other men. And now this final act of treachery. Yes, as always, she has placed family second; it's friends and lovers that count for more than any of us, like they always did.

Why must this rude man, who was just one of many and probably counted for little, if he only knew, get everything that should rightfully be mine? I have had so little and lost so much. How could Kranti ever know what it means to have a child, a boy, and then to lose him? A searing wound that never heals, where the skin just about closes, waiting to be picked to start bleeding again. No travel. No holidays. Just the drudgery of making two ends meet and bringing up the girls.

Her infant son, lost at two months.

But he still lives in me. He is more alive than the girls. If they find out I talk to him, they'll think I've taken leave of my senses. Yet, when I first saw Peter, I thought of my child. Because Peter is so beautiful and so kind. The way my Girish would have been. He is a star up there somewhere, smiling down at me. Oh Girish, you would have been thirty-two today, had you lived. Just imagine, thirty-two. I am the mother of a thirty-two-year-old. You would have loved this place, these boats, this river ... maybe even your aunt.

The beauty of Paris is simply breathtaking. Clean, smooth, efficient. But also cold and unfriendly, haughty like its people.

She has never seen such graceful, stately buildings, nor met such surly, sullen, unsmiling people. They're elegant all right, especially the women, but hard, jewel-bright, calculating and pragmatic. No wonder Kranti loved the place. She fit right in, snug as a kitten. Diamond hard, my sister was, whatever they say.

How could she have amassed so much wealth without going crooked somewhere? She used to be such a sunny, happy child, almost angelic. How much I loved her, walking on the side of the traffic so she wouldn't get run over. All that love and affection, the care I showered on her, kicked back in my face.

This has been a miserable week. That first day, she suddenly felt so drowsy and tired, she lay down, sari, coat and all and fell instantly asleep. A flaming thirst and an insane desire to urinate had her stumbling out of bed, dazed and disoriented in the early hours of the morning. The flat was dark. She felt her way along the corridor to the bathroom. Her watch, still on Indian time, told her it was 7:00 a.m. in Chennai, well past her usual hour. Hugging her coat closer around her, she made her way to the living room in the creepy early morning semi-dark. Sitting there, she wished she hadn't come, hadn't been so stubborn, overruling all of Raja's objections and declaring: 'After all, I'm the blood relative. I'll get it out of him, you'll see. It will be money well spent.' She was no longer so sure. A free legal-aid association in Chennai had put her in touch with a similar NGO in Paris and an encouraging letter from a certain Marty Weinstein has given her hope.

I am functionally illiterate here, able to read individual letters but unable to understand words or pronounce them.

She is out of her depth, afloat in a strange and hostile universe where nothing makes sense, from the constant smell of scented candles and pot pourri, the unaccustomed opulence of her surroundings, to the single bathroom, albeit luxurious, that must be shared with a stranger, with no one to do the cleaning or washing up. Thank goodnes she has remembered to bring her khus attar with her: that penetrating, clinging smell gives her a sense of familiarity and protection.

Her hands, her one real vanity, have become rough from an excessive use of washing-up liquid. She hasn't forgotten Peter's patronizing remarks about the microwave, so there is no question of admitting she can't use a dishwasher, so she has been washing away, pretending it's cleaner, purer, a part of her Bramhin ritual, receiving the expected, withering look from Robert-Pierre.

He would rub her into the dust if he could. Shanti feels his resentment and disdain like a bad smell. Once it gets into your nose, it's difficult to shake off.

Everything about her irritates him, she knows. Just as his pomposity and air of self-importance irritate her. He has made no effort at all to be nice or welcoming and even when he smiles, his lip seems to curl up in disdain. More than that, it's his distrust she can't bear. Locking his bedroom behind him each time, as if keeping it safe from a burglar. She is in her sister's flat and has more right to it than he does. Well, he'll be sneering from the other side of his face when he gets the legal notice. Then we'll see who's annoyed and who sneers!

She can feel his ire rising to the surface like oil in her cooking pot as she sets about making upama, khichadi or poha for breakfast while whooshing up lentils for the day's two main meals; he is contemptuous of her waking up at 4.30 a.m. to do her ablutions and say her prayers; he despises her little temple in one corner of Kranti's studio, where she burns incence sticks, ringing a small bell while chanting early morning slokas. The pressure cooker whistles and sputters, spattering bits of dal on the immaculate stove and the smell of asafoetida fills the kitchen, wafting towards his bedroom.

She tries to tread softly, creeping out of her room while he's still asleep, finishing her chores, gulping down her breakfast at breakneck speed, scuttling back into her bolthole before he wakes up to brew his coffee, shower and leave for the day.

But when the cat is away, the mice are bound to play, it's as simple as that, Shanti smiles. I might look poor and unsure in comparison, but I'm not a nobody. I have a Ph.D and a will of steel and I'll show them. It's going to be difficult, but I too don't give up easily, she thinks with an unconsious lift of her chin.

Twice already, she has taken a taxi to the legal aid office in the 8th district. Marty Weinstein is an earnest young carrot-topped American lawyer who deals with sticky immigration issues for his compatriots wishing to live in France. He's not all that familiar with inheritance laws, but he knows enough to warn her that it won't be easy.

'Of course you can challenge the will, especially if you think your sister was unduly influenced or pressurized in any way. But you must first verify if the will was notarized and if the notary read it out formally. There is some jurisprudence about this in France; a decision handed down in 2002, if I remember right, by the First Chamber of the Court of Cassation. But for that, you'll have to consult a lawyer. Our association gives free advice only in cases of genuine distress – people who are homeless or about to be expelled and your case, I'm afraid, does not fall into that category. I'm really not a specialist, so I guess you'll have to hire a lawyer and those guys cost plenty. But it's worth a try if you're willing to spend some money and I could help you get a couple of names and free help if possible, or at least minimal cost,' Marty Weinstein assured her. She has a definite case, he said.

For the past two days, she has called Raja twice a day, pouring out her anger and frustration, telling him about her conversations with Marty, arguing about why she should stay on.

'When do you plan to return? When are you going to talk to him about the ashes and the property? That's why you went there in the first place,' Raja keeps reminding her. 'Is any of this worth it? Why don't you just get the ashes and come back? After all, she did make a will and leave it all to him. Do you want to get into a fight you are not sure to win? Just think of the expense.'

'But it's so unfair. And you should see him, Mr High and Mighty. I think they suited each other perfectly. Mr and Mrs Snob.'

'Why don't you just come home? This fight is beyond us. Just leave it, let it go. The girls don't need the money. We don't need it. So what are you after? Just give it up and come back. As that lawyer said, there are rules and jurisprudence. Just think, what do we do if we lose? How long do you plan to stay on? Legal business is usually very long. I was against your going in the first place. But do you ever listen? You've always done what you want. Anyway, this conversation is costing too much. We can't afford it. '

'Let him pay! I'm not paying. After all, he's managed to grab everything,' Shanti tells her husband, who makes his usual clucking sounds as if soothing a fractious child. It infuriates her. 'Why don't you please shut up,' she says. 'You never have the guts to do anything. Mr Mild, you are. Never taken a decision in your life. Well, I've decided to stick it out!'

'Listen to me Shanti, don't be so stubborn. What are we going to gain from fighting like this? We are losing our inner peace. Just look at the state you're in. I have rarely seen you so agitated. The longer you delay, the more difficult it will get. It's best to get the essentials out of the way as soon as possible and then you can really enjoy Paris with an easy mind. And if it doesn't work, just let it go. Will you talk to him tomorrow?'

'Stop lecturing me, Raja. An injustice has been committed and I want to make it right. I am only asking for what is mine and I am not ready to give up. Nothing ventured, nothing gained, remember? I must pin him down somehow, but he's a slipperry customer and he's been avoiding me. But I shall find a way. Maybe a legal way, if it's not too expensive.'

'Yes, but how?'

'How? I don't know just yet, Raja. Just stop going on about it, will you? I call you up for support, not so you can discourage me. How? I don't really know. So stop asking again and again.'

The question has not stopped pursuing her. It was easy to be belligerent and demanding in writing and over the telephone. But now that she's met Robert-Piere, she feels somewhat cowed. And he has made no effort to make her feel wanted, shown no sympathy whatsoever for her loss. After all, she has lost a sister. It's her sister who's dead. She committed suicide in a decidedly morbid way, Mrs Savic has made her understand.

The old lady has been her only real support, taking her down to the metro station, travelling a few stops with her, helping her change lines while explaining in her broken English how it worked. Peter, who was so nice that first day, has vanished. 'He's shooting. Film.' Mrs Savic explained miming a camera shot, to Shanti's irritation.

Even I can understand the word film. Why do these people

treat me like a mental retard? But at least the old lady's been helpful, which is more than what can be said of her son or that ogre, Robert-Pierre.

Paris is not that difficult to navigate, she has discovered. Mrs Savic circled the Louvre, Eiffel Tower and other monuments on her map, telling her with shrugs and and many '*pardonnez-moi*'s that she would not be able to accompany Shanti because her husband was very ill.

These buildings are sheer poetry, with their mellow stone facades and wonderful wrought iron balconies, similar and yet so different. Unity in diversity, like we say in India, she smiles to herself, her footsteps quickening in anticipation of the dal, rice and ghee waiting for her. There is some kheer too, that she cooked this morning with plump raisins and vermicelli. A large bowl of the sweet, warm, thickened milk would be most comforting. She expels a long breath between a sigh and a sob.

Walking home in the semi-darkness, she can see the lights of pleasure boats as they cruise down the river. She was tempted but the ticket price, forty euros for the hour-long ride, was just too much to pay. 'You get a glass of wine. Free,' the lady behind the ticket counter had coaxed. But sensibly, she had refused. Taxi fare to the lawyer's office was the only permissible expense. For the next meeting I'm taking the metro, she tells herself.

I'm spending money like water. But what have I bought? A couple of bloated, tasteless aubergines, onions, ginger, garlic and coriander, a carnet of ten metro tickets, a booklet of postage stamps, a few postcards of Paris, and the better part of the hundred euros Peter gave me has gone, evaporated. That's nearly eight thousand rupees, she calculates afresh.

Raja shouldn't nag so much. She has tried to pin down Robert-Pierre, looked for a proper moment when she could engage him in conversation. But hasn't been possible. And she's not being totally fair. He did invite her to join him for dinner once and brought her a mug of disgusting, under-brewed, very milky tea. And she did go to the dining table where he had laid their places, very prettily indeed, with shining cutlery and fresh napkins. She took some steaming dal and rice to the table as a peace offering. But the sight of the blood oozing out of his steak made her stomach turn. So she stood up and left the table before she threw up all over him. She couldn't very well tell him his food was nauseating.

How does one explain these things? Why couldn't I have told him that I didn't mean to insult him? Raja is right. If you let the opportunity slip once, it never comes back again.

He became quite openly hostile after that and he continues to lock his bedroom before leaving for work each morning. She knows almost nothing about him, what he does, if he's single or married, or maybe divorced.

He could be a teacher or professor. He's always got his nose stuck into papers and documents. Maybe he's a writer. No. Not scruffy enough for that. And he goes to an office everyday, carrying that awful, worn out leather briefcase. A lawyer, a journalist? I must ask Peter.

But when she tries to worm information out of Peter, he clams shut like an oyster and says he has to leave, he's vey busy. Too busy even to exchange a few words with her? What was it about Kranti that demands such loyalty? Couldn't any of them see through her?

She is sure there is something Robert-Pierre is hiding inside that locked bedroom. It's not just the fact that he wants his privacy. There's something more to it.

So, the moment she hears the front door slam behind Robert-Pierre, she starts rooting around the flat. Her fingers longingly caress glass and silver, run along book spines. Some of the paintings have a dark, velvety quality, others are gay and full of light. Thick leather-bound volumes contain Kranti's fashion sketches. There are labels she recognizes, others she doesn't. Hermes, Rati, Lacroix, Tango, Cardin, Rainbow, Jeanette et Shapiro ... There are designs for dresses, scarves, coats, hats and Indian bridal dresses including saris and ghagra cholis.

In a cupboard in the studio, she discovers their mother's saris carefully preserved in tissue paper.

She must have stolen these when she left home. Aayee would never have given them to her. So, she was just like Baba. Like father like daughter. Thieves, the pair of them.

But Shanti has the grace to recognize that these fragile materials have survived this long thanks to her sister's meticulous care. In my hands they wouldn't have lasted beyond a year. Oh God, why have you made me clumsy and fat and ugly and untidy? Why have I remained the ugly duckling? What did I ever do to deserve this? But one day, all this will be mine. I only have to be patient and stop Raja from nagging and discouraging me.

Shanti prowls through the flat restlessly, rifling through her sister's possessions. She stumbles upon photo albums of them as children, opens almirahs stacked with china, silver, clothes and jewellery, but she does not find the key to Robert-Pierre's locked door.

She feels weepy, looking at the pictures of them as children. Pleasant, innocent times, especially in Babuji's Poona house. Staring at the locked door, she fancies herself in Bluebeard's castle and wonders where all this is leading.

17

The Black Notebook

Berguenstock, Switzerland

20 December 2006

I'm not a skier. What a mad idea then, to come here in the dead of winter. But the very thought of spending Christmas alone in Paris, knowing R is in town, probably devouring oysters and truffles with his wife, quaffing champagne with her, is too much to bear.

Somewhere close, not too windy, not too touristy. And then suddenly I thought – the mountains, why not the mountains? Like the Himalayan ranges stretching out before us at boarding school in Musoorie. Switzerland seemed just right.

Far below me, I can make out the frozen contours of Lake Lucerne. The little funicular that ferries guests up and down the mountainside is shut for the winter. I sit by the fire in the lounge all day, going for short desultory walks to help me digest the gigantic meals I consume with such relish. Beef and cheese fondu, rostie, the lot gulped down with robust Italian wine. And I pretend to write or sketch, surrounding myself with a semi-sacred aura. The waiters go by on tiptoe so as to not disturb the genius at work!

They make me pay, my parents, and pay and pay and pay. I want to break the silence, tell it all, declare it to the world, give it a life of its own, free myself of the past. They won't let me. So long as the truth remains trapped in my head, it's all right. I can relive it, run it like a film, visualize it over and over to my heart's content. But the moment I try to put it down on paper, they punish me. And I am hungry for punishment; I deserve no better.

I can feel them perched within me, a pair of bats hanging upside down on my brain's tallest branches, their talons holding fast, waiting, watching – Aayee-Baba, Motherpuss and Sourpuss. Tai is there too probably, a smaller bat on a lesser branch, penetrating the dark that fogs my brain, picking up each desperate thought which, like a dropped stitch, tries to escape.

But this time around, I have really gone and done it, allowing myself to be robbed at Zurich station. Allowing. A subconscious desire to be punished. Because I had seen the man hovering around as I waited on the platform to take my train. He had noted my mink, my chic suitcases and the jewellery box in my hand. And yet, I didn't even bother to hide it. Child's play it was for him to wrench it out of my unresisting fingers. Gone before I even knew what had happened. All my gorgeous, gorgeous jewellery – my dangling uncut emeralds, the Lorel family solitaire, those stunning diamonds, rubies and pearls, gone before I could even blink, let alone shout. Gone before I could reach this lonely hilltop hotel that is my retreat. But now that I have paid, I've no intention of getting sidetracked. I shall not be held back this time. I shall say my piece even if it means a great washing of dirty linen.

Our move to Pune was the subject of much secret discussion between my parents, possible only during Aayee's lucid spells. We knew what was going on, of course, Tai and I, having by now become master eavesdroppers, listeners at doors. Did he really want to go back? Could he face Poona society again after what had happened? It was so long ago, people probably didn't remember any more, he shrugged. Again that nagging mystery. What had happened? Why had he run away from Poona in the first place? Had he really been married before?

People did have long memories, they did remember, as it turned out. My first day at university in Poona. A philosophy class taught by an ageing Gandhian scholar who wore khadi jackets and held up his rough homespun trousers with bicycle clips to keep them clear of eczema-afflicted shins. 'Are you related to Engineer Goray?' he asked me during roll call.

'Yes, sir, he was my grandfather.'

'So which of the brothers is your father? Is it Vijay Goray?'

And when I nodded, he said, 'I hope you are not a firebrand like your father. I knew him well during our student days. He was a real hellraiser. I don't want that sort of behaviour here.'

So he was a 'hellraiser', was he? I liked that, but I also found it vaguely disquieting.

Baba's past became an obssession. With scraps of information culled from cousins and acquaintances, I began to piece together his story. Who was the woman he had married before my mother? A certain Miss Abhyankar, first name Shakuntala – the spurned beauty in Indian mythology. But here, she was the one who did the spurning.

She was his second cousin. My dead grandmother with her heavy nose ring and Shanti garden pots, was her great-aunt. Shakuntala was beautiful, someone whispered, and like Baba, a communist. But there was more, I knew. Something shameful and untellable that remained unspoken.

At family gatherings, when the Gorays got together in the crumbling old wada that belonged to my grandmother's tribe, Aayee received curious, often pitying glances, accompanied by solicitous enquiries like: 'Is everything going well now? Are you happy that your husband has a fine job at last and your daughters have grown up?'

You poor, sick, wretched creature, we know all about your dreadful past and of course about his shameful past, they seemed to say. At once a taunt and a threat, these seemingly harmless remarks made my mother retreat into silence, and she appeared dumb, stupid, confirming their worst presumptions about 'the poor, illiterate widow from Kolhapur that Vijay – so handsome isn't he – married in desperation'.

I wondered if Shakuntala and Baba had grown up together, if it had all started with them playing 'doctor-doctor'. I wondered if that old family house, hidden away behind high walls, its balconies overlooking a central courtyard with four ancient coconut palms and a large well where they once bathed elephants, had ever echoed their childish laughter, absorbed their adolescent pain. What was it that made their names so unmentionable?

Baba's Poona relatives, very conscious of their superior caste status – for all that it was left unsaid – pushed Aayee further into loneliness and isolation, until she became a virtual prisoner in the house, handicapped by her illness and increasingly dependent upon Baba.

Her frustration and rage found their outlet against us and she railed and ranted. Rarely leaving her bed any more, she whiled her days away watching television, occasionally gossiping with the servant of the day, pecking at the food brought to her in bed, waiting for my father's return every night.

Her gums had rotted, her mouth gave out a foul smell and she reminded me of hospitals, fetid odours, kidney trays with soiled dressings, blood and injection needles. I found it hard to bend down and kiss her, afraid I would get a blast of her breath. My mother had become a repulsive, smelly creature and it was easy to dislike this new person, so unlike the mother that I loved and remembered, the Aayee of my childhood, who smelled of cardamom- flavoured supari, Pond's Dreamflower talc and fresh mogra blossom. Easy to hold her in contempt, to ignore her needs, leave her to the mercy of servants and our negligent father. She found so few reasons to happy. And then I spoilt her rare, innocent pleasure at Vasudha's wedding by creating a commotion and making a show of myself.

The atmosphere in the house on our return was sheer poison. Baba hobbled about in an exaggerated manner, making much of his bandages, conducting business from the house, lapping up sympathy from his office staff. Aayee was like a smouldering volcano, glaring at me from her bed, her mutton eyes accusing, blazing with manic rage, following me with a fixed stare each time I came within view. Which was often, considering their bedroom opened onto the kitchen and dining room. She snapped at me, I growled at her.

Finally I said to him, 'Baba, I want to move to the hostel. I can't live with Aayee any more. I've had enough of her. I can't stand her stares and her accusations. Nothing I do is right.' He caressed my cheek softly and said, 'We'll talk.'

And a couple of days later, when he could walk normally again, he took me out for a drive, stopping the car on the side of the road opposite the green expanse of Saras Bagh. It was a lovely evening, cool after the day's rain although the monsoon had yet to break, and we sat in silence for a while. 'Do you want to walk in the park?' he asked. I refused.

My eyes were already swimming with tears. So we sat there in silence some more and then he said quietly, matter of factly, 'I can't let you leave. You're the only one who understands me. Life would be unbearable without you. How can you leave me like that? Do you think I could survive without you? I love you. You're my special girl, aren't you? You are the one that keeps me going, understands my needs. Aayee needs you too. You must never forget she's a sick woman.'

The dam burst. Sobbing hard, I slid across the seat to cry into his shoulder. A strange, deep warmth awoke within me. The tips of my breasts strained to touch his arm and I could feel my face and neck suffused with the blood rushing madly through my body. My love for him became a sharp physical ache. I was crying so hard that passers-by gave us curious looks. Little by little, a small, restless crowd gathered, peering at us through the windows, wanting to know. 'Move on, what is there to see?' Baba said, rolling down his window. They shuffled their feet, but stayed rooted to the spot, and with an annoyed frown Baba started the car, scattering people as he revved the engine to take us back home. Someone thumped the rear window. A voice shouted an obscenity. I felt embarrassed, sullied, diminished as I climbed the verandah steps.

I was going to do this for him, only because he had asked me to. My heart ached for him. I understood it was not easy for him to have a wife like Aayee – sick in mind and body, vile and violent. Still, it took me an hour to go to her. Holding my breath, I bent down to peck her cheek. 'Hello Aayee,' I said.

She looked up. 'Where were you, my Kuka,' she said, drawing my head towards her chest, her voice trembling with tears. And then we were weeping in each other's arms. She called me Kuka, Soni, Babi, and all the other baby names she once used, and I was no longer seventeen but five and this was the mother I loved and needed so.

We were extra nice to each other over dinner. She made a special effort and came to the dining table where we sat close together and held hands. And then it was time for bed, time for her to take her medicine, her nightly doses of largactyl, pacitane, dopamine. Did I imagine it, or did I see Baba pouring out a second spoonful of largactyl into her medicine cup?

I lay on my mattress on the carpeted floor of the dark living room, the notes of Beethoven's 4th Concerto cascading around me. I slept there because that was where my parents had placed their large stand-up Revox with its 11-inch spools. Recorded off LPs borrowed from the British Council Library, the music had become a real need. Those glorious, gurgling notes helped me get to sleep, keep my demons at bay. I imagined water, mists. Delicate droplets, majestic waterfalls, thundering storms, pearly curtains of monsoon rain, dazzling expanses of snow, fresh and soft as baby's down. I did not like the power and the glory of The Emperor, the 5th. I wanted the tensile strength and delicacy of the 4th.

I did not hear the door open. He must have been there for a while. His pyjama bottoms lay in a heap beside my mattress and his kurta stood out like an erect tent. Without a word, he lay down upon me, tugging at my nightgown, pulling up his kurta, pushing my legs up and back until my knees almost touched my shoulders. And I accommodated him, dutifully lifting my bums so my nightie rode up to my armpits, displaying my newly discovered breasts. No preliminaries, no words, no sounds, not a kiss. Just his fingers absently rubbing my nipples. Beethoven, loud and strong, enveloping me, transporting me away from the shame of that room with its shabby maroon sofas, its chipped peg tables banged about from one move to the next, his whiskey-sour breath.

This was not the way it was supposed to be. Where was my dream hero with his velveteen eyes and scented breath, his broad shoulders and whispered sweet nothings? That unkown surge of desire I had felt earlier now fled, leaving me cold and unresponsive. But I lay there inert, lifeless, not protesting, not resisting. Please God, I am not here, I am somewhere else, in a world of gilded elegance peopled with fine ladies and honourable gentlemen surrounded by art, music, cherubic angels, engaged in gentle flirtation.

The unfamiliar, suffocating weight of a man's heavy body. Then a short, sharp stab, the feel of rubber, a slight pause, several quick, thick thrusts. Gathered and congealed within his sheath. His muffled groan.

He left as soundlessly as he had come, his juices in their rubber pouch dangling pitiably at the tip of his flaccid member, his pyjama bottoms clutched in his hand, too ashamed or too afraid of discovery to take the time to put them on.

I do not remember sleeping. Beethoven. Just Beethoven. But the sound of rain had gone. Instead the music was harsh, unrelenting, a clash of cymbals, ominous rumbles of thunder.

The next morning, my thighs hurt. They felt stiff and hard, as if beaten with a mallet. Eyes blank, face numb and frozen. It was difficult to talk. My vagina was sore, my body wooden, slothful. There was a terrible din in my head, like the sounds that emerge from a temple at saandhya arti – human voices, babbling and shrieking, bells and cymbals crashing, music and chanting mingling with car horns and the sounds of traffic. I could not hear my thoughts over the racket, and the buzzing in my ears grew louder as I strained to hear.

What were they saying, those raucous, accusing voices? My fault, not my fault? Rape, not rape? Incest? Had he not invaded my dreams? And those locked looks at Vasudha's wedding? Had I not wanted it and not wanted it? And then again, what was IT? A quick stab in the dark, an ungainly coupling, dread, guilt, fear? Was that IT?

I kept away from Baba, avoided looking at him. He took my arm in the corridor but I brushed him aside locked myself in my room. I found a note on the dining table. In his neat, precise hand he had written out a list of medicines I had to buy for Aayee from Bhogilal's Chemists and Druggists. With it, five hundred rupees. I did not need money for Bhogilal's. We had an account there. This was money for Lolita's trinkets. Money for sevices rendered.

This was not how I had imagined it in my wildest, most secret dreams. Not those smells, not that weight, not the quick mechanical brutality of the act of copulation. Tortured by shame, I went about with a blank, hangdog look, guilt writ large all over me. How could anyone fail to notice? I was like a large boulder of misery planted in the middle of the road.

A two-day lull, and then the attack. Tai spoke first, a frontal thrust. She had seen him tiptoe into the living room and divined the rest. 'So what does your Ambabai say, now that she's had a taste of the real thing?'

Ambabai, Kolhapur's famous fertility goddess, was how our grandmother referred to the female sex organ. There was no point denying anything. She knew it all.

Aayee could only hurl abuse. He was a pimp, a whoremaster, lying with his own daughter, whereas I was a raand, a bitch who had stolen her husband, a snake who held him fast in her serpentine coils.

I stopped going to college, took to wandering the streets of Poona, wearing out my thin leather sandals. In the sweltering pre-monsoon heat, I walked all the way from Gultekdi through Rasta Peth, to Camp. Up Main Street, down East Street to Quarter Gate, peering into shops at Sarbatwala Chowk. I would take a number 4 bus back down to Deccan Gymkhana to gape at Babuji's old house, now sold and under renovation. Then late evening, sweaty, sunburnt and foot-weary, I would come home to confront Aayee, who lay sharpening her anger like a knife at the wheel, watching, waiting to pounce.

Most nights, the door would open and I could hear him, panting as he entered, sodden with whiskey, the nauseating smell of booze and cigarettes. Three minutes of jing jing and it would be over. Never a word, no acknowledgement of what had happened and only the sound of his heavy breathing punctuating a terrible, strained silence, glossed over by Beethoven's dancing notes. I learnt to blot him out. Blot out his large beer belly slapping against my concave stomach. Learnt to turn my face away, hold my breath, count up to twenty, catapult myself into another world, Vienna or Versailles, where I would walk down mirrored corridors in silken robes or sit at an escritoire writing letters, chestnut ringlets on my head and Belgian lace at my lily white throat, a Chopin nocturne drifting into the flower-filled morning room bright with mild June sunshine...

But I did not protest, run away, speak out, complain to or side with Aayee.

The money.

I took.

And hoarded.

Carefully putting the crumpled notes into a plastic bag that I buried deep inside a flour tin full of wood ash from the old brass samovar once used to heat our bath water, now abandoned at the back of the garage. Before Vim detergent came on the scene, the ash was used to clean our dirty kitchen pots and dishes.

And then, with my little hoard, when I could, I left.

Pierre asked me the other day about how I came to Europe, met Guillaume, married him. What could I tell him? Got raped; ran away; found not one but two morons in succession to marry? First, out of the house; then, out of the country et voilà me voici?

I think those years wrenched out my soul – what little was left of it. Baba's guilt and guile meant he left money lying around for me to pick up. Which I took with just one aim in life: to get away.

Tai left to teach at a college in the north and if her barbs and taunts were no longer there, I lost some of the protection her presence provided me. There was Baba trying to turn me into a substitute wife, issuing endearments that made me sick to the stomach. Was it not enough that he visited me a couple of nights a week? Did he have to make this shameful secret public?

'Beta, how are you feeling today, you look a bit off-colour?' The first time he asked me that, I could have slapped him. In a roundabout way he wanted to know if I had my period, which meant he would not be able to 'visit' for a couple of days. Before it all began, I would have welcomed his endearments as those of a loving father. Now I knew better.

I left just five weeks short of my eighteenth birthday. I had five thousand rupees in the kitty – a pretty sum – a mediocre BA degree, and admission to the J.J School of Arts in Bombay. I told no one. I had hired a PO box at the central post office in Pune near the railway station and from there, for almost a year, I sent and received mail in utmost secrecy.

It was raining hard the day I left, taking a window seat in a third-class carriage of the Poona-Bombay Mahaluxmi Express. Aayee was asleep and Baba was at the office when I sneaked out of the house carrying his best leather suitcase filled with my few belongings and some of her best, oldest, most beautiful saris. A couple of things for everyday wear, trousers, T-shirts, make up. That was all I possessed.

Had I waited the five weeks to my birthday, I could have walked out legally and Baba would have been able to do fuck all about it. But school had already started a couple of months ago and I was being admitted with a 'late fee'. My artwork had pleased the admissions committee, so I was being treated as a special 'outstation' case.

I was seventeen though, still legally a minor, and a couple of days later the police tracked me down to the girls' hostel I was living in near Girgaum. I had forged Baba's signature on all the papers – for the hostel warden, for the college principal – and I saw my dreams collapse before they could even begin to take shape.

He was nice, the principal of JJ. He called Baba and asked why the family was so set against a career in art. Baba couldn't tell him the truth, of course. He also wanted to appear progressive and it was artful how he pulled his chestnuts out of the fire.

'Oh, I have nothing against her doing a degree in Fine Art, Professor Vij,' he said. 'She already has a BA degree. But with a family as open and progressive as ours, I wonder why she felt she had to hide it. Why did she imagine we would say no? Of course, her mother is very ill and she is really needed in the house, and I do think it was selfish to think

only of herself when the rest of us are making such an effort. Perhaps I said that there was no money in art and that must have stayed in her head. We would have said yes, of course, even though it will be difficult to manage with my wife so sick. But just imagine the worry it caused us to find her suddenly missing from home.'

I know Prof. Vij sensed there was something amiss. Baba was too sweet-tongued, too accommodating, too 'let's make up and go home' and not enough of the bewildered, angry parent he ought to have been. There had to be something more and I saw the puzzled frown upon the professor's face. He saw me weep and shake my head as the two of them spoke as if I were completely absent from the room, a mere piece of furniture. I think my evident distress moved him. There was more here than met the eye. And though he was too bureaucratic to probe further or to get involved, he understood he had to keep me there.

Also he was genuinely interested in having me as a student, even though I had forged signatures and lied about almost everything.

'Then, if you agree, Mr Goray, we can tear up these forms and your daughter can fill new ones with your real signature. The sketches she sent in were considered very good by the selection jury and we even awarded her a scholarship. We would like to have Kranti as a student if she promises to abide by the rules and not run away.' And that was that.

But then came terrible hardship. Money evaporates in a place like Bombay. My scholarship was just about enough to pay the school fees and rent at the hostel. For the rest, I had to fend for myself. I began doing little sketches for magazines. It was lowly paid work – thirty rupees here and there – which would tide me over a couple of days. And then I began modelling for newspaper advertisements, and won the Smile India photo contest.

At least that brought my lean and hungry days to an end.

18

A Division of the Spoils

As she goes through the drawers of Kranti's roll-top desk, pushing her hand as far back as it will go, Shanti's fingers touch a small packet. She draws it out, a mounting excitement convulsing her. A thrill of triumph goes through her as she fingers a bunch of keys held together with sello tape.

It is 10 a.m. She is alone.

She double locks the front door, moves quickly to try the keys on Robert-Pierre's room. First one, then another, then another, until finally, the key turns. She pauses, almost not daring to go in as the heavy wooden door swings back under the pressure of her hands.

Compared to the untidy mess in the studio where Shanti's bags and yawning suitcase display bunched up saris and underwear, his space is neat as a pin and spare as a monk's cell. The bed, a beautiful art deco piece in polished acajou, is covered with a stark damask bedcover, its headboard topped by Russian icons, the holy trinity arranged in a semi-circle. Golden points of light radiate outward from the sacred trio's crowns. An embroidered Kashmiri durree drapes the wall opposite while wooden logs piled up in the chimney await a match. A door at one end leads to a walk-in closet where more of Kranti's clothes hang alongside Robert-Pierre's suits.

The bedside table closest to Shanti holds a glass and a water jug on a lacquered tray. Beside it, a pile of typed-up papers in French. Squinting without her reading glasses, Shanti makes out several medical terms. The article has been corrected in red ink.

So he's a doctor, as I suspected, and these are case studies.

She goes around the bed to the other side. Almost reverentially aligned, next to a gilt table lamp, she finds two thick artist's notebooks, blank on one side, ruled on the other. The deep crimson notebook is unnaturally bloated with photos, clippings and drawings. The other, a slimmer volume, black in colour, is filled with page after page of diary notings.

So this is why the door has been locked all these days. There is something more than just privacy at work, something in here that he does not want me to see.

She rushes out to the living room, places the notebooks on the glass coffee table. Her hands are tingling. Chappals flapping, she rushes to the kitchen to cook a dense brown brew, loose tea leaves boiled up with cardamom and generous lashings of milk and raw sugar. She kicks off her open slippers and sits back comfortably, tailor-fashion, her thighs warming her feet. The first hot satisfying sip goes straight down to her freezing toes.

Aaah, says Shanti, propping her reading glasses on her nose, bringing into focus the hundreds of lines of squiggles written in thick sepia ink.

She reads steadily into the afternoon, dipping into first one notebook, then the other, forgetting to eat or drink. Occasionally she bends down to pull another tissue out of the box of Kleenex now lying at her feet. Her vermillion mark is smeared; her eyes have become puffy, red, reduced to slits. She has been weeping copiously, occasionally crying out loud, other times burying her face in her sari pallu, lying prostrate on the sofa, her glasses clutched in her outstretched hand.

Long ago, Kranti had pressed on her a book called *The Children of Sanchez* about a Mexican family living in a slum. 'Spanish and other cultural differences aside, the Sanchez remind me so much of us. They are dysfunctional, just like us. The parents don't care, the children hate them and each other, and fight constantly. There are four of them and they're miserable and they never see eye to eye on anything. Best part is how they remember identical experiences in completely different ways. Read it, Tai, you'll really enjoy it. It will remind you of us and our failings, our blinkered existence,' Kranti had urged. But Shanti had not bothered, dismissing it as just another of Kranti's many fads, a fact she now regrets. She certainly does not remember things quite the way Kranti describes them.

She has barely budged from the sofa. The red notebook moves her beyond grief, beyond tears. It seems to have a magical power on her, the pictures captivate her, send her hurtling back in time. She finds herself becoming the Shanti of those early years and feels a tide of love for little Kranti.

Others might find it banal and dull. But there is somethig so poetic in the way our story has been written, even though she has given me the role of the wicked and sly elder sister. I don't mind so much. It's a fairy tale, our fairy tale. I know how much I cared for her and looked after her when we were young. But again, what an abominable fairy tale. She has given it that never-never atmosphere, yet there's no hiding the underlying sorrow. Aunty Cou-ee's baby, I wonder if that was true. Aayee's misery was real enough, as were our moves from town to town, school to school. Nevertheless, there is something soothing, beautiful, about the way it's written.

But did she have to be so deliberately cruel in her diary? Who was she trying to impress? Her psychoanalyst with whom she wanted to start an affair? Kranti was always twisting things around, spreading poison. All those awful things about Ram Singh and me, about me making that dirty pass at her. Lies, just lies. Imagine me shirking hospital duty. That's so nasty, somehow. Where was Kranti when Aayee became paralysed? She just cut us all dead. Understandable maybe, given what happened with Baba and all, but she played along, didn't she? Why didn't she kick up a fuss? I would have, if he'd tried that on me. Taking all that money too. She was just a whore, even with her own father. She went her way, I went mine. I did not approve of the way she lived, but at least I had the guts to tell her so. She thinks that gives her the licence to run me down and say awful things about me. How manipulative she is! Leaving behind this terrifying bunch of lies to damn everyone in her family. Aayee and Baba are ash already. And I, the one she most damned, am unable to defend myself against a corpse. The bitch isn't even alive, for me to be able to speak in my defence. I understand now that Robert-Pierre's reading of me has been coloured by a dead woman's tale.

Shanti has lost her sense of time. She jumps at the harsh peal of the doorbell. She had meant to put the notebooks back just the way they were before Robert-Pierre returned, but now he's right there, framed in the doorway, and she has been caught with her hand in the cookie jar. In a split second, she decides to brazen it out.

Robert-Pierre is staring at her, his leather office case at his feet, the housekeys dangling from his hand.

'*Bonsoir*, what are you doing with that?' he says coldly as his eyes take in the notebook in her hand, her dishevelled appearance, the used Kleenex scattered on the carpet.

They exchange a cautious look. 'If you ask, I will show,' he says, advancing into the room, throwing his briefcase onto an armchair. 'This not good way to do. Not right, *pas bien*.'

'Would you have shown me if I hadn't found out? Day after day you have been hiding this, locking your door. I knew there was something strange. I am in my sister's flat, after all. I am not a thief. How dare you treat me this way?'

'I not thinking you steal. This is my room, my life, *mon intimité*. I not ask you to come. You decide to come, to live in my house. Why you come? What do you want? I know what you want. Not ashes. You want all this. The money, the apartment, the *objets d'art*. You have no love for Kranti. You hate your sister and your sister hate you. Why is she leaving her money to me, not you?'

Shanti glares at him, but does not reply.

'And today I receive this,' he says, drawing a folded letter out of his pocket. As he unfolds it, Shanti sees it's a legal notice sent by her new lawyer, Louis Michel, a thin man with parted teeth and strictly parted hair. 'Why you need to send this? We talk. That is simpler, *non*?'

'No, it's not simpler. Because these past ten days, that is what I have been trying to do. Talk to you. But you leave early in the morning and lock yourself in when you return. Yes, you ask me to join you for dinner, but I can't stand the sight of your bloody meat. So where is the opportunity? I am a civilized person, not the under-developed savage you think I am.' She is shouting now.

'Please stay calm. *Tranquille*. Your sister was a wonderful woman. She never shout like this. Never make spectacle, no crisis, no caprice. You are like a child.'

'My sister loved you and died because of it. You treated her coldly, indifferently. It's all over her diary. Don't think she didn't want to shout out too. She was desperate.'

'What you know of my relation with her, *hein*? You see how she talk of you in her journal? I do not understand why you are here. You write to me saying I am coming. No talking. You want to see bank books, accounts? Why? Why I must show you? Why you are so angry with me? I do nothing. Your sister gives me her money, her flat, her paintings, everything, yes. But what I did to you? What wrong I did? Okay, you want property. Okay, you send me legal letter. But not good shouting like this, opening my room when I am not there.'

He strides up to the coffee table and Shanti shrinks back, her arms going up instinctively to fend off a blow that does not come.

'I am not violent man. Not like your father.' He picks up the notebooks with great deliberation, tucks them under his arm. 'This is my property. And now, you don't touch,' he says with finality.

'Wait,' she says, 'I haven't finished reading.' But he ignores her, puts the notebooks into his briefcase and walks out.

Robert-Pierre calls Sophie's family lawyer, Alain, and meets him for a drink at a nearby café.

'Well, you are in a delicate position. What is it you want? You have to first decide what you want. Do you want to keep all this and leave your home and Sophie for good, or do you want to rebuild your relationship? She was telling me that you call her every second day, that you want to go back and patch up. How do you expect to keep the property as well? Have you thought of that? Anyway, that's not my business. Have you got a copy of the will? And the legal notice?'

Stroking his wispy beard, Alain studies the will carefully, examines the notary's stamp and seal, the signatures of the lawyer and his assistant. 'Well, clearly, she was in her right mind. She did this on her own. No one else was present. It was made out in the lawyer's office. So we can argue there was no undue pressure. The terms of the will have been clearly set out. She has named you her artistic executor. So there is no ambiguity there and if you want to fight it, this will stand up in court. However, remember, there has been a police enquiry and Louis Michel can always dig that up. I would, if I were handling the case. I know Michel well. After all, we're not that many senior advocates called to the *Barreau de Paris*. Not a very nice man. He could be dangerous. Knows the inheritance laws backward and has cracked many a difficult case. He's threatening to get the assets frozen and move the *juge de referé* so the case can be heard immediately on the grounds that his client lives far away and cannot afford to stay in Paris.'

Robert-Pierre snorts. 'But she's living in my flat at no expense whatsoever! All she eats is vegetarian rubbish, yet she's always complaining about money and how much everything costs.'

'Maybe she really doesn't have any money. Imagine, with an inheritance like that, easily over three million euros from what I see of her assets listed in the will, would you let it go unchallenged? Michel is probably not charging her a fee. He works *à l'américaine*, on a commission basis. He has probably asked for fifty per cent of recovery. And if they lose, she pays only the court costs.'

'Fifty per cent? But that's exorbitant!'

'I know, but for someone in her situation, it's a pretty decent deal given there are no legal fees and in any case, she's getting something for nothing. If she loses, the costs will be minimal. So it makes sense from her point of view.'

'What do you advise me to do?'

'It depends on what you want, my friend. It's your future that's at stake. I have been the Taquet family lawyer ever since I took over the practice from my father. I've known Sophie since we were this high. Don't try to pull one on her. She won't take it. And once she decides it's over, that's it. So think it over carefully. In any case, now that you've received a formal legal notice, I suggest you move out into a hotel or something for the rest of this lady's stay.'

'Wouldn't that be like running away? Leaving the entire field open to her?'

'I'm not sure you have a choice. After all, she is a very close blood relative, immediate family, and under French law, she certainly has a claim. Remember, sending someone a legal notice is an act of hostility. I don't think I would be able to live in the same flat with someone like that. If you want to stick it out, go ahead. There'll be tensions, I'm warning you. And don't expect your wife to understand if she finds out that you're now *en ménage* with the sister.'

'How can you even suggest such a thing! You haven't seen her. She wears some very strong, sweet perfume that clings to everything she touches. The other day, she found a set of duplicate keys and entered my bedroom and helped herself to Kranti's notebooks. It's a total invasion of privacy. Never heard of please or may I, a real *Madame sans gène*. She has opened every drawer, trunk and cupboard in the house, touched everthing. And now it all reeks, especially the notebooks, which have sweat marks on them. You don't know the hell I'm living in.'

'Which is why I say, move out. But you're stubborn, Pierre, always have been, and you usually get what you want. I remember when you were chasing Sophie. You were a poor student like all of us, but you stopped at nothing. A hired car, a hired suit, dinners on credit. Anything to impress. You haven't changed that much, I see. Anyway, I've got to run. I'll look up the jurisprudence for you, but I'm sure this woman can challenge the will and my hunch is that the judgement could go against you. In any case, I'll send a letter to her lawyer. And you are not to speak directly to her about any of this. From now on, it's the lawyers who talk to each other.'

'But if Kranti left everything to me, it was with a reason. If you read her journals and her stories, she paints a terrible picture of her family. She hated her sister. So why should any of this go to her?'

'Since when has an inheritance been decided on whether the beneficiary deserves it? Do you think you deserve it? Don't be naïve. Your friend may have been in sound body and mind when she made the will, but that still does not negate her sister's claim.'

'You never met Kranti. You did not even know of her existence. She was extraordinary, quite special. She had beauty and talent, a sense of fun, and she had endured. Lots. *Elle en avait encaissé.* I'm discovering what a miserable childhood she had. She had reason to loathe her family. I won't go into the sordid details. And yet, she overcame it all, came here, made a success of her life.'

'Then why did she kill herself?'

'I am still trying to understand. But I think sometimes a person reaches a tipping point, when everything appears futile. When there's no strength left to fight. I think it was her past catching up with her. Everything she had managed to suppress welling up in a massive tsunami. That's the only explanation I can find. But I think I shall never really know.'

'Well, that's for you to figure out. Just let me know what you want me to do. If you want to contest or let it go, or seek a compromise. That too is possible. Now I'd better go, I'm late as it is.'

That night, listening to Pavarotti's vocal maestria in Rossini's Barbiere di Siviglia, Robert-Pierre goes over his conversation with Alain.

Perhaps there is a way out. I could give up the flat, keep the paintings, the cash. Establish a prize which will give the magazine a much-needed boost, perhaps even endow it in Kranti's name. Surely her sister can't want a fight to the finish? Does she have that kind of staying power? Will she be open to a compromise? That lawyer Louis Michel is no fool apparently. He might get a bit less through a compromise, but he won't have to do any work. The sooner this gets done, the better. A compromise is in everyone's interest. He knows I could make it drag on, as Alain said. He'll want his fee. This flat alone is worth over a million euros. He'll get almost half a million for doing absolutely nothing. She'll get about the same, less the tax. Maybe she'll be happy with that? Who knows? There's no end to human greed. Alain must get this Michel fellow to settle quickly. Tell him we'll go into appeal if the decision goes against us. Where will she go if the judge decides to freeze the assets and the property pending judgement? After all, how long can she live here like a poor refugee?

19

The Black Notebook

Pune, 14 July 2007

Bastille Day. The day I first met Guillaume, in the ballroom of the Taj Hotel in Bombay, exactly thirty years ago.

Had an invitation to the French Embassy celebrations in Delhi tonight but declined, pleading pressing family business in Poona. Prudence probably dictated the invitation. I still count for something, I suppose. Even ex-wives have their uses and Guillaume is an MP, a centrist rising star, bound for high ministerial office. I have no wish to relive past Bastille days amongst Delhi's chattering glitterati in their finery and fakery. I know they continue to gossip about me. 'Did you know she's twice divorced? Married for money the first time and for a title the second. Ditched them both to live the high life.' I am quite the sexy siren, the scarlet woman. Why, even my own cousins wish to protect their progeny from my corrupting influence. So, with no one to trust, my social intercourse remains terribly superficial. Oh for the likes of Olga Savic. Unquestioning, affectionate, slavish – like a puppy dog panting for love and affection. She is staunch, little Olga, the funny old thing with her terrible taste in clothes and that greasy-haired look. But I do love her, truly.

So I have given Bastille Day celebrations the royal boot. Instead, I have come away here, to the more authentic Deccan Gymkhana, where caste still reigns supreme, where upwardly mobile computer experts, engineers and entrepreneurs, academics and bankers (Brahmins most), continue to pronounce atmosphere the way Aayee did, with an inner jet-engine thrust as if the word needed to be blown outward. It's the one unasked, hinted-at question, lying just beneath the surface in every conversation. Between Maharashtrians, that is. Once your caste has been ascertained, your credentials established, the terrain tested, there are at first oblique, then freer, references to X or Y being a 'shed'. As in Scheduled Caste – untouchable, Mahar, Bhangi, Chamar – same thing.

Why do I say nothing, appear to go along, hide my discomfort? Truth to tell, it's faint, my discomfort. There isn't that feeling of outrage I get when secularism is under attack. Were such things said against the Muslims or other minorities, I would speak out, surely. So why am I benign about caste?

Where is R? Rome? Orvieto? Florence? I think of him because it's his day, Robespierre's Day, in a sense. I do not care to imagine him, though, walking the streets of those magnificent cities, hand in hand with his wife.

What a contrast. His swank hotels – I mustn't be jealous, I do get the luxury of the Gritti once a year – compared to the shabbiness of mine. A Poona Brahmin hotel run by tight-fisted Chitpavans of my father's clan. Light-eyed and calculating. Where every penny is extracted in advance and hardly a thought given to the shabby curtains, the water rings on the bedside table, the accumulated grime around electric switches.

Why then am I here? Why am I not parked at some posh, airconditioned five-star hole in Koregaon Park? God knows I have the money. I made a killing with the last portfolio. Jewellery and bridal wear for India's grasping spendaholics. You could sell them anything. It's a game I've begun to play. I design some hideous clothes with huge price tags, mix them with my trademark understated creations. The ugly ones always go first. The pricier the better, it seems.

No, it's not money constraints that have brought me here. I am on a mission. An Aayee–Baba mission. Desperate to fill in the blanks. It's been a painful journey, but not fruitless. I have made some startling discoveries.

Baba's secret with Shakuntala lies revealed, in the form of a small yellowing newspaper clipping that one of my great-aunts, my grandmother's younger sister, hands me by way of explanation. It has taken a lot of cajoling to worm it out of her. 'Why do you want to revisit the past? What's done is done and your father and mother are both dead now. Why should it matter so much?' But I will not leave well enough alone and in the end she pulls out the clipping from an old file filled with family pictures of the entire clan, me and Tai included, wedding invitations and old newspaper cuttings.

One year's RI for jewellery, arms theft. Single column, 11 point, Times Roman with a one em indent. Dated 2 December 1944, it reads:

> *Vijay Goray, son of Engineer S.G. Goray, was condemned to one year's rigourous imprisonment for stealing the service revolver of his father-in-law Major S.K. Abhyankar of the Maratha Rifles. Jewellery and money were also missing from the Major's house. Handing down the sentence, Justice P.R. Scott said the highly educated young man from a prominent Poona family had 'compounded his crime' by stealing the fire arm of a serving officer in His Majesty's Imperial Army and betraying the trust placed in him by his father-in-law. The stolen items were recovered by the police. The sentence will be served out at Yeravda jail in Poona.*

Baba was born in 1923. He was just about twenty-one and already married. To Shakuntala, his cousin and first wife. So that's what it was. That's what they all whispered about. He was no communist freedom fighter, my father, no brave revolutionary hero, no firebrand student leader imprisoned by the wicked British as I had been given to believe. He was just a low-down thief, a common-law prisoner, a felon. A petty pilferer, gutless enough to steal from his own family.

They had lived together in sin, my great-aunt gives me to understand, in my grandfather's half-completed house in Deccan Gymkhana, where Tai and I would first see the light of day over a decade later. Where a gate with a dropped hemline made deep grooves in the soil on its journeys back and forth, where the drawing room stuck its pointy nose out into the drive, where chopped cosmos heads would one day be whipped off their stems before my bewildered eyes.

Shakuntala was beautiful and intelligent, my great-aunt says, but selfish too, and after the trial, she threw him over. 'He wanted that revolver for his terrorist activity. But the jewellery? That was Shakuntala's doing. After all, she gave him the key to her father's house with instructions to steal her inhritance. Major Abhyankar had cut her off when she married your father and Shakuntala was afraid her father's mistress would grab the lot. Vijay paid the price while she went scot-free. That is why I feel so bad for your father. Vijay was an idealist, essentially a good boy and very generous. Damaged for life,' she sighs.

But a bigger shock awaits me at Babuji's old house in Poona, which has passed into new hands. Nice enough people, the Gokhales, distant relatives of ours, but no taste to speak of.

The house has completly lost its old-world charm, its colonial character. The round verandah, where we played as children, has disappeared, to be shut in by an ugly pink wall with glass windows. The rambling roses that surrounded it have been uprooted – too many mosquitoes, Mr Gokhale says regretfully, and the drawing room no longer pokes its nose into fragrant mogra bushes. But the garden is there, large, rambly and drowsy, as I've always known it.

'Did you know that the police would come by regularly to ask if we had news of your father? Very regularly, up until a few years ago, almost until his death. I did not see the point of it. He was already an old man. But that's bureaucracy, I suppose. Once you get into the police files, they never let go of you. I knew of the case, of course,' old Mr Gokhale tells me with an apologetic, almost mournful air. 'Your father was such a hero at one time. And then such a terrific fall from grace. So sad.'

He means terrible, of course, a terrible fall from grace. But after all these years working in HR at Tata Motors, Mr Gokhale's English has remained resolutely Maharashtrian. 'He was of my generation, I was two years younger to him, and we were in Fergusson College together. What a fantastic personality he had, and so bold. I don't know what happened, how he slipped into crime or terrorism. We never really understood what it was exactly – but it spoilt a brilliant career as a lawyer, even as a future politician. Come, I have something to show you. But be prepared for a shock,' he says, leading me into the ugly, pink-walled living room.

It's so changed inside I cannot connect this to the place where I played hide and seek with Tai. 'Do you remember,' he cuts into my thoughts, 'that there was a wall here, a sort of half partition that separated the drawing room from the dining room? Well, when we redid the house, we pulled down that wall. And guess what we found? Look here, down on the floor, the marks are still here. We are going to re-do the floor next year. So you are lucky to see it.'

My mind is reeling. What I see is the outline of a loop. The wall once encircled a small hiding place, just large enough for a person to sit, stand or lie down. Like a priest's hole.

'This wall was over six feet high and your father hid in this space when the police came looking for him. Your grandfather had an old

gardener called Haribhau, who still worked here when we bought the place. He told us how your father would climb up a ladder to jump in there when the police came knocking, and how your grandfather or his cook would help him go in and out.'

I imagine Baba, young, handsome, insouciant, reckless beyond belief, hunted like an animal, cowering on the floor of that tiny space, sweating it out until his trackers left.

The discovery of the hidey-hole leaves me shattered. I do not remember saying goodbye to old Mr Gokhale. I know he wants to talk more, 'discuss the case' as he calls it, and I regret having rushed out of the house. I should have asked pointed questions, flushed out details, raided his mind and scooped up, vaccumed out, all his memories. 'I hope you don't mind my saying this. But no one knew for sure whether he was a terrorist or a freedom fighter, a hero or just a thief. So people, as usual, chose to believe the worst. Which is why I think your parents left Poona, to escape all the gossip. But there was no doubting his utter brilliance.'

I weep for Baba. For the brilliant young man wanted by the police, abandoned by a faithless wife, spurned by polite society, his career in tatters. He had no option but to marry my mother, a semi-literate widow and like him, another bit of discarded flotsam.

I feel peculiarly torn between love and pity, hate and anger. The visit to the Poona house has brought home the fact that as a small child, I knew only one side of Baba – the kind, gentle, loving father, who punished only when we did wrong. The lecherous, corrupt, self-serving male predator made his appearance much later.

And now I also weep for poor Aayee, who paid the heaviest price of us all. Who leapt from the frying pan into the fire, just so she could stop being a widow. She was dealt a raw, brutal hand – fatherless and betrayed by her brother, who married her off to a homosexual. Then widowhood, followed by marriage to a lecher who raped her daughter. Unlettered, unable to fend for herself, she became the object of contempt within her own family, derided by us all – Baba, Tai and me.

20

The Good Doctor Perrin

Robert-Pierre whistles as he ties his white bow tie, pats Eau Sauvage on his cheeks. He is looking and feeling wonderfully sartorial in his wing-collared shirt and his mother-of- pearl studs, a wedding gift from Sophie's father. Gently he fingers the paisley weave of the white satin waistcoat he wears under his dinner jacket. Kranti had ordered it for him from Burlington's tailors in Bombay.

It's right that a bit of her goes with me tonight, he thinks.

He's been preparing for this evening, writing and re-writing his keynote address, rehearsing before the mirror. There's a nervous flutter at the pit of his stomach, but he's confident that the evening will go well. He has complete mastery his material and his case studies contain a wealth of documentary detail that fully bears out his theory.

After months of pain and uncertainty, he is beginning to see a tiny light flicker at the end of the tunnel. Alain's call this evening has been a real pick-me-up, even though a great deal still remains to be done.

'You really owe me one, you bastard. It was tough and I've had to push real hard. But Louis Michel's been quite cooperative. Apparently he thoroughly dislikes his client and thinks its best for everyone if a compromise is worked out quickly.'

'So what have you settled for?'

'She's taking the flat. Michel says she's an argumentative bitch and very greedy; wants it all. But he's managed to convince her this is the best she can get. It will be a private agreement between the two of you, an out-of-court settlement. That way, we avoid all the court fees as well. First she wanted the money. But when she was told the flat is worth more than the cash, she quickly changed her mind. I think she'll just sell it through an agency and transfer the funds to India or stash them away in a Swiss bank if she's clever. It's also the easiest way out for her. She doesn't have to bother with getting rid of all the stuff. She tried to hold out for the jewellery too, but I told Michel, no way, it's the flat versus the rest. She'll have to pay an inheritance tax and Michel will handle that for her. He's going to make a quick killing, he's quite happy. So remember to be at the notary's at 11 a.m. tomorrow.'

'I'll be there, but what else must I do?'

'Well, you've got a huge job on your hands. You have to decide what you want to keep. The money and the contents of the flat come to you, so you'd better contact Drouot or some other auctioneer to classify and remove the stuff. I sent an assessor around last week to make an estimate and I must say you've got the better deal of the two, although I admit it's a big hassle. But at least you don't have to pay that much in taxes, and you'll be stunned if I tell you what you're getting.'

'So how much?'

'About a million two at least, I would say, less fifteen per cent as my fee.'

Robert-Pierre whistles.'And that's net, after the tax deduction etc.?'

'Yes. The entire estate is worth about three million. You get a little over half, but then the state takes its share in estate duties and taxes.'

'That's enormous. No wonder people are taking their money out of the country.'

'Strange to hear you talking like a bourgeois. I thought you were a revolutionary republican through and through! But that's not the end of it. From next year, you'll have to pay wealth tax because you'll have a personal fortune.'

'It's Sophie who's rich, not me. Everything we have belongs to her. I just scratch out a living. And in any case, the money will go into a trust. I plan to endow a prize in Kranti's name. I shall remain dirt poor as ever.'

'No more, Pierre, no more! But if you do establish a trust, you'll pay less tax. The amount will be drastically reduced.'

'Well, it's still a project and I haven't told Sophie. So not a word to her, Alain, at least not just yet.'

'Come on *mon pote*, don't be daft, do you take me for a fool?'

The news couldn't have been better. All good things come in threes, so this evening will be the final icing on the cake. Even Shanti's annoying presence, her fads and foibles, the unbearable, overpowering smells that emanate from the kitchen, have faded into oblivion. She has been suspiciously conciliatory of late, but he has held his distance. He cannot resist one last act of revenge – or is it pity, he wonders. As he lets himself out of the flat, he leaves the notebooks on the coffee table where Shanti is sure to find them. Let her read that last devastating bit and begone. She wanted to know the whole truth. Well, now she will. It will rock her off her silly, flat feet: knock that smugness.

His heart is singing as he drives home to pick up Sophie, hoping she will wear the royal blue cocktail dress that suits her so well, with the rope of perfectly matched pearls he gave her. It was an extravagance, but he's never regretted it. The pearls come alive each time she wears them, glowing warm and luminous against her creamy white skin.

He was nervous when he called to re-confirm the evening's programme. She seemed shocked and reproachful that he could have doubted her. 'I promised. It was decided months ago, when they first invited you. It's an honour that you've been asked and I'm not going to back out now. That's not my style, I would have told you otherwise. You know that.'

Darling little soldier. Word of honour and all that. What an elegant family they were. What a contrast to Kranti's weird parents and my own simple folk. How lucky I have been and how daft not to know it. Why can't I be the good husband when I have such a decent, wonderful wife? It's the sex, he muses. I need it too much and there isn't any of that with Sophie. If only I didn't fall in love with whoever it is I'm seeing. But just sex is never enough. Maybe I should go to Pierre Keller, he thinks jocularly.

Sophie looks her usual no-nonsense self with straight-cut hair and a hint of lipgloss, the rope of pearls her only adornement. She has a quiet inner beauty that shines through the little black cocktail dress, obviously bought for the occasion. It has a high collar and a long slit down the back that falls tantalizingly open when she bends. He has never seen his wife try on the sexy look before.

No bra. I could slide in my hands to cup her breasts in front.

But his hands stay mutely by his side as they exchange chaste kisses on the cheek. 'You look well and very handsome,' she says with a quick smile.

At the hotel, he takes a peek at himself in the rear-view mirror before handing the car keys to the parking valet. The Grand's lobby is massed with flowers. A discreet panel announces the annual dinner of the French Psychiatric Association on the first floor. Robert-Pierre checks his pocket. His keynote address nestles safely in there. His powerpoint presentation was sent by email yesterday.

The ballroom looks and smells wonderful with its gilded mirrors reflecting the twenty-odd tables glittering with crystal and silver set for a formal banquet. He and Sophie will be seated at the head table.

He makes his way to join Sophie in the antechamber where a pre-dinner cocktail is in full swing. This is the very best of the closed, discreet world of phsycians of the psyche. Neurosurgeons, psychiatrists, psychoanalysts, therapists, academics, all top drawer. And I know almost all of them, Robert-Pierre thinks as he joins his wife and a few Fellows. Pierre Keller is part of the group and there is a short strained silence as he strolls up to them. No cheerful *Bonsoir* this evening, he notices, just an awkward nod or two.

Not surprising, they're probably jealous as hell at not being asked to speak. And Keller? Perhaps he has put two and two together and knows I'm Kranti's secret lover? Certainly, Keller is giving him a distinctly odd look.

A glass of champagne lifts his mood and he finds himself smiling as Eric Moulin, the president of the association, beckons him to one side of the room. He is a gloomy man, literal minded and singularly lacking in a sense of humour;

dry as dust, stooped, with old-fashioned spidery whiskers and gold-rimmed glasses.

Playing at being professorial and only half succeeding, thinks Robert-Pierre with a happy smile.

The two men have been enemies forever. But it's been a fair fight. Moulin lacks Robert-Pierre's charisma and has seen his younger colleague replace him as professor and head of psychiatry at the *Hôpital Sainte-Anne*. Now Moulin rarely gets invited to international congresses whereas Robert-Pierre has presented several papers abroad on his work with anorexic adolescents, which is the subject of his lecture tonight.

Moulin leads him out of the room and lets out a slight, embarassed cough. 'I have to speak to you urgently, my dear Perrin, you seem totally unconcerned. What is your explanation?' he asks.

'You'll hear it when I speak. It's a highly complex subject. There are many reasons for adolescent anorexia, as you know, but the driving impulses appear to be power and guilt.'

Robert-Pierre remembers how he first started specializing in the field. His earliest patient was a certain Mademoiselle Sophie Taquet, shattered by the death of her twin, punishing her own emaciated body, starving herself to death. Both guilt and power were at work there too. He remembers her as the thirty-four-kilo semi-skeleton he treated all those years ago and is engulfed by a tender pride at his wife's robust health and understated beauty.

'What are you talking about? I'm not referring to your paper, Perrin. I'm sure that's very good. I'm talking about this morning's reports in *Closer* and the *Le Canard enchaîné*.'

Robert-Pierre stares at him, a frown on his face. 'You mean you don't know? Oh *mon Dieu*! The whole room is agog with the news and you are completely blank? As they say, the cuckold is always the last one to know.' He laughs drily.

As Robert-Pierre opens his mouth to speak, Moulin waves a couple of clippings under his nose, then thrusts them into his hands. 'I thought someone must have phoned you. We tried to call you all day, but your secretary said your personal phone was off and she didn't know where to get you. I thought you were in hiding, avoiding the press. But here you stroll in completely unaware of what's been going on. This is ridiculous.'

But Robert-Pierre is barely listening. He is speed-reading the lurid clipping from *Closer* magazine. *Did the Good Doctor Help Her Die?* says the highly suggestive headline. There's a glamourous semi-nude photo of Kranti and one of himself in dark glasses, taken at her funeral. He seems to be shying away from the camera, looking decidedly glum and shady. It's a slanderous little article full of innuendo that identifies her as Guillaume de Lorel's ex-wife, part of Paris' scabrous demi-monde. The *Canard enchainé* piece is more factual but equally damaging. Quoting anonymous sources close to the police, it slyly hints that the 'famous Dr Perrin' could be guilty of seducing a patient and driving her to suicide. A police investigation carried out was later dropped, the paper says. The articles are perfectly timed to cause maximum hurt and humiliation.

It has to be Laporte. Who else knew of the investigation and the details? Did he sell his story? He's obviously been paid. The *Canard* pays quite well, but that rag *Closer* must even better.

Robert-Pierre is trembling with anger and there is a strange tightness in his chest, nearing panic. He has an urge to turn on his heel and walk away. But he remains rooted to the spot, only a stain in his cheeks betraying his emotion.

'I think we'd better skip the post-speech questions from the floor. It would be too embarassing. It will make us look like fools. This is a public occasion and the press has been invited. There are television cameras in the room. I want to avoid any unpleasantness both for you and for the association.'

Robert-Pierre has gone very pale. He is fighting to stay calm and concentrate on what Moulin is saying.

'So you see, we must decide immediately how to conduct the evening, what must be done. Of course there will be an enquiry, that goes without saying, and I have called a meeting of the Ethics Committee next Monday. This is not the first time an analyst has been charged with having relations with a patient.'

'I did receive a couple of calls from journalists today. But I didn't respond. I thought they wanted some advance dope on this evening's speech. I wanted it to be a surprise. I had absolutely no idea it was about this utterly scurrilous and vicious attack.'

'We've had complaints of this nature before. After all, the patient-analyst relationship is delicate and does occasionally tip over into something else. We have seen this often enough. But this charge of suicide is very serious. In your case, it's more complicated because you are both an analyst and a qualified medical psychiatrist. So the question of drugs assumes greater significance. Also, there's your professional position to consider.'

'I understand all that, Eric, *je comprends*,' snaps Robert-Pierre.

But Moulin drones on. 'You are, of course, innocent until proven guilty. So, this evening, the programme shall go ahead as planned. But I just wanted to make sure you'll take no questions from the floor, contrary to normal practice. Could you speak a little more than the alloted forty minutes? I shall ask them to bring the entrée before you begin speaking. Perhaps you could leave immediately after?' It's a statement, not a question. '*Courage*, Perrin. We've all got to see this through. So just avoid the press at least until the event is over, will you?'

Robert-Pierre has crushed the clippings, jammed them into the pocket along with his speech, making his dinner jacket bulge. Of course he'll do as Moulin says, that's obvious, but his first thought is for Sophie. He has to tell her before someone else does.

He strides back into the party, only to be waylaid by his wife, who whispers urgently: 'Where were you, Pierre? I've been looking all over for you. Something terrible has happened. It's some article on the suicide and it's all about you, and it's very nasty.'

'I know. Eric Moulin has just shown me the clippings. They're bad and completely false. He wants to cut out the after-dinner questions. Valérie from *Libé* and that fellow from *Psychologies* magazine called several times today. I didn't know it was about this.'

So she knows. I don't have to tell her. But what exactly have they told her? What does she think? He swings between relief and fear, tight-lipped and disoriented.

'Anne told me. You've got to face this. We'll sort it out later. Never mind now. Just go and lock yourself in the toilet and I'll come and get you when it's time. Then you come in from the door at the other end, near the top table. I'll tell them something. Now go. Just go.' She almost pushes him towards the door, stepping forward gracefully to ward off a journalist moving purposefully towards him.

Later, he does not remember how they got through the evening. He found it difficult to concentrate on his speech, but long practice meant he was cruising on auto-pilot. The applause was muted. Instead of waiting to discuss his findings with his peers, explain his method of treatment, savour the compliments, or dish out little quips and sound bytes to the press, he sidled out with Sophie just before the dessert was served. They stole away like thieves in the night.

He is ruined, facing dismissal. That's all there is to it. There will be an enquiry. He knows Moulin and the others will contact the police. The whole sordid tale will out. The hospital will sack him on charges of professional misconduct, without pension benefits or severance pay. His explanation that his long-term affair with Kranti started in earnest long after their first dalliance ended will cut no ice with them. Thank God for the money. He'll never be able to set up the prize or create a trust. It will have to keep for the lean, hard days that are bound to come. It will remain a guilty secret. He'll never be able to tell Sophie.

Like a drowning man clinging to a flimsy bit of plywood, he winds himself around his wife. It's an unhappy homecoming. In his own bed at last, his wide, practical bed, large enough to accommodate his full height, naked and entwined, he begins to talk. He talks, she listens, murmurs something now and then.

She starts moving under him, gently at first, then with more urgency. Her perfume wafts up from her heated earlobes. It's Kranti's perfume, just a little different on Sophie's skin. It's the body chemistry, he thinks, it changes the way the perfume smells.

Sophie moans, her hands are on his back, her mouth on his, hungrily seeking his tongue. It's been years since they made love. He closes his eyes, goes with the flow, allowing her to take the lead. He tries hard, wills himself to respond, but finds he cannot harden. Until he sees Kranti's face, her pearly teeth, wide, luxuriant smile, earrings glinting in the sunlight. He suddenly goes from soft to rock hard but before he can enter Sophie, he ejaculates all over her stomach. Mortification. This has never happened to him before. 'I'm so sorry, *chérie, pardon, pardon,*' he says, burying his head in her shoulder. 'It's been so very long I just couldn't control myself.'

'Its all right Pierre,' she says, smiling in the dark, running her fingers through his hair. 'We have all the time in the world. We've been given a second chance. Just relax now and go to sleep. You've had a terrible day. And there will be more terrible days to come. But I'm here with you and we'll see it through. So just let go.' Her foot moves up and down his leg and he has a vision of a purring cat rubbing itself against his skin.

He goes slack in her arms, relief flooding through him. But it's early light before he finally drops off to sleep.

21

The Black Notebook

10 August 2007

My dear Pierre,

Perhaps you may never get the chance to read this and offer your usual, valuable comments. We may never meet again to say our final goodbyes or talk about what I am just about to tell you.

I owe you an infinite debt of gratitude. You have held my hand every inch of the way. I am ready to unburden myself at last, get rid of this weight I carry around. I want to offer you my deepest and most profound thanks for making it all possible.

I must take a deep breath before I can go on.

It happened a long time ago. I was still in Bombay, recently married to the man who would soon become my first ex-husband, a wealthy alcoholic, a pickled dunce. My career as a model and designer was taking off. But I was deeply depressed. A violent, terrifying anger inhabited me. I wanted to flaunt my new-found wealth, to show my family I had made it big without an inch of support from them. But neither my parents nor Tai had found it in themselves to attend my wedding.

The drill of what I would do had run through my mind several times over and what transpired was entirely premeditated.

I took an early morning train to Poona where I arrived a little after 10 a.m. I knew Baba left for the office around then. I slowly made my way home, stopping the autorickshaw two lanes away. In the morning heat, I entered the garden through the side door and the house through the kitchen which was always unlocked.

The maid who came to wash and clean would be gone by now. The cook would arrive at 12 p.m. to make chappatis, some dal, a couple of vegetables. I had timed it exactly right. She was alone, lying on the bed with her eyes closed. She seemed asleep. I tried to make as little noise as possible, but something startled her. Her eyes flew open and she struggled to sit up, giving me a truly happy smile of surprised welcome.

'When did you come? How are you, Kuka?' And when I kept on advancing, still saying nothing, 'Is there a problem?' Poor creature, she could not have imagined what was to come. 'Why are you looking at me like that? What do you want, Kuka? I must call your father.' The childhood endearment almost undid me. But I did not falter.

As she turned towards the telephone near her, I picked up a cushion and pounced, pushing her back on the bed, pinning her head against the pillow, pressing hard with all my might. There were muffled noises. Her hands clawed mine. She tried to kick her legs, but they were trapped by the sheet, working sideways, like a pair of useless scissors.

I held on, pressing hard for long agonizing minutes, and slowly, after what seemed an eternity, her hands went slack, her head stopped moving. Her body lay still. It was finally over.

There were deep scratch marks on my hands and forearms where she had tried to pinch and prise with surprising strength. I felt lightheaded. The stone on my heart had been lifted at last! Looking neither right nor left, I tiptoed out the way I had come, walking away quickly to catch the No. 6 bus to the station. I met no one and saw no one who could have recognized me.

I waited to hear news of my mother's death. None came. Then, through a chance meeting with a cousin, I learnt that she had survived but was paralyzed and incapable of speech – thank God!

I never saw my parents again. Aayee died the year my divorce came through. Tai phoned to summon me to the funeral, which I had the grace not to attend. Baba went to his grave quietly in his sleep, a decade later. Grey and shrunken, he had lost most of his teeth along with his fatal charm.

I see my sister sometimes. I know I continue to embarrass her and the last time we met, she quite plainly told me I was a manipulative whore. 'You have slept your way to the top! The only way you know how is by parting your thighs.' I wonder what sparked that puritanical streak in her despite the liberal arts degree, the research on T.S. Eliot, the Ph.D on Britain's war poets.

She's jealous, I know. The dumb younger sister who turned into this elegant swan, who gets written about in celebrity mags, while she herself has become a dumpy, boring, middle-class Amma, her intellectual achievements buried in the fat of her double chins...

Yes, I am bitter. I don't think I have ever received real love or been able to give it. You have to receive in order to give. I was loved by my parents once, a long time ago, as a very young child, but it all blew away like sand upon the wind. I think I became as much a monster as Baba and if he killed Aayee or at least tried to poison her, I am guilty of the same crime, just slightly differently executed.

Now that I pine for R's love, now that I'm insanely jealous of Sophie, I can begin to understand what Aayee must have gone through. Her looks destroyed, her body wasted, her mind crawling with suspicion, it was inevitable that she should lose her reason.

Matricide. I have committed murder, Pierre, never mind that I failed. The intention was to kill. Wherever I go, I think people are looking at me knowingly, accusingly. 'You murderess,' a woman's eyes seem to blaze as I brush past her at the supermarket.

Strange, is it not, that women turn against other women, never against the men? It was my father who raped me. Yet, it was my mother I hated. She made me feel soiled and ashamed. She treated me like a competitor; not like the daughter who needed care and love but like an alien woman who was her husband's mistress. She gave me no protection, no succour. Looking back, I ask myself how she could ever have protected me, being so weak and vulnerable herself.

I can analyze my actions now. Then, I was acting out of blind rage and a feeling of terrible injustice. I don't think I ever forgave her for falling ill, for her inability to take his infidelities in her stride. If she hadn't lost her health and her mind, her beauty, her allure, his predatory eye would not have fallen on me. So many ifs. She failed in her 'wifely' duty towards him and in her 'motherly' duty to protect me. A parent must give protection, it's a sacred duty.

Now that I have put it down, what next? The cat's out of the bag, the genie released. Will I have to confront you? Tell R? They say every murderer, rapist, child molester, killer reaches a point where he wants his secret discovered. It's a relief, they say. This is certainly a kind of release, but what about the consequences? How do I continue to live now, what do I tell myself? I suppose I can ask you to keep it to yourself. The secret of the confessional.

I know you will understand. You are the only one alive who now cares what happens to me. A professional psychiatrist. What a sorry, lonely existence. There is Olga, of course, poor, sincere, striving, pattering Olga. But her very mediocrity kills me. As does Tai's. At least Olga is kind and non-judgemental, though she is such a plodder. And who else is there for the final goodbye?

I only hope I don't get it wrong. I don't wish to remain a cripple, a half-alive vegetable. I don't want to be like my mother. I must make sure and doubly sure. Cannot make the same mistake twice. That would be unforgivable, if not fatal.

I have been listening to Margaret Price singing Ave Maria. The purity of her voice, the extraordinarily plaintive Schubert lied, an ode to Mother Mary, the protector of all things broken, has me sobbing like a child and I yearn for that encompassing, loving embrace. I want to be that child again who held Aayee's hand, nestled in her lap.

I look at the Holy Trinity above my bed. Mary's love for Jesus pours out of her eyes like a thousand points of light. How delicately she holds her infant son. I know that's how Aayee once loved me. Tai may not admit it, but I know how she feels about losing little Girish. There is a special word for mother love in Sanskrit. Vatsalya. It's the infinite sea of love a mother has for her child. That Yashodhara had for Krishna. I know Aayee had it for me. Oceans of it. I want my mother. I need her to console me, blow upon my scratches to make them stop hurting. I feel her beckon, call out to me. My mother, young and beautiful, smelling of scented supari and Pond's Dreamflower talc. She is the only safe haven I shall ever know.

22

Adieu Paris

Pale and drained, with violet pools under his eyes, Robert-Pierre arrives late at the notary's. He has switched his phone off, asked his secretary to deflect all calls, and warned Shanti to remain tight-lipped if the press turns up at the door. He is sure Kranti's flat has been beseiged by a flurry of hungry reporters. His fall from grace made the morning news on France Info, he knows.

It's all very business-like and is over within an hour. Louis Michel accompanies Shanti, whispering translations of what the notary is saying while Alain sits close to him, their chairs touching, as if to protect him from further harm.

'Put your initials on each page and sign on the last one with the date and the words "read and approved",' the Notary says.

Shanti is leaving that night, her bags and bundles already packed. It seems she can't get away soon enough.

'There is one final matter to be settled,' Robert-Pierre says, turning to her. 'The ashes. Right now, they are kept in my ivory sculpture. I could easily transfer them into a small box or an envelope and give them to you this afternoon.'

Shanti stiffens, sits up in her chair, looks him straight in the eye for the first time since her arrival. 'She was an evil woman, a murderess who tried to kill my mother. I cannot and will not pollute the holy Ganges with her ashes. I don't want those ashes.' A visible shudder goes through her body. 'You keep them since you all love her so much.'

'But you are happy to take money of this evil woman? How do you know what she is saying, it's true? How do you know it was not *fantaisie*? Human psyche is very complex. I have seen it before. Patients feel *culpabilité*, guilt, which is not real, all in the head. They think, feel, tell things that never happened. And they are sure that is how it happened. But in fact it never happened. It is common psychological delusion born from *culpabilité*. How you can be sure what she said is the truth, *la verité absolute*? I knew her. She was not a killer.'

'So why did she kill herself then? You tell me. I have read her diary. I have known her all my life. From the moment she was born. She was cold and calculating. She looked like an angel but she was an evil devil-child, a born manipulator. Why should I feel guilty about taking her money? I've paid for her existence throughout my life.'

'*S'il vous plaît*,' the notary interrupts, 'please take your quarrels outside my office. My job is done. *Madame*, you will receive the papers through your lawyer. The cheques will be sent directly by my assistant. *Monsieur*, your affairs will be handled by your counsel and we shall be in touch. Now I wish you all a good day.'

As they emerge on the landing, Robert-Pierre suddenly has a vision of Shanti hurtling down the stairs. I'd like to see her fall. He imagines her body, lying broken at the bottom, her sari pooled around her.

Shanti clutches her bag and begins to walk down, one hand on the bannister. Robert-Pierre turns to thank Alain, who says he'll see Shanti into a taxi. He lets them go, takes the steps slowly, one by one. Out in the sunshine, he looks at the cloudless blue sky, the mellow stone buildings, as if seeing Paris for the first time. Then he strides off to the nearest café and a tiny cup of strong double espresso. '*Serré, s'il vous plaît*,' he tells the waiter.

Epilogue

'I have checked the ephemeris. We should know the position of the planets and the exact time of sunset. That's the most important thing,' Peter says. They are standing at the river's edge, Olga, Robert-Pierre and Peter, down the steps from the Pont d'Iena,.

'It's bizarre,' says Olga. 'The sun has been out every single time. The day she died. The day of her funeral and now, today, when we are sending her away. What a beautiful sunset too. Like always. It's as if she wanted to go in a blaze of light.'

Peter has bought an antique miniature wooden galleon complete with masts, sails and rigging, about four feet long. The figurehead on the ship's prow is a busty female with rosy cheeks, streaky blonde hair and billowing skirts. Highly polished, the boat has a blue and gold trim and Peter has fixed Indian and French paper flags to its tallest mast. Kranti's ashes lie in a slim Japanese papier-maché box, tacked firmly to the deck. Peter has looped marigold garlands around the vessel, making it look festive and peculiarly Indian.

The sun is beginning to sink as they stand together in quiet communion. Curious passers-by gather around.

'What a beautiful boat. Are you serious about sailing her?' someone asks.

'Oh, he's probably got a remote control somewhere to bring it back to shore. It's a costly boat, you can see,' another voice says.

Peter carefully places the craft in the lapping waters of the Seine as Olga begins to cry, softly at first, then loudly, her Parisian control giving way to long-suppressed Slavic emotion. Robert-Pierre holds her close, comforts her. But this time, unlike at Kranti's funeral, it's no distant embrace. He holds her fast, a family member in distress.

'*Maman, regarde, le bateau part*. It's going, it's really going,' a little boy shrieks to his mother, clapping his hands in excitement.

The current quickly catches the gallant little vessel, carrying it first west, then north, as the Seine meanders, gently bends. The setting sun is turning the ripples of water into liquid gold. The boat's white sails reflect the light and it appears to be dancing on the waves.

'It will turn over, it will fall.' Robert-Pierre clutches Peter's arm.

'No, it won't. It's completely seaworthy. Fashioned by a master craftsman. Unless there's a storm or a collision, it will reach the sea.'

They watch in silence as the little ship sails on, becoming smaller, more miniscule with each passing minute. A mere dot. And then, as the last rays of the sun go dipping down, it takes a graceful turn further west. Its sails, now tinged a brilliant orange, send out one last conspiratorial signal, a final wink of light, before it disappears from view.

Acknowledgements

The prologue of this book came to me ready-written, like *bani-banayi chai*, when I was in hospital during an illness some years ago. I realized later that this was my way of dealing with the question of mortality – I had to metaphorically kill my alter ego in order to survive.

As I got well, the manuscript lay around, untouched and gathering dust. But Olga Savic had already made her appearance, as had Robert-Pierre and Sophie, and it seemed a pity to let them go. Friends urged me to carry on and if it had not been for them, this novel would never have been written. I owe them all a huge debt of gratitude. The list of persons who read early drafts and made valuable suggestions is long and if I forget to mention any of them, it is because of my own failing memory.

Olivier Bétourné, steadfast friend and former boss, wrote me a personal cheque saying: 'The fact that you've received an advance will force you to work!' I can finally pay back that debt with added dollops of gratitude.

Indrani Vidyarthi and Ayesha Kagal cheered me on right through and never complained about having to read the same material several times over.

Others who gave invaluable inputs include Mariam Ram, Catherine Bernard, Rakesh Sood, Moira Dineen, Erin Mella, Urvashi Butalia (whose upstairs garret has housed many a struggling writer), Jayapriya Vasudevan, Janine Krause, Sudhir Kakar, Lola Barroso, Anne Michel, Lorenz Bolliger, Roma Tearne, Gillian Slovo and Curtis Sittenfeld.

A very special thanks to Anita Roy, my 'personal' editor and friend, who did a lot of encouraging, hand holding and rooting from the sidelines.

And of course without V.K. Karthika's love, faith, friendship and patience, this book would never have materialized.

Finally, where would I be without our animals, whose constant attention-seeking evokes such irritation that it sometimes overtakes love? So to Ppons, Zoz, Caillou and the Touris family, to les Kas, Apu-Papu, Grandmère, Caperon, le Loup, la Fouine, Canard and la Grosse Citrouille, a big hug. Thank you all.